COUNTRY HAM

COUNTRY HAM

John Quincy MacPherson
& Mikeal C. Parsons

RESOURCE *Publications* · Eugene, Oregon

COUNTRY HAM

Resource Publications
An Imprint of Wipf and Stock Publishers
199 W. 8th Ave., Suite 3
Eugene, OR 97401

www.wipfandstock.com

PAPERBACK ISBN: 978-1-5326-1864-2
HARDCOVER ISBN: 978-1-4982-4439-8
EBOOK ISBN: 978-1-4982-4438-1

Manufactured in the U.S.A.   04/27/17

For all those in whom the MacPherson blood runs,
and for all those MacPhersons yet to come . . . .

CHAPTER 1

First, Ham had to pick up his tux—black trousers with a lime green jacket with long tails to match Nora's dress. Since it was 1976, almost everything and everybody would be decked out in patriotic red, white, and blue. But Nora decided to go with a lime green dress, because it went well with her features. So, of course, Ham would have a matching jacket. After the tux, Ham had to swing by Snow's Florist to pick up Nora's corsage. Then back home to wash the Studebaker.

He opened the door to JoAnna's Boutique. A little bell over the door rang, announcing his arrival. Mrs. Joanna Weaver came from the back to the counter.

"Hi, Miss Joanna. I came to get my tux," Ham said.

"Hello, Ham. Just a minute." Mrs. Weaver went to the back and emerged a moment later with a plastic covered hanger. "All paid for, I see," she said, as she lifted up the plastic cover. "Pink jacket and matching cummerbund and tie. That right?"

"No ma'am. It's supposed to be a lime green jacket with matching cummerbund and tie," Ham replied.

"Hmmm, well, the ticket order says, 'pink.'" She held the paper out for Ham to examine. "Do you remember who helped you?"

"Some young woman I never seen before."

"That might have been Julie. We have a lot of temp help during this time of year. I'm afraid there's nothing I can do about it now, Ham. Winter Waltz is tonight. I'll give a 10 percent credit toward your next purchase, but you really should have come in earlier in the week to make sure the order was right."

"Yes ma'am. My mama said the same thing 'bout coming in early. All right, then, thank you Miss Joanna." Ham took the hanger and left the shop. The little bell announced his departure.

Things went better at the florist. Nora's corsage was ready, and it was just what Ham (or more accurately, his mother Nina) had ordered. By the time he stopped for lunch at Arby's (he loved their roast beef sandwiches) and got home, it was nearly two o'clock. He went in to the house and took a catnap. A little after three o'clock, Ham pulled his 1948 Studebaker closer to the garden hose to start washing it, despite the slight chill in the air.

After fifteen minutes or so, he looked up and saw a strange sight coming down the driveway. A gray and black Pontiac hearse with black tinted windows was rolling slowly toward the house. Ham watched, puzzled. What was a hearse doing here?

As the hearse came to a full stop, the driver turned the flashers on and sat on the horn. Then Uncle Carl opened the door and got out. In his early forties, Carl Calloway Brookshire was tall and thin, and he had a black goatee and ponytail to complement his balding head. He had on his trademark white T-shirt and bib overalls.

"How do you like your ride, Ham?" Carl asked.

"What the hell is that thing, Uncle Carl?"

"Why, it's a hearse, of course. I call it Mr. Ed." Then Carl began to sing. "A hearse is a hearse of course, of course, and no one can talk to a hearse, of course, that is of course unless the hearse is the famous Mr. Ed."

"Uncle Carl, have you been drinkin'?"

"Ham, what kind of question is that? It's the weekend and I'm your Uncle Carl. Of course, I've been drinkin'."

"I can't take Nora to the Winter Waltz in that thing!" Ham shouted.

"Why not?" Carl asked. "It's the same length as a regular limousine. I checked myself. Besides, Nora is goin' to love it!" Carl winked.

"It's for carryin' corpses, not dates." Ham cried.

"In my experience, Ham, sometimes it's hard to tell the difference." Carl quipped. "Ham, this is a real classic. It's a 1954 Pontiac Barnette two-door hearse, for Christ's sake. And did you know that there are Hearse Clubs where owners drive in parades just like they do classic antique cars?"

Ham ignored those comments. "Where in tarnation did you get this?"

"From a colored funeral home." Carl said. "It was a real bargain, too. Plus, there haven't been any corpses in the hearse in over two months. Business was bad, which is why, I reckon, they sold it."

"What in God's name made you decide to buy a hearse, Uncle Carl?"

"Why I've always wanted a hearse, Ham."

"I never knew that. Why?"

"Well, don't you know people are dyin' all over the place to get into a hearse?" Carl laughed at his own joke until he started coughing. He reached inside his overalls and retrieved an inhaler. He inhaled the medicine, waited a moment until his lungs cleared, and then said, "Seriously, Ham, I've always liked the look of a hearse, and when this one came available, I jumped on it. Ridin' in a parade next weekend. But you get the honor of bein' the first one to take it out in public."

"What happened to the limo you were supposed to get?"

"Oh, my buddy Jimmy knew a fella with a limo, but that deal kinda fell through. I should've known not to trust Jimmy."

Yeah, thought Ham, and I should have known not to trust you.

Carl changed the subject. "Ham, why are washin' your car in this cold?"

"Because I figured this would happen."

"What would happen?"

"You wouldn't come through with the limo, Uncle Carl, that's what! I'll just take the Studebaker. She's all cleaned up now."

About that time, Jimmy rolled up in his red, flatbed truck. Carl opened the passenger side, jumped in and rolled down the window. "Well, the keys are in the ignition if you change your mind."

"I thought you were goin' to get us a driver."

"Only room for two in the front comfortably, and I'm bettin' you don't want to ride in the back by yourself! I'll be back to get it tomorrow afternoon either way. Have fun tonight, Ham! And be safe."

Before Ham could reply, Carl rolled up the window, and he and Jimmy took off down the road.

Ham looked at the hearse in disgust. He had to admit it had a certain air about it, and it was very clean. But he knew there was absolutely no way Nora would go to the Winter Waltz with him if he showed up in Mr. Ed.

Ham went inside and showered. He put on his hot pink, long tailed jacket and black trousers, topped off with a pink bowtie and cummerbund. He was in the kitchen drinking a glass of water when his mother came in the back door. She had been preparing the ground in the garden for the spring planting and had missed her brother's visit altogether. "Hammie, why are you wearin' a pink tux?" (His mother was the only one he'd let get away with calling him "Hammie.")

"They got the order wrong, Mama."

"Oh Hammie, I told you to go earlier in the week so this wouldn't happen."

"I know, Mama, I know. I gotta go."

He put the glass down in the sink and headed out the front door. He got into the Studebaker and turned the switch, but the car didn't turn over. "Crap," Ham said. He turned the ignition key again. No sound. Either the starter or the battery, but either way it was too late to do anything about it. He looked over at Mr. Ed, took a deep breath, got of the Studebaker, and walked over to the hearse.

He could hear his mother yell through the screen door. "Hammie, where did that hearse come from?"

He pulled out of the driveway and turned Mr. Ed in the direction of Nora's house.

Just as Ham feared, Nora took one look at the hearse and declared, "Ham, I'm not ridin' in that thing!"

"Nora, I know. I'm so sorry. I shouldn't have trusted Uncle Carl. But the Studebaker won't start, and we don't have anythin' else to drive, except the farm truck, and it's filthy."

"Well, I'd rather go to Winter Waltz in a filthy truck than in a hearse!"

"Oh come on, Nora, it'll be unique." Ham knew he was sounding like Uncle Carl. He began singing, "A hearse is a hearse of course, of course . . . "

"Shut up, Ham MacPherson!" With that Nora got in the passenger side of Mr. Ed and slammed the door shut. She folded her arms across her chest and looked straight ahead.

"And why are you in a hot pink suit?"

"They got my order wrong."

"You should have gone earlier in the week!"

"I know. That's what Mama and Miss Joanna said," Ham said. "You look real pretty, though, Nora."

Stone silence.

"Tonight'll be fun, Nora, I promise."

"Shut up and drive, Ham!" So down the road they went: Ham in a pink tux and both of them in a hearse. The slight smile of amusement that crossed Nora's face did not go unnoticed by Ham. It was a look Ham had seen before.

The dinner and Winter Waltz were uneventful. In the last slow dance of the night, Ham whispered in Nora's ear. "Notice anythin' different 'bout this year from last?"

"You mean besides the fact you're in a pink tux and we came here in a hearse?"

"Well, yeah, besides that. There warn't no cats with firecrackers tied to their tails runnin' through the gym."

Nora giggled. "Well, that's true." In fact, it was true. But the real fireworks this year came after the dancing was over. By then, Nora had relaxed; she loved to dance, and Ham had been extra thoughtful, always making sure she had a refill of her coke and dancing every dance, even the fast ones (which he usually balked at). But tonight that was part of his penance.

Around midnight, they got into the hearse, and Ham drove to their "make-out" spot, a pullover spot near the top of the Brushy mountains that overlooked the Yadkin River Valley and the lights from Wilkesboro and North Wilkesboro. It was one of a dozen such "lover's lanes" tucked into the back roads of the Brushies.

Ham looked at Nora in the passenger seat. Small, petite, thick blond hair, with piercing green eyes and a killer smile. They had gone steady for three years. Ham and Nora had never done "it," though by Ham's reckoning, they were standing squarely on third base. He wondered who came up with the baseball analogy for making out, but it was well known in Wilkes County:

first base = kissing
second base = light petting on the outside of the clothes
third base = "heavy petting" underneath garments
home run = going all the way, doing "it"

Football really didn't have any kind of equivalence. Basketball either. No wonder baseball was America's favorite pastime!

The hearse had an after-market eight-track tape player and a bucket of Soul and R & B cartridges on the floorboard of the passenger side, presumably from the previous owner. Ham pulled out a tape.

"How 'bout the Staple Singers?" Ham asked.

"I never heard of them," Nora replied.

Four versions of "Let's Do It Again" played while Ham and Nora made out. He shut down the engine; the tape deck continued to run on auxiliary.

The front of the hearse was not very conducive to heavy petting.

"This thing was made for the dead not the livin'!" Ham declared as he hit his shin on the tape deck. Somehow Ham had managed to get his hand down Nora's spaghetti-strapped dress and was fumbling with her bra strap, feeling around for the clasp.

"It's in the front, Ham," Nora gasped.

"What's in the front?" Ham heaved.

"The clasp!"

"What the heck is it doin' up there?"

"It's a strapless bra with the clasp in front."

"Well, that's confusing," Ham grunted, as he freed the clasp and simultaneously hit his funny bone on the steering wheel and his head on the overhead interior light. Curtis Mayfield was crooniing through the speakers,

> *If you will count up to ten*
> *That'll give me a chance to get my breath back*
> *Then . . . we'll do it again an' again!*

They looked at each other and then both looked at the tinted sliding glass window separating them from the back of the hearse. Ham opened the sliding glass, wondering why a hearse driver would ever need to communicate with the back of the hearse.

"Wanna go back there? There's more room." Ham asked tentatively.

"The back of the hearse?"

"Sure why not?"

They hopped out of either side of Mr. Ed and met in the back of the hearse. Ham threw open the back door. They both stared inside, then turned toward each other and began laughing. There was a mattress with a fitted sheet in the back of the hearse. A thick, neatly folded blanket sat in the middle of the mattress. Ham recognized it as one Uncle Carl had purchased on the Cherokee reservation years ago.

"Did you put this in here, Thomas Hamilton MacPherson? Pretty presumptuous of you!" Nora demanded, trying to feign an indignant tone.

"No, I promise I didn't," Ham said. "It must have been Uncle Carl."

"What did your Uncle Carl think we were goin' to do?"

"I'm sure it warn't for us, Nora. You know, Uncle Carl'll sleep off a drunk spell in his car. He probably put this back here for him next time that happens." Ham tried to sound convincing, but he certainly wasn't sure what Uncle Carl was thinking. He did remember his wink and his words, "Nora's gonna love it."

"Aren't you just dying to try it out, Nora?"

Nora giggled and took Ham by the hand and led him onto on the mattress. They shut the door to the hearse. There wasn't much vertical room, Ham thought. Nobody was expected to sit up in the back of a hearse. But he decided there was plenty of horizontal room, and the mattress was soft. He covered them with the blanket. The Staple Singers continued to sing. By the time they got to the seventh song on the tape, Ham and Nora had reached "home." Ham had hit his head on the hearse's ceiling more than once, but now they were lying close together, arms and legs entangled listening to the melodic instrumentals of "After Sex."

"I love you, Nora."

"I love you, too, Ham, but we shouldn't of done that."

"Do you regret it?"

"Of course not, but we can't do that again til we're married, okay Ham?"

"Okay, Nora." The tape ended with "Chase." Ham listened to Nora's steady, rhythmic breathing, and his mind wandered. He thought about the warning his baseball coach gave the day before every game. "Don't have sex, tonight, boys," he said, "it'll mess you up." Since Ham wasn't having sex, he didn't pay much attention. What was it Coach Maynard said after that. You'll lose your edge? You'll lose your legs? Ham couldn't remember. But Opening Day wasn't until the following Friday, so he thought he surely would recover by then. He was scheduled to be the Opening Day starting pitcher.

Then he thought about Miss Turnage's English class. She recently introduced the class to "Freudian psychoanalytic" ways of reading literature. Best Ham could make out, psychoanalytic readings were all about sex and death. Wonder what a psychoanalytic critic would make of him and Nora having sex in the back of a hearse? "That's what literary critics would call 'irony,'" he could hear Miss Turnage saying. Kinda like dying of a heart attack in a whorehouse, he mused.

They slept soundly for a couple of hours; to a casual observer they might have passed for corpses. At 3:00 a.m. they both awoke abruptly.

"We gotta go home, Ham." They put their clothes on and got back into the front seat of Mr. Ed.

By now the Staple Singers' eight track had looped back around back, and they began again singing seductively, "Let's do it again."

"Turn that off, Ham!"

"Sorry Nora." Neither of them had been prepared for tonight; "good" Southern guys and gals seldom were.

CHAPTER 2

Ham slept through Sunday school. He didn't drop Nora at home until 3:30 a.m. But he knew Nora would be at Sunday school and church because she loved to go. Ham dragged himself out of bed, showered, and ate a bowl of cereal. He could hear his father snoring in the master bedroom. His mother, Nina, had left with his younger siblings Diane and Michael Allen over an hour ago; she taught the elementary age girls' Sunday school class every week. Ham walked outside toward the Studebaker and remembered it wouldn't start. He thought about taking the hearse to church but knew his mother would be mortified. Looking at the hearse, however, reminded him that maybe he needed to do something with the now soiled fitted sheet in the back of the hearse. He thought about washing it but was afraid his mother would ask about it. So he just crumpled it up and threw it in the very back of the hearse and figured Uncle Carl would deal with it and not ask any questions. He got into the farm truck and drove to the Second Little Rock Baptist Church. Ham was a few minutes late for the service and slipped in on the back row next to JC where they always sat. JC MacPherson had been Ham's best friend since they were eight years old. They were not related, so far as anyone knew, but folk called them the "MacPherson twins" nevertheless. Ham was white; JC was black.

The services on that Sunday were like most every other Sunday since Second Baptist Church and Little Rock Baptist Church had merged—blacks and whites worshipping together. The church had co-pastors: Brother Bob Sechrest, who had led the two congregations to merge a decade earlier, and Brother Matthew Zimmerman, a young African American preacher. During Brother Matthew's prayer, Ham furtively scanned the congregation trying to locate Nora. She was with her family on the second row. Almost as though she felt his eyes on her, she glanced back over her shoulder, smiled shyly and gave a little wave. Ham smiled back and blew her a silent kiss, hoping nobody else's eyes were open during the prayer. He would see her that afternoon; they needed to talk. The choir sang a rousing version of "Swing Low, Sweet Chariot," and it was time for the sermon.

That Sunday there was a guest preacher, a fellow named Martin England who had been a missionary to Burma and was, along with Brother Bob, another white minister who was active in the Civil Rights movement. In his introduction, Brother Bob said Rev. England was also good friends with Clarence Jordan, co-founder of Koinonia Farms in Americus, Georgia, whom Brother Bob often spoke of. He told the congregation Rev. England had convinced Dr. Martin Luther King Jr. to buy a life insurance policy just weeks before he was assassinated, and that money had helped his family in a very difficult time. Dr. King had given his famous "Letter from a Birmingham Jail" to Martin England to make sure it was released to the public, which, of course, everyone knew it was. At that, some of the congregants said, "Well!" "Thank you Jesus!" "All right now!" Brother Bob ended by saying Rev. England was one of the most unassuming and humble persons he'd ever met, and he was honored to share the pulpit with him.

Rev. England stepped to the pulpit. He was a small man of medium build, black hair, and piercing black eyes. He thanked Brother Bob for the warm welcome, and said self-effacingly with regard to the Birmingham letter that he'd "just been in the right place at the right time." He also said Brother Bob had been a good friend since they met during their time as Civil Rights activists.

"Your pastor was there for the Freedom Rides that Ella Baker organized in Raleigh, sponsored by the Congress of Racial Equality. Blacks and whites rode Greyhound buses together to challenge segregation on the buses and in the bus stations. Brother Bob worked closely with Durham activist and attorney, Floyd McKissick, and he participated in the successful campaign against the segregationist policies of Howard Johnson restaurants. Your congregation is a beacon on a hill for so many of us in the South."

Rev. England then read the parable of the Good Samaritan from Luke 10, closed his Bible, and said, "That is the question today, brothers and sisters, 'Who is my neighbor?'" Then he told this story:

> "My grandfather, Jasper Wilson, was drafted into the Confederate army and was at Fort Sumter in the early stages of the

war. He was badly wounded and thought he was going to die, and his tent mates thought he was going to die, too. And he wanted to die at home, which was a good many miles away from Charleston, back up in the mountains of western North Carolina. And his tent mates put him on a train, sewed up a lot on Confederate money . . . in the lining of his coat so he would have enough money for his needs on the way home. Train crews lifted him off of one train onto the next when he had to change. Finally, he got to Walhalla, the county seat town of Oconee County, that was the end of the railroad. It was about forty miles, I suppose, further on to his home in the mountains. And he lay on the station platform in Walhalla two whole days, begging anybody who could to take him to his home in the mountains and also, if anybody could, to get the word to his family, that he was there.

Finally, a black man who had a horse and wagon, hauled freight from the station to the stores in town, picked him up and put him in his wagon and took him home. When they . . . got to his home, the road crossed a little creek, below the house on the mountainside and he called out to Jeanette, my grandmother, his wife, 'I'm home' and 'Bring clean clothes and towels and soap, but don't come near me.' From his wounds, the pus and the blood, and from insects that all soldiers in most wars . . . know about, he said, 'I'm lousy and don't come near me, but bring these and throw them across the creek.' She did that. The black man very gently undressed him and bathed him there in the creek and dressed him in clean clothes and then took him carefully up to the house.

'Who is my neighbor?' My neighbor is whoever will help me in my time of need, when I'm in the ditch—that person, regardless of race, religion, or creed, is my neighbor. And it may be the person I would least like to receive help from. It certainly was for the man in the ditch. A Jew receiving help from a Samaritan? Unheard of in the first century! What about today? Who is your neighbor? In the Kingdom of God, all barriers are broken down. We are called to love God and our neighbor as ourselves. Amen."

During the communion that followed, Ham reflected on the Rev. England's homily. He knew exactly what he was talking about, not wanting help from somebody who has offended you or annoyed you. His daddy, Thom Jeff, called it his "shit list." Ham was pretty sure the list was mental, but Thom Jeff kept it up to date. Ham thought he'd be surprised if Jesus or even Rev. England called it a "shit list" (though Jesus at least did have a lot of harsh things to say about some of the Pharisees), but they both definitely knew what a "shit list" was. "Which of these would I least like to receive help from?" In other words, "Who on my shit list would I least like to help me when I'm in the ditch?" Ham was sure he got the point.

He thought of his own shit list. Usually at the top would go his daddy, but Ham dismissed him almost immediately on the grounds that at this point in his life he cared so little for Thom Jeff he couldn't imagine mustering up enough resentment to put him on the list. There were several other candidates. There was JC sitting beside him. Certainly they had their struggles over the years. The better you know someone the more clearly you see and know his faults. But Ham knew in his heart JC was the person Ham would most easily accept help from. And JC was not on Ham's shit list—that was unimaginable.

He turned his gaze to the front of the sanctuary where people were receiving communion. Communion at Second Little Rock Baptist Church was observed by intinction, in which church members came to the front and dipped the bread into the wine. And they used real wine. There was Sarah Elizabeth Corn receiving a piece of torn bread from Brother Bob. She had made fun of Ham's name in the seventh grade. But he harbored no real resentment toward her.

Next was Carolyn Leggett. Ham thought about her for a long while. Carolyn used to be church treasurer until she was caught embezzling money from the church a couple of years earlier. But the church had arranged for her to pay the money back, and Ham really had no personal animosity toward her. She might be on somebody's "list," but not Ham's. By the time these thoughts had run their course, everybody had gone to communion except the row in front of Ham and Ham's row. As he stood in the line forming down the middle aisle, Ham saw Uncle Carl dipping bread into the wine. Where did he come from? It must have been a blue moon last night, Ham would tell Carl after church, because that's when Carl came to church. Carl was now in the crosshairs of Ham's "least like to receive help from" list. Ham would have plenty of reason not to want help from Carl. He was unreliable, and when he was drunk, he was an embarrassment. Wine dripped down Carl's chin onto his white t-shirt. He grinned at Brother Bob and then started coughing. When he sat, Carl pulled the inhaler from his pocket. Yes, Ham thought, Carl would surely be on the list of people he didn't want help from, even if he didn't always rise to the level of the List.

With only five people in front of him in line, Ham realized he really didn't have any enemies in the church or really either at school. So he thought of the "Sylva Streak" Bobby Skeeter, the star of the Sylva Baseball team they would play next Friday. Skeeter was an excellent athlete, and Sylva had beaten Wilkes Central in nearly every game of every sport during Ham's career. Yeah, he definitely wouldn't want any help from Bobby Skeeter. Not that he considered him an enemy per se, but he was certainly an adversary—even a nemesis. Ham couldn't imagine a situation in which he'd want help from Bobby Skeeter. So as he approached Brother Bob holding the bread and the co-pastor, Brother Matthew holding the chalice, he thought, yea, it'd be a tossup between Uncle Carl and Bobby Skeeter for the title of "Person I'd least like to receive help from." He could feel the Vin Santo slide down his throat into his stomach. It was cool and left a sweet taste in his mouth.

That afternoon he picked up Nora and they drove to the Dairy Queen for a chocolate dipped ice cream cone. They sat side by side in a booth in the back with no one else around.

"Ham, I feel so guilty about last night. I meant to save myself for my weddin' night. I didn't sleep at all after I go home, worryin' 'bout what we did."

"I know, but it just sorta happened. Besides, we're gonna get married. You know I would marry you right after graduation if you'd say 'yes.'"

"We don't have any money, and we both want to go to college, Ham. And, everybody says we're too young."

"We can make it work, Nora, I promise. I'm hopin' I can get a baseball scholarship 'fore the end of the year. And I can get a part time job."

"Well, that worries me, too, Ham. What if you get a scholarship some place far away, some place where I didn't apply or can't get in?"

"I'm hopin' UNC will offer me; we can both go there. Or we'll stay closer to home. I want us to be together."

"We just can't be together again like we were last night, okay Ham? Not til we're married. It goes against everythin' we've been taught at church and in our family."

Ham couldn't remember hearing exactly that at church, at least not under Brother Bob. But certainly Nora was right about family; his mother would not be happy if she knew he and Nora had sex. "Okay Nora. But it was wonderful, warn't it?"

"Yes, Ham, it was."

Ham leaned down and kissed Nora on her cheek. He thought about how much he loved the girl.

CHAPTER 3

"Top of the seventh, Ham struck out the side! I think Ham just threw a no-hitter, Jesse!" Roy looked up from his scorebook, which he kept every game. It was "unofficial," but generally more accurate than the book kept by the official scorer up in the booth who had been known to check his stats against Roy's on more than one occasion

"No way, Roy, we're behind 1–0," Jesse replied.

Jesse White and Roy Martin, North Wilkesboro's barbers, were sitting behind home plate, like they did every home game. The two barbers from North Wilkesboro were avid baseball fans and diehard Wilkes Central fans, even through the lean years, which had been many. They cut the hair of most of the boys on the Wilkes Central team, including Ham.

Roy scanned his book. "Yeah, but that one run was unearned. Don't you remember? Ham walked that kid in the fourth. Then a sacrifice bunt moved him to second and a stolen base moved him to third."

"Oh, that's right," Jesse said. "And he scored on that passed ball JC should've stopped."

As the Eagles came into the dugout for their last at bat, Jesse said to Roy, "This black kid, Skeeter, is pretty good, huh?"

"Oh yeah, Bobby Skeeter is the real deal. He's got a perfect game goin'." Roy knew it was bad luck to mention a no-hitter, much less a perfect game, while in progress. But that's exactly what he was hoping for; some bad luck for Sylva and its pitcher, Bobby Skeeter. "They call him the 'Sylva Streak.' He's signed with Carolina to play football next year. That don't keep the baseball scouts away though. Helluva an athlete."

While they were talking, Skeeter struck out the first two batters in the bottom of the seventh inning.

"Well, here comes ole' JC! Let's see if he can make up for that mistake he made earlier," Jesse said. "Big ole' boy, that JC. Say, didn't I hear he signed to play football down at the State University in Raleigh?"

"Yep. Offensive line. He's listed at 6'4" and 265 in the program, but I'm guessin' he might be a bit bigger than that," Roy replied. JC took the first pitch for a strike. "C'mon JC," Roy yelled. "Don't see many coloreds playin' baseball anymore," Roy observed, watching the two African Americans battle each other.

"How big is Ham?" Jesse asked.

"Well, he's grown right smart since last year. I'd say a shade taller than JC, maybe 6'5" and a bit lighter." JC swung at Skeeter's curve ball and missed. Strike two.

"What's he goin' do next year?" Jesse asked.

"Don't nobody know yet. He ain't had no offers, but judgin' from the way he's throwin', he's quite a bit faster than last year. And he's a lefty; everybody loves those southpaws. Him and JC are the only two athletes with any chance of playin' at the next level. Rest of 'em of good enough high school athletes, but that's about it." JC fouled off a changeup.

"C'mon Skeet. Set him down, and let's go home," someone shouted from behind the visitor's dugout.

With one foot in the batter's box, JC went through his batting ritual again: he tugged at his uniform, pulled up his pants (which were always sliding down), and spit tobacco juice over his left shoe. He stepped into box and struck an imposing figure. Nor was it all looks. JC had considerable power and had already set the Wilkes Central record for career home runs with twenty through his junior season. But there were to be no heroics from JC tonight. JC struck out looking on the next pitch. Game over.

Roy, who prided himself on being something of an historian of North Carolina high school baseball said, "I believe that's the first, or maybe the second, time when neither team got a hit!" Roy's memory was confirmed the next day when the *Wilkes-Journal Patriot* reported the only other time in state high school history a game ended with no hits by either team was back in 1957 when Clayton beat Apex 1–0.

Ham would always remember Opening Day, 1976, as the no-hitter he lost. Ham walked off the field, disgusted. "Figures," Ham muttered to himself. "The day I throw a no-hitter; Skeeter throws a perfect game." Ham

16

walked silently toward the locker room to shower and change. He sure would like another shot at Bobby Skeeter and Sylva High. But Ham knew that could only happen if both teams got deep into the playoffs, and nobody expected Wilkes Central to do that.

When Ham came out of the locker room, Nora was waiting. She knew better than to approach him immediately after the game, especially a game like *that*. He leaned down and gave her a kiss. She smiled up at him and said simply, "Sorry, Ham." MacPoochie, the MacPherson dog, was with Nora. Nora brought him to every game since Ham won his first game pitching as a sophomore and MackieP, as they called him, was there. Ham was no more or less superstitious than any other baseball player, but clearly MackieP was a good luck charm. He leaned down and rubbed the German Shepherd's head. MackieP wagged his tail and licked Ham's hand.

As he raised up, Ham felt a hand on his shoulder.

"Helluva game, kid." Ham turned to see Walter Rabb, head coach of the University of North Carolina baseball team. They had met last summer, and Coach Rabb had appeared interested in Ham but did not make him a scholarship offer.

"Thanks Coach. That's a tough one to take."

Ignoring Ham for the moment, Rabb turned to Nora and stuck out his hand. "Hello, ma'am. Walter Rabb, University of North Carolina."

Nora nodded shyly. "I'm Nora."

Rabb turned back to Ham and smiled. "You had what we call a 'quality start.' Hell, it was more than that. You threw a no-hitter!"

Ham shrugged, "Yeah, but we lost the game."

"I know. I know." Rabb had a soothing manner. "I'm over here because we've got a game tomorrow against Appalachian State, and I couldn't pass up the opportunity to watch the marquis Opening Day game in the state of North Carolina."

Ham knew Rabb was trying to convince Skeeter to play baseball once he got to Chapel Hill; it had been in the papers. He glanced over to the other side of the field and saw Skeeter still surrounded by scouts and fans; his teammates and coaches were waiting patiently for him on the bus.

"Just gettin' tired of losin' these Openin' Day games, Coach."

"Say, I think you've grown a bit since I saw you last summer!" Rabb eyed Ham up and down.

"Yes sir. I grew four inches and gained thirty-five pounds. Mama says Grandpa Dubya did the same thing when he was young," Ham said.

Rabb whistled. "That a fact? And I think your fastball has picked up a lot of velocity, too."

"Yes sir. My cousin, Leo Jr., is a highway patrolman. He brung his radar gun over couple of weeks ago and clocked me at ninety-two."

Rabb smiled. "What were you throwing last year, about eighty-five?"

"Yes sir, at least accordin' to Leo Jr.."

Coach Rabb also glanced toward the other dugout.

"Look Ham. We're very interested in you. You've grown. You've gotten bigger. You're throwing harder. We just don't have any scholarship money left; I've committed everything for next year. But things change. Kids get drafted out of high school and pass up their scholarships. So if something opens up, you're going to the top of our list after tonight. You keep pitching like this and you're going see the offers start pouring in. I'll stay in touch."

"Thanks Coach."

Rabb turned away and began sauntering toward Skeeter. Ham liked Coach Rabb. It seemed like he had been the coach at UNC forever. Ham quickly replayed the brief conversation with Rabb in his head. Would he get college offers to play baseball? Why did he have to wait til his senior year to start growing and throwing harder? He knew a scholarship was probably the only way he could go to college. Not that Thom Jeff couldn't afford tuition and fees, which at the state school was less than $500 a year—expensive, but certainly doable. But Thom Jeff couldn't really see the benefit of college for making a living. If Ham had a scholarship—even a partial one—perhaps he (and his mother) could convince his father to shell out the difference.

Ham felt a tug on his sleeve.

He turned to Nora and said, "Let's get out of here." They walked over to the Studebaker. Ham had taken it Moore's garage and had the starter replaced. Ham opened the door for Nora, then folded his large frame into the seat behind the wheel. He coaxed the car to start. He, Nora, and MackieP took off into the chilly evening of the North Carolina Brushy Mountains.

CHAPTER 4

Ham woke up on the morning after Opening Day to the smell and sound of bacon frying. His left arm was throbbing. It was Saturday. Some Saturdays Ham had to go to the sawmill with Thom Jeff, to "catch up" on sawing logs. Most Saturdays, though, his dad was out looking for the next tract of timber for his sawmill. Even after a night of heavy drinking—which was most Friday and Saturday nights—Thom Jeff was up and out of the house. Ham loved those Saturday mornings when Thom Jeff left early. He got to sleep in til 8:00 a.m. Some mornings he would go fishing or hunting with JC. Some mornings he would lie in bed and listen to Casey Kasem's "America's Top Forty" on his transistor radio. Some mornings he would just lie in the bed "simmering," as Grandma Cornelia called it, thinking about the game the night before or plans for the weekend. This morning he simmered, thinking about the game the night before, but then, in a more reflective mood for some reason, he started thinking about his name.

Thomas Hamilton MacPherson. Ham had asked his mother when he was about eight years old where his name came from. She had a simple answer.

"Hammie, your daddy's family is a proud family, so the MacPhersons have a tradition of namin' the first born male after presidents of the United States. Your daddy's name is Thomas Jefferson, and Grandpa Dubya's name is George Washington. And you are Thomas Hamilton."

"What was Grandpa Dubya's daddy's name?" the young Ham asked.

"Nobody knows."

"Grandpa Dubya doesn't know his own daddy's name?"

"Well, I reckon he knows it, but he ain't never told nobody. Dubya's daddy died right after he was born, so I 'spect nobody much remembers him anymore," his mom replied. Then she added, "And if anybody else does know, he's sworn them to secrecy too. There was, I believe, a Benjamin Franklin MacPherson sometime before that."

Ham thought how that answer satisfied him for several years, though the mystery of his great-grandfather remained. Then Ham thought about the seventh grade, when he took U.S. history and was required to memorize the presidents' names up to Teddy Roosevelt. He confronted his mother one morning at breakfast. "Mama, you said we first born MacPhersons was all named after presidents, right?"

"Yes, that's right Hammie."

"Well, I've been studyin' up on the presidents." He then reeled off the names he knew:

"George Washington, John Adams, Thomas Jefferson, James Madison, James Monroe, John Quincy Adams, Andrew Jackson, Martin Van Buren, William Henry Harrison, John Tyler, James K. Polk, Zachary Taylor, Millard Fillmore, Franklin Pierce, James Buchanan, Abraham Lincoln, Andrew Johnson, Ulysses S. Grant, Rutherford B. Hayes, James Garfield, Chester A. Arthur, Grover Cleveland, Benjamin Harrison, Grover Cleveland, and William McKinley."

"Why, Hammie, that's wonderful!!" Nina exclaimed.

"Yeah," Ham said proudly. "We learned them all up to Teddy Roosevelt. Next week we're goin' to learn the rest from Roosevelt to Gerald Ford. We get extra credit if we memorize their dates, too, but that's way too much trouble!"

"Well, I just think that's amazing!" She hesitated. "But Hammie, didn't you say Grover Cleveland's name twice? Will the teacher count off for that?"

"No, Mama, he was president twice at two different times, so we have to list him twice." Then Ham remembered why he recited the list.

"Mama, there's no Thomas Hamilton who was ever president."

"Well, maybe he's in the list you haven't learned yet Hammie."

Ham leaped to his feet and pounded the kitchen table. "No, Mama, I looked ahead. There's no Thomas Hamilton. And Sarah Elizabeth Corn made fun of me. 'Ham, we thought you were named after a president.' 'I was,' I said. 'Well, apparently you warn't!' Then everybody giggled. So I looked ahead and sure 'nough. There's no Thomas Hamilton anywhere. I was embarrassed Mama. Kinda like when I got in the fight on the school bus when I was seven with Dennis the Menace Pinnix because he said Santa warn't real, and I said he was. I was wrong about that, too." Ham took a breath and sighed.

"Hammie, sit down." Ham sat back down in the chair at the kitchen table. His mother sat beside him, and took his hands into hers. "I should have told you this a long time ago, I guess, but it never seemed like the right time. You had an older brother, Hammie. He was born six years before you came along. He only lived a couple of days; he had a lot wrong with him—congenital defects the doctor called them. Anyhow, he lived long enough for us to name him, and we did. Alexander Hamilton."

Ham sat in silent disbelief. He had a brother? He had a brother he never knew and never knew about? He felt numb. He knew his daddy was a little older when he was born. Thirty was ancient to father your first child by mountain standards. And twenty-six for his mother was not much better. He had always thought—in fact, he had always been *told*—that his parents wanted some time together alone before they had children, and that's why they waited seven years to have children. But that was a lie! He had a brother! What else haven't his parents told him, he wondered. Then it came to him.

"Mama, Alexander Hamilton warn't no president either!"

"I know, Hammie. Your daddy was so upset about how sick the baby was, and I wasn't well either. It was a hard delivery. So when they asked for the baby's name, your daddy tried to honor the MacPherson tradition and said the first name that came into his head: 'Alexander Hamilton.' He told me later it was the only name he could remember from U.S. history, and he was sure he had been a president. When we tried to change the name later, it was too late. It was Alexander Hamilton on both the birth and the death certificates."

"Daddy couldn't even get the damned name right," Ham half muttered to himself. "Probably drunk."

"Thomas Hamilton MacPherson! Do not use language like that in my house. And your father was not drunk!" She paused. "And though he warn't a president, Alexander Hamilton was a very important American. He was the first treasurer of the United States or somethin' like that. In charge of the country's money."

Ham tried to let all this sink in. Finally, he spoke again. "So where did the name Thomas Hamilton come from?"

"Well," his mother hesitated. "We wanted to honor the memory of your brother, so we kept the Hamilton part. Neither of us liked Alexander very much. And Thomas is your daddy's name, of course. So we chose Thomas Hamilton. There were a bunch of Thomas Hamiltons in the seventeenth and eighteenth centuries. All of them some kind of Earl in Scotland. I looked it up in the *Encyclopedia Britannica*. And your daddy's family is Scottish, so it seemed right. Plus, the name *sounds* like a president's name. Fooled everybody in North Wilkesboro all these years."

Dazed, Ham rose from the table and wandered back upstairs to his room and crawled into bed. The same bed he was lying in the morning after Opening Day thinking about that day. The day he had his presidential credentials ripped from his self-identity. Five years later and it still stung, and classmates from school still ribbed him about it, especially Sarah Elizabeth Corn, whom he didn't like, and JC MacPherson, whom he did.

"Hammie, breakfast is ready!" His mother called up the stairs.

"Comin' Mama." Ham rolled out of bed and put on his slippers. When I have a son, he thought, I'm gonna name him Ulysses S. He knew Grant was a Yankee general so that would piss off Thom Jeff—an added bonus— but from Miss Turnage's English class he knew Ulysses was a Greek leader in some big war. Plus, he really liked the way the name sounded. Ulysses S. Then Ham paused on the bottom step of the staircase to ponder: Wonder what the S. stands for?

He entered the kitchen, hugged his mother and said, "Smells delicious, Mama!"

CHAPTER 5

Grandpa Dubya's eightieth birthday celebration was that same night—Saturday night—and it began with a surprise. Carl showed up in the hearse to take Dubya and Cornelia to the Hillbilly Hideaway. Carl was not a blood relative, but Dubya refused to ride with Thom Jeff, and neither he nor Cornelia drove after dark anymore. Carl had the same proclivity to drink as Thom Jeff, but unlike Thom, he recognized when he should not be behind the wheel. So Carl recruited Ham to go with them as the designated driver on the way home. Dubya was fine with these arrangements; he liked Carl and enjoyed his offbeat sense of humor.

So Dubya and Cornelia were not surprised when Carl and Ham showed up to drive them. But they were surprised to see Mr. Ed.

"Whatcha drivin' Carl?" Dubya asked tentatively. Cornelia didn't say anything.

"My new hearse!" Carl exclaimed. "Well, it's not new, but it's new to me."

"Happy birthday, Grandpa Dubya," Ham said, trying to change the subject.

Dubya turned to Ham and gave a broad smile. "Thanks Ham."

"Okay, everybody ready to go?" Carl asked.

"Where are we all goin' to sit?" Cornelia asked. Ham hadn't thought of that when he agreed to ride with Carl.

"Well, goin' up, Ham can ride in the back. I'll ride back there comin' home."

"That okay with you Ham?" Cornelia asked.

Before Ham answered, Carl said, "Why sure, Miss Cornelia, Ham has been back there before." He turned and winked at Ham.

"That right, Ham?" Dubya asked.

"Oh, you know Uncle Carl, Grandpa." Ham said as he headed to the back door of Mr. Ed.

When he opened the door, he saw Carl had removed the mattress. He tried to position himself between the grooves that would hold a coffin in place.

"Don't raise up too quickly, Ham, you might hit your head." Cornelia offered.

The ride to Hillbilly Hideaway was nearly an hour, but it felt like ten hours to Ham. He couldn't hear the conversation in the front seat, but he did think he heard Al Green singing "Let's Stay Together" on the tape deck until it was abruptly shut off, probably at Cornelia's request.

By the time they got to the reserved room at the Hillbilly Hideaway, all of Dubya's family was there, at least those still living. Aunt Nora, his oldest daughter, was there with her husband Wilson and their two children. They lived in Chapel Hill, and Aunt Nora was a deacon at Pullen Memorial Baptist Church, one of the first women to hold that position in the state of North Carolina. Thom Jeff and Nina were already there with Diane and Michael Allen, whom Dubya called "Mike Al."

Dubya's youngest daughter, Edith, was there with her step-husband, Bill Lovette, and her three boys. Bill was the younger brother of Fred Lovette, who started Holly Farms Poultry in North Wilkesboro in the 1940s. Thom Jeff said Bill and Edith were "well off." Ham had gone to basketball camp with Edith's boys when he was fourteen. They went to the camp at Campbell College run by Fred McCall and Press Maravich. UCLA Coach John Wooden was there and taught them how to put on their socks so they wouldn't get blisters. But the star of the show was "Pistol Pete" Maravich. By that time, Pistol Pete had finished his storied collegiate career at LSU and was playing professionally for the Atlanta Hawks. Each night after dinner he would give a shooting and ball handling clinic in the Campbell gym, which consisted of him spinning and dribbling two balls every way imaginable and then shooting from way beyond the top of the key swishing jumper after jumper after jumper, all the while talking to the campers about shooting technique. He was amazing. Edith's youngest son, Pat, had been the star of the Taylorsville High School team that year and probably could have played NAIA basketball. But he was called to the ministry and went to Freedom University over in Virginia to study with the faculty that the fundamentalist preacher Gary Farmwell had assembled. Pat, who was a couple of years older than Ham, didn't think much of Ham's church. "Way too liberal, Ham. God will spew that lukewarm church right out of his mouth come Judgment Day." Ham and Pat got along fine so long as they avoided the subject of religion and especially religion as it was practiced at the Second Little Rock Baptist Church.

Conspicuously missing from the celebration were Dubya's other three sons: Harold, Atwell, and Leo. They were missing because they were, well, deceased. Dubya believed it was the "MacPherson Curse" that had been put on him when he was a kid and was somehow transferred like original sin to his male offspring. When Dubya was eighteen—before he met Cornelia and therefore still drinking—he went to the Wilkes County Fair with some buddies. On a dare, he went in to see Lady Godiva, Palm Reader and Fortune Teller. Her reading was rather predictable and vague: Dubya would marry, have kids, lead a mostly normal life. When she finished, Lady Godiva said, "That'll be fifty cents." "I don't have it," Dubya confessed over his shoulder as he ran out of the tent. While still in earshot he heard Lady Godiva shout, "YOU will not live to see fifty, young man!"

Dubya mostly forgot the Curse until the night before his fiftieth birthday, when he told Cornelia about the Curse. "Oh Dubya, don't be superstitious. Nothing's goin' to happen to you." And, of course, nothing did. But the same could not be said for his male children.

The first to die was Atwell, the fourth of Dubya and Cornelia's children (after Nora, Thom Jeff, and Harold). Born in 1932, Atwell joined the Navy at eighteen and was shipped off to Korea. Dubya and Cornelia were sure Atwell would die in the war, but he came home on furlough for Christmas in 1952. Like most of the MacPherson men, Atwell was a heavy drinker, a habit he continued to cultivate in the Navy. He went to a poker game in Asheville on Christmas Eve. The story that came back to Dubya was that Atwell was accused of cheating in the game and a heated argument erupted, which ended with Atwell being shot and killed. No one was ever arrested; Atwell was dead at the age of twenty. Dubya was sure it was because of the Curse. Rumor had it Atwell was holding Aces and Eights, the dead man's hand, at the time of the shooting, but Ham was pretty sure that was just a tale told to embellish the story.

Leo, the next to youngest child, was thirty-four when he died, also the victim of a gunshot wound. He had followed a woman home from a local bar to her trailer park. Turned out the woman was married (or at least living with a man), and the man didn't take kindly to a stranger standing outside his trailer in a drunken stupor yelling for his woman to come outside. The man warned Leo to leave, and when he didn't he threatened to shoot him. And when Leo still didn't leave, "by God, I shot him," the man told the sheriff. Leo died hours later at Wilkes General hospital. Leo left behind a wife and two boys; all three were at Dubya's party. Leo Jr. was a highway patrolman who had clocked Ham's fastball with his radar gun.

The last to die was Harold at the age of forty-two. Harold was two years younger than Thom Jeff; he never married. Harold loved baseball, but he wasn't a very good player. So he umpired all the games in the county—high school in the spring, American Legion in the summer, men's open and church league softball in the fall. In his early twenties, Harold attended the Bill McGowan School for Umpires in Ormond Beach, Florida. The school ran for five weeks, and when Harold returned home Mr. McGowan arranged for Harold to umpire in minor league games across the state of North Carolina. After several years of umpire school and minor league umpiring at a pittance pay, Harold was called up to umpire in the American League in 1970. That year he joined the Major League Umpires Association (MLUA), a union formed to lobby for benefits for umpires. After the one-day strike of the championship playoff on October 3, 1970, the MLUA negotiated a labor contract that set the minimum salary of $11,000—over double what Harold had made during the season and more than he possibly could have hoped to make in North Wilkesboro. He umpired two more seasons. He died of a brain aneurysm on New Year's Eve, 1972. Dubya was convinced Harold was another victim of the Curse. That left only Thom Jeff, who had turned forty-eight that February. Ham thought the deaths of the MacPherson men, with the exception of Harold, were due more to liquor and stupidity than to any kind of cosmic Curse.

The Curse was the last thing on anyone's mind that night at the Hillbilly Hideaway. Along with family members, Cornelia had invited a large number of folk from church, and everyone was in a festive mood. After a dinner of salad, mashed potatoes, green beans, sweet corn, short ribs, and fried chicken—all served family style—the "program" that evening consisted of a few words from Cousin Magnum Fox and Brother Bob Sechrest. Magnum Fox lived in Seattle, Washington, but he made the trip to North Carolina at least once a year, usually at Christmas when he would recite from memory Dr. Seuss's "The Grinch Who Stole Christmas" to all the children's delight ("Every Who down in Whoville loved Christmas a lot / But the Grinch who lived just north of Whoville did not . . . "). He was the family's "genealogist" and would update everyone on his most recent discoveries of the MacPherson family history. Ham was sure that one year Cousin Magnum would announce that the first MacPherson had come to America on the Mayflower.

Tonight, as with every other visit he made to North Carolina, Cousin Magnum gave each child a silver dollar and to each adult he gave a copy of his latest reconstructed MacPherson family tree and a calendar—with the MacPherson crest and clan motto, "Touch Not the Cat Bot a Glove." Ham was not quite sure what the motto meant; something about being prepared he guessed, since he knew from experience how badly a mad cat could scratch. Ham was disappointed that this year he fell into the adult category and got the family tree and calendar and not the silver dollar. Best Ham could figure, Cousin Magnum, who must have been close to Dubya in age, was Dubya's first cousin, son of the sister of Dubya's father. Dubya, of course, remembered neither his father nor his aunt. Ham checked the family tree to see how Magnum had listed Grandpa Dubya's father. It said simply "R. E. MacPherson."

"Cousin Magnum, what does the R. E. stand for?" Ham asked, as he did every other time Magnum Fox distributed a genealogical tree.

Magnum looked at Dubya and winked. "Ask your grandfather, Ham."

Brother Bob gave a short devotional about how wonderful it was to celebrate together a long life well lived. He talked about the parable of the Prodigal Son, not so much about the sin of the Prodigal or even his repentance, but more about the party the father gave the son. And how much God wants to give a party for any and all of us. Then he smiled at Dubya and Cornelia, threw open his arms to those gathered there and whispered, "Don't miss the party!"

A much smaller group gathered at Dubya and Cornelia's house for cake after the dinner. As planned, Ham drove home. Carl could be heard snoring in the back of the hearse, even through the tinted glass. When they pulled in the driveway and up to the front of the house, they could see through the front window that people were already gathering in the dining room. Dubya looked at Cornelia and said, "What's *he* doin' here?" Cornelia looked up to see her younger brother, Roosevelt Brookshire, looking out the front window at them.

"He's my brother, Dubya. I had to invite him. But I promise I had no idea he would come."

Dubya didn't dislike Roosevelt. But he knew that "Rose" and Thom Jeff despised each other. The conflict was mostly over the fact John Jr., Rose's older brother, had refused to let Rose join Dubya and himself in the sawmill business, despite the fact Dubya had made it clear he was happy to have Rose as part of the business. That, of course, meant Rose was cut out of the furniture business deal that later proved so lucrative to John Jr. Rose couldn't be mad at his brother because John Jr. had hired Rose to work in the furniture company. And he couldn't really be mad at Dubya because Dubya hadn't opposed him working with them at the sawmill; furthermore, Dubya had benefitted even less from Brookshire Furniture than Rose had. So for whatever reason, Rose's wrath had landed on Thom Jeff. And being no wilting flower, Thom Jeff had reciprocated the dislike word for word and action for action.

That night it looked like they might make it through the cake and ice cream and go home in peace. Thom Jeff and Rose, both inebriated, had managed to stay on opposite sides of the room. But in the blink of an eye, which is often the case in these kind of squabbles, Thom Jeff and Rose were standing toe to toe yelling at each other at the top of their lungs. Ham had no idea what they were arguing about, and later neither did the two of them. Thom Jeff was poking Rose in the chest with his finger, when all of a sudden Rose produced a pistol and began waving it around the room.

"What the hell are you doin', Rose!?!" Thom Jeff shouted and lunged for the gun. They struggled, and the gun went off and the front window of the dining room exploded. Everybody froze.

An eternity later, a disheveled and disoriented Uncle Carl threw open the front door and surveyed the room, inhaler in hand. He saw the gun still in Rose's hand.

"Godammit, Rose. You shot Mr. Ed!"

"Dear Jesus! Who's Mr. Ed?" asked Edith before she passed out and crumpled to the floor. Aunt Edith always did have a flair for the dramatic.

As he rushed over to relieve Uncle Rose of his weapon Ham had two thoughts. First, the Curse of MacPherson stupidity had been narrowly avoided this time. And second, this probably wasn't the kind of party Brother Bob or God had in mind.

CHAPTER 6

No charges were filed. As far as the MacPhersons were concerned, it was just another family "incident" of which there had been many and no doubt would be many more. Cornelia would arrange to have the front window replaced. Aunt Nora and Wilson spent the night with Dubya and Cornelia and went to church with them the next day. Nora was curious about how the Little Rock Baptist Church—now the *Second* Little Rock Baptist Church—had changed since she was a girl growing up and attending there. From what she had heard it had become one of a handful of progressive Baptist churches in North Carolina, similar to Pullen Memorial, the one she attended in Chapel Hill. It even had women deacons like Pullen! Because of family, church, and business commitments, she hadn't been able to attend services there since Brother Bob had become co-pastor, and that had been nearly ten years. Even on holidays, she and Wilson made it a point to be back at Pullen on a Sunday morning where the two of them had taken turns rotating on and off the deacon group. But curiosity had finally gotten the best of her.

She was not disappointed in the service. There was something there for everyone, and she loved that communion was observed every week. The highlight of the service was Scotty Moore's baptism at the end of the service.

Scotty was a cherished treasure in the community. He had been diagnosed during childhood with a hydrocephalic condition. His skull was enlarged, and shunts failed to reduce the swelling caused by an accumulation of cerebrospinal fluid in the brain. Scotty suffered from other physical and cognitive disabilities associated with hydrocephalus, including seizures and tunnel vision that left him virtually blind. Scotty was now twenty-two years old and had lived longer than any of the doctors thought he would. Most everyone concluded Scotty's longevity correlated exactly with the will and determination of his parents, Cecil and especially Peggy, to keep Scotty alive. Inactivity had caused his weight to balloon, and it was now difficult to move him from bed to wheelchair, but Peggy and Cecil did it every day, bringing him to the garage during the week and making sure he was in church at Second Little Rock Baptist every week.

Scotty sat in his wheelchair at the front of the church, singing to himself under his breath. According to the doctors, Scotty could not see much more than outlines and shadows. Brother Bob spoke:

"Brothers and sisters, a few weeks ago we voted unanimously to accept Scotty Moore as a candidate for baptism."

"Amen," someone said.

"As you know, we generally practice believer's baptism here by immersion, but the church council approved sprinkling as an appropriate mode in this case. I think they didn't want me to drown Scotty in the baptistery!"

"I don't wanna drown, Brother Bob," Scotty said.

"You're not going to Scotty," Brother Bob reassured him. "I'm going to sprinkle the water on you. Scotty, do you accept Jesus Christ as your Lord and Savior?"

"Oh yes, Brother Bob!" Scotty began to sing his second favorite song, "Jesus loves me this I know. For the Bible tells me so." The congregation joined in. "Little ones to him belong. They are weak and he is strong. Yes, Jesus loves me. Yes, Jesus loves me. Yes, Jesus loves me. For the Bible tells me so."

"Scotty, my brother in Christ, I baptize you in the name of the Father, and the Son, and the Holy Spirit." Brother Bob sprinkled Scotty's head with water, which proceeded to run down into his eyes. Scotty wiped his eyes and confessed that "the Holy Spirit done got into my eyes, Brother Bob." Then he began to sing "Jesus Loves Me" again. When he finished, it seemed the Holy Spirit got into everybody's eyes that day.

Ham cried, too, and marveled at what he witnessed. God has a special place in heaven for Scotty, Ham thought, and it meant a lot not just to Scotty's family, but also to the church to be able to participate in publicly welcoming this child of God into the family. Second Little Rock Baptist Church had accepted members from other denominations "upon statement of faith" regardless of their mode of baptism ever since Brother Bob had been pastor. But folk who made a "profession of faith" in the church and "accepted Jesus into their hearts for the first time" were immersed. Ham received believer's baptism by immersion when he was twelve years old. Scotty's baptism was the first time anyone could remember at Second Little Rock when a new convert's baptism was done by sprinkling. But nobody objected to the mode of Scotty's baptism.

Nina had invited Wilson and Aunt Nora to join the MacPherson clan and Brother Bob for Sunday lunch. The family and Brother Bob were about to sit for lunch following the morning services, and Brother Bob excused himself to go to the bathroom. Everyone was horrified when Brother Bob re-entered the room, wet hands raised like a surgeon about to operate— Nina had forgotten to take the sign down!

"I didn't want to die, so I didn't know what to do," Brother Bob said.

Nina looked horrified. "Ham, you didn't take down the sign in the bathroom?"

"I forgot, Mama," Ham said, realizing his mother's warning, "Touch these towels and die!" written on an index card, must still be hanging on the bathroom mirror.

"I'm so sorry Brother Bob. It's hard to keep the house clean for guests when you have four children," she said, cutting a glance over at Thom Jeff, who had not attended services but did manage to put on a clean shirt and pair of trousers in place of his usual faded jeans.

"Don't worry about it, Nina. Everything is fine," Brother Bob said and smiled.

Aunt Nora was looking forward to finding out more about this unusual pastor and how he ended up back in North Wilkesboro, so while they were eating, Aunt Nora began her inquisition.

"So Brother Bob, Mama and Daddy tell me you are from around here? I wonder why I don't remember you. Honey Ham, would you pass those green beans, suga'. They are delicious, Mama." Ham passed the beans, and Aunt Nora dipped a few on her plate, all the while looking intently at Brother Bob.

"Well, I was a few years behind you in school, but I remember you Nora." Nora was hard to forget. Head cheerleader. Winter Waltz Queen. And, even at fifty-two, still a good-looking woman.

"Oh that's right, you were big buddies with the Brookshire twins, right?"

"That's right. Jimmy and J. B., and there was Rick Sutton, too. We all went to UNC together. J. B. is the reason I ended up back here."

"Well, you've all done quite well for yourselves. I believe I remember that you were a Morehead scholar?" Brother Bob nodded. Nora continued. "And now J. B. is a successful lawyer and helps run the Brookshire Furniture company. Jimmy teaches English at the college and is an aspiring author with a growing audience, I hear. Did I hear that Rick Sutton recently became the Sports Commissioner of the Atlantic Coast Conference?"

"You did indeed."

"Chapel Hill is a small place," Aunt Nora smiled. "Did you go to seminary after UNC?"

"Yes, I went to Yale Divinity School."

"That's impressive. And Mama said you got a doctorate there too?"

"Yes, in Christian ethics."

"But the church folk here call you 'Brother Bob' instead of 'Dr. Sechrest'?" Aunt Nora asked.

"Oh I know why that is," Ham volunteered. "In one of his sermons, Brother Bob told the story of a man who used to travel once a year to hunt coons. From a local hunter, he borrowed a dog called 'Preacher' who was the best huntin' dog in the county. One year he returned and asked for Preacher and the owner said that they didn't have a dog by that name anymore. 'Did he die?' the man asked. 'No,' he said, 'he's still here, but you don't want him.' 'Why not?' the man said. 'Well, a city slicker came through the year before and started callin' the dog "Doctor" instead of Preacher, and the dog hadn't been worth a darn ever since.' So we took it from that story that Brother Bob preferred to be called 'brother' rather than 'doctor.'"

"And you took it the right way, Ham!" Bob said and smiled.

Grandma Cornelia picked up the conversation. "Brother Bob studied with a very famous theologian. What was his name Brother Bob?"

"Richard Niebuhr. Yes, he was very influential, though most folk in the churches haven't heard of him."

Cornelia laughed and said. "I remember what Mabel Sturgill asked you when you met with the pulpit committee."

"Were you on the pulpit committee, Grandma?" Ham asked. He didn't know that or had forgotten it.

"Well, yes I was. Anyhow, Mabel said to Brother Bob, 'Who did you study with at Yale?' As if she would have recognized anybody's name. When Brother Bob said 'Richard,' what was it?"

"Niebuhr," Bob supplied.

"Oh right. 'Niebuhr.' Mabel looked at him straight in the eye and asked, 'Is Neighbor one of them theologians what loves God, or one of 'em what don't?' Brother Bob assured her that he was one what loved God!" Everybody laughed.

"And then remember when Sally Perkins asked you if you smoked, Brother Bob?"

"I do, indeed. I admitted that I did, and she asked me how much, and I told her I had cut down to three cigarettes a day," Bob said.

"And then, Sally said, 'Well, every little bit helps, Preacher!" Cornelia recounted. "You know Sally and her husband Steve raise fifty acres of tobacco, don't you, Nora?"

Aunt Nora continued her line of questioning. "So how in the world did you get from New Haven to North Wilkesboro?"

"I took a detour in Raleigh at University Baptist. Actually, they fired me. J. B. heard about it and offered his family's guest house. That was ten years ago. I'm a terrible mooch!"

"So what did you do to get fired?" Aunt Nora asked, rather impetuously.

Cornelia intervened. "Let me tell this story, Brother Bob, from a layman's perspective." Brother Bob nodded, amused.

"Well, Nora, you know that Brother Glenn dropped dead in the pulpit in 1965? That was just after Brother Bob moved back here. J. B. convinced Brother Bob to preach for us while we was searchin' for a preacher. We all loved his preachin' so much that the pulpit committee decided we had the preacher we wanted. So after a couple of months, that's when we met with Brother Bob and told him we wanted him to be our pastor."

"What did he say Grandma?" Ham hadn't heard this story before.

"Well, he was very reluctant. He had a bad experience in Raleigh. Got involved in the Civil Rights Movement, and the monied folk at the church warn't altogether happy about it. They liked havin' a preacher with a fancy degree, but they warn't so happy when he turned activist."

"Can't really blame them, can you?" Thom Jeff interjected.

Cornelia ignored Thom Jeff's remarks.

"Well, we told Brother Bob we didn't have a whole lot Civil Rights stuff goin' on in North Wilkesboro. Then he says, if I agree to be your pastor, I have a couple of conditions. Course that didn't settle too well with Charlie Snow, chairman of the committee. 'What kind of conditions, Brother Bob?' 'Well,' he says, 'first off, I won't take any salary. I just took a teaching job over at the college and don't need any more income than that. So my compensation could be living in the parsonage and having my utilities paid.' Charlie looked around at us and winked and said, 'I reckon we can live with that. What else?' Brother Bob continued, 'I'd like for us to have joint worship services once a month with Second Baptist Church in Wilkesboro.' 'Do you mean on a Sunday evening?' Charlie asked. 'No, I mean on a Sunday morning,' Brother Bob said. 'Where would we meet?' somebody asked. 'There one month and here the next.' 'What would we do about the offerin' on those days?' 'Split it, I reckon. Remember I'm not taking a salary,' Bob said. Mabel asked, 'What if one of those "co—, I mean black folk want to join our church?' Bob said, 'What if they do? That wouldn't be the purpose of the joint services. The purpose would be to get to know each other better. If a black wanted to join the church we'd cross that bridge when we come to it, just like they'd have to do the same if one of our members wanted to join their church.' Somebody said, 'Not sure we're ready to have coloreds join our church, Brother Bob.' So, the committee looked around at each other, but this time we warn't smiling. After a little while, Charlie said. 'We probably ought to take that up at the next business meetin' if it's okay with you.' 'Sure. I expect that'd be the right thing to do,' Bob said and stood up. The meeting was over. Well, what do you know, two weeks later, we met in business session, and voted to call Brother Bob as pastor. He began on the first Sunday in January, 1966." Cornelia paused.

"You have a wonderful memory, Mama," Aunt Nora said. She turned to Brother Bob and said, "When did the two churches merge?"

"Well," Brother Bob began, "that sorta evolved over time. The two congregations enjoyed worshipping together from the beginning. After a year we went to two services a month and after a couple of years, the two congregations simply decided to merge. It just seemed to make sense. Brother Willie and I served as co-pastors, and we took turns in the pulpit and alternated locations."

"Brother Willie was a little too long-winded for my tastes," Grandpa Dubya remarked.

"And Brother Bob was a little too liberal for mine," Thom Jeff chimed in.

Nina shot him a dirty look, but Brother Bob said, "I'm sure you weren't the only one in that category, Thom Jeff!"

"I was a little surprised that the most difficult transitions in the merger came in the area of food, though I guess in hindsight I shouldn't have been.

Blacks and whites weren't accustomed to eating together, so dinner on the grounds was a challenging event in those first couple of years. Coaxing members to mingle with each other and share food was difficult. It helped, Nora, that both whites and blacks were marvelous cooks, like your Mama and sister-in-law." Cornelia and Nina simultaneously blushed and looked down. "So that anxiety soon melted away like butter on Cornelia's hot biscuits.

"We met more resistance when we asked the congregation to share the holy food of communion. From the beginning, Brother Willie and I agreed that the church should observe communion every Sunday. Perhaps it would have been less of a big deal if we had used unleavened chiclets and individual plastic cups for the grape juice, but we used real wine and served communion by intinction."

"Oh that's where you dip the bread into the wine?" Aunt Nora asked. "We do that at Pullen, too."

Bob nodded and continued, "It was a bit messy, and to old timers it was tantamount to drinking after each other, a taboo more than a century in the making and not easy to break."

"It warn't just tant'mount, it was exactly like drinkin' after each other," Thom Jeff interjected. Nina meant to kick him under the table, but hit Ham instead. Ham grunted. Oblivious, Thom Jeff said, "Ham, could you pass the mashed 'taters?"

"But after a few months, only a few diehards refused to come forward for communion."

"Me bein' one of them," Thom Jeff said, spooning a second helping of mashed potatoes on his plate.

"Like Thom Jeff, not everyone, was happy with these changes. That was no surprise. What was surprising was who the majority of these folk were. A large contingent of faculty and staff from Stearns and Marshall College started attending Little Rock when I started preaching. They liked the *idea* of attending an integrated church. Turned out, many of them didn't care for the *practice* that an integrated church entailed. They could tolerate worshipping together once a month, but they really didn't like 'black church music' and they didn't like the fact that when Brother Willie preached, it was often for forty-five minutes and often on themes of racial and social justice that made them more than a little uncomfortable. And if the truth were known, they didn't like sharing food around a table, whether picnic tables or the Lord's Table, with members of Second Baptist Church. Despite their head knowledge about racial equality, their hearts—conditioned by generations of prejudice—were not fully open to those who were not like them. So when the two churches merged into one, many of the educated, middle class white members quietly migrated back to First Baptist Church, Wilkesboro. That left the rednecks, the blue collars, and a few professionals, like the Brookshire twins, who had been in Little Rock Church all their lives to 'do church' with their black counterparts, and also blue collar and some professionals whose roots likewise went several generations deep into Second Baptist Church. And they were bound and committed to make it work."

"A few of us rednecks went the way of the educated white collars," Thom Jeff muttered through a mouth full of mashed potatoes, just loud enough for everyone to hear. Nina kicked again. This time she hit her mark, and Thom Jeff grunted. They exchanged glares.

Bob ignored Thom Jeff's comment. "The next big change had occurred in 1971, when Brother Willie died. At that time, the congregation called Matthew Zimmerman, one of the first African American graduates of Duke Divinity School as co-pastor, and we decided to hold worship services at the Little Rock Church and to convert the Second Baptist building in downtown Wilkesboro into a day care and community center to serve the children and youth of the community. And we decided to incorporate into the Second Little Rock Baptist Church, even though there was no First Little Rock Baptist Church. As one member put it, 'We must decrease in order that Christ might increase!' I liked that sentiment," Brother Bob admitted.

Aunt Nora finally spoke again, "That's a fascinating story. And how is it that a handsome fellow like you is still single, Brother Bob?" She smiled sweetly and batted her eyes at him over her glass of iced tea.

"I was married once."

"Widowed or divorced?" Ham was amazed at Aunt Nora's forthrightness. It was unusual in North Wilkesboro to be so straightforward.

"Divorced."

"Oh dear, what happened?" Aunt Nora pressed.

"Pulpit committee went through this with Brother Bob, and we was satisfied that Brother Bob's divorce was in line with biblical teaching," Cornelia interjected.

"Oh was your wife a pagan or a cheater? I believe those are the two 'biblical exceptions'? Not that it matters really. We have divorced ministers and deacons galore over at Pullen, don't we Wilson?" Wilson grunted.

"Brother Bob warn't involved in no affair or nothin', Nora, if that's what you're gettin' at. Like I said, the pulpit committee went over that with him." Cornelia raised her eyebrows to indicate the interview was over.

"Things just didn't work out, Nora. I prefer not to talk about that. It was a long time ago, and I think it important to honor what's left of the relationship by not dragging it through the mud," Bob said.

"Who's ready for dessert?" Nina asked, rising from the table and filling the awkward silence.

"Your pecan pie, I hope, Nina," Aunt Nora said. "Let me help you." She left the table and joined Nina in the kitchen.

When she was out of the room, Cornelia whispered to Brother Bob. "I'm so sorry about that. Nora has always been headstrong and a little forward."

"That she has, that she has," her husband Wilson said. It was the first and only time he spoke during the meal.

Everybody ate their pecan pie, and Wilson and Aunt Nora got in their Cadillac de Ville and headed to Chapel Hill. Brother Bob got on to his Harley Davidson and headed back to the parsonage. Dubya and Cornelia went back to their house. Ham and Diane washed dishes while Michael Allen dried. Nina put them away, Thom Jeff fell asleep in his easy chair and snored. Ham had learned things about Brother Bob he didn't know even after ten years. And he liked and trusted him more now than ever before.

CHAPTER 7

On his way to school Monday morning, Ham saw Uncle Carl had already left the hearse for repair at Moore's Garage, the same place Ham had left the Studebaker for repairs (turned out to be the starter). He pulled over to the side of the road and walked back to Moore's shop. It was just after 7:00 a.m. so the Moore brothers hadn't arrived. Ham found the bullet hole in the passenger door about two inches below the door handle. It was a small hole matching the .22 pistol Uncle Rose had brandished Saturday night. Ham whistled, got back in his car, and drove to school.

Ham parked in his familiar spot in the student parking lot. It was raining, so he walked into the gym, which was the shortest route to his first period class. Across the gym, he saw the assistant football coach, Trey Groves, about to enter his little cubbyhole of an office. They were the only two in the gym at the moment. Ham yelled across the gym, "Coach Groves." The natural intonation of his voice caused the second word to come out louder than the first. Across the gym, Coach Groves heard only his last name. Irritable and tired from the long fight the night before with his estranged wife, Coach Groves took immediate offense at the apparent infraction.

"Ham, get over here right now!"

"Yes sir." Ham was taken aback by the obvious anger in Coach Groves's voice.

"Dammit Ham, how many times have I told y'all not to call me by my last name? It's disrespectful and I won't tolerate it!"

"But Coach Groves, I did say Coach. You must not have heard me across the gym. I'd never disrespect you like that."

"Bullshit Ham! I know none of you athletes respect me."

"Coach, I played football for you for four years. 'Course I respect you. I never done nothin' like this before. I promise you I said 'Coach.'"

By now Coach Groves had become unhinged. "Nah, you boys think I'm just a washed up teacher and all. Ever since my wife took up with that damned quarterback over at Starmount High, I've been the laughin' stock of the county. I'm gonna teach you a goddamn lesson, Ham, you and everybody else will never forget!"

Coach Groves went behind his desk and pulled out his paddle. The paddle was actually a baseball bat with the barrel end shaved and smoothed to make a flat hard surface. Ham had heard of the baseball paddle—it had a name, but he couldn't remember it—but he had never actually seen it or knew anyone who had ever been on the receiving end of it.

"Pull your pants down and bend over the desk, Ham."

"Sir?"

"I said, 'Pull your pants down and bend over the desk,' dammit."

"But Coach—"

"Just do it."

Ham complied.

"Boxers, too."

Ham pulled his boxers down below his knees and bent over Coach Groves's old school issued oak desk. Ham could not believe what was happening to him.

WHACK. Coach Groves brought the paddle down on Ham's exposed buttocks with violent force. Ham grunted.

WHACK. A second blow harder than the first landed on Ham's backside. For a reason he would never be able to explain, Ham snickered. Maybe it was because of the absurdity of the situation, him standing with his jeans and boxers down around his ankles in Coach Groves's cubbyhole office. Maybe it was to keep from crying. Maybe it was because at that moment he remembered the name of Coach Groves's paddle—Jose, after Chicago Cubs outfielder Jose Cardenal, whose signature was engraved on the unshaven portion of the barrel of the Louisville Slugger bat. Kids used to say, "Jose, can you see Trey?" He even remembered the model number—C271; that bat was known for its large sweet spot.

Ham may not have known why he snickered, but Coach Groves did. "Makin' fun of me again, you big oaf?" Groves shouted. "I'll show you!"

Coach Groves grasped the handle of Jose with both hands and swung at Ham's hams as hard as he could. WHAMMMM!! His feet left the floor as the bat struck Ham's backside with a sickening thud. An instant later and the bat splintered into several pieces. Ham gave out a blood-curdling cry that caused the kids who had gathered for first period gym to come running over. Coach Groves shooed everyone way, saying to mind their own business.

He turned back to Ham, "Pull your pants up, boy, and get to class. AND DON'T EVER CALL ME THAT AGAIN!"

"Yes sir." Ham said weakly, gingerly pulling his shorts and trousers up over his throbbing buttocks. He thought, "I don't think anything's broken or I wouldn't be able to walk." Actually, he was *barely* able to walk, and he certainly could not sit. He stood whenever he could, and when a teacher asked him why he was standing, he just said, "Tryin' to stretch my legs." Or "Got a Charlie horse, Miss Turnage." When forced to sit, he tried to make as little contact with the chair seat as possible. He didn't tell anyone what had happened, not even Nora. He was embarrassed and ashamed. He drove home that day by leaning back against the upright seat without having to put his bottom on the seat.

When he hobbled into the house, his mother immediately wanted to know what happened. He knew he couldn't fool his mother, so he didn't try. Standing on one foot and then the other, he began to sob and through the tears told his mother what had happened. Nina hugged Ham and rubbed his back.

"Let me see where he hit you, Hammie."

"Okay, Mama." Ham pulled down his pants so his mother could see. Nina gasped at the huge, angry whelp that went from one side of Ham's butt to the other. Blood blisters had already formed. And the very center of the whelp was white as if there were no blood there at all.

"Good Lord, Hammie, we've got to get you to the doctor." Nina told Ham to pull up his pants and said simply, "Let's go."

Nina put down the back seats of the station wagon and told Ham to lie down on his stomach if he could. He obeyed, and she drove him to the Wilkes General Emergency Room. When they got out of the car, Ham noticed Nina's eyes were red.

"Have you been cryin', Mama?"

"A little, Hammie. I can't believe somebody would do this to you!" She squeezed his hand.

The doctor ordered x-rays, which came back negative for any broken bones. He gave Ham two large pills and handed Nina the rest of the bottle and an ointment to apply to the wound. Then he said, "He can stay home from school for a day if you like." Then he added, "Your son is very lucky he was not hit higher across his backside; the damage could have included skeletal fractures or nerve tissues."

Relieved, Nina said, "Thank you Doctor. I'm so glad Hammie's gonna be okay." By the time they got home, the painkiller had taken the edge off the throbbing, though the pain was still there.

Ham could see his dad was home. He pushed through the back screen door and headed up to his room. He lay down on his stomach across the bed. He could hear muffled voices as his mother presumably explained where they had been and why there was no dinner on the table. Thom Jeff let out a yell; Ham wondered if it was because of his whoopin' from Coach Groves or because Thom Jeff had no dinner. He heard his mother rustling around in the kitchen; he knew she was putting leftovers out for dinner. He knew his father hated leftovers.

Nina called out, "Diane and Michael Allen! Dinner's ready. Wash up and come to the table." His mother knew he wasn't coming down for dinner.

His mother came in to check on him before she went to bed. "Hammie, are you okay?"

"Yeah, I think so Mama. I didn't call Coach Groves by his last name, Mama. I promise."

"I know you didn't son. Coach Groves has a lot of family problems and what not. Ought not to be workin' at the school in my opinion. He nor nobody else has the right to hit a child like that."

"What's goin' happen, Mama?"

"I don't know, Hammie. We'll figure it out. You just have to concentrate on gettin' better."

"Can you sit for a while, Mama, and maybe sing to me?" Ham felt a little foolish, asking that. His mother hadn't sung to him since he was a small child.

"Sure Hammie." Nina sat and sang Peter, Paul, and Mary songs, "Puff the Magic Dragon," "Leaving on a Jet Plane," and "Stewball." The last words he remembered before falling asleep were

> Old Stewball was a racehorse and I wish he were mine
> He never drank water; he only drank wine.

In the morning when Ham came down for breakfast, his father was sitting at the kitchen table drinking coffee.

"You all right, Ham?"

"Yes sir."

"Well, I'm goin' to school with you today to have a word with Coach Groves."

"You don't have to do that, Daddy." Ham knew when his father "had a word" with someone it never stopped with just a word. "I'druther just let it go."

Thom Jeff ignored that statement. "Can you sit or do you need to ride in the back of the truck?"

Ham took a quick inventory of his current physical condition. "I think I can sit, but probably shouldn't drive."

"Okay, then eat your breakfast and let's go." Ham woofed down a bowl of cereal while standing beside the sink, and kissed his mother, who had been carefully observing the interaction between the two. He gingerly made his way to the Studebaker.

When they got to the school, Thom Jeff and Ham headed straight for the gym. Coach Groves saw them coming, and began walking toward them with his hands raised. "Hold on now, Thom Jeff. Let me explain."

Thom Jeff ignored him and walked straight into Coach Groves's office, turned and glared at Coach Groves. Ham followed his father and stood behind him. Groves sighed and went into the room. There was barely enough room to close the door.

"Ray, nobody hits my boy but me." Ham knew the latter part of that statement was true. He thought about the whippings he had received from his father with a variety of instruments—switches made from Weeping Willow branches, flyswatters, and Thom Jeff's favorite, his leather belt.

"Thom Jeff. Ham disrespected me. He knows the rules and called me by my last name with no 'Coach' or even 'Mr.' in front of it."

"The boy says he said 'Coach' before he said 'Groves,' but you didn't hear it."

"Yeah, he told me that too. But like I told him, if I didn't hear him it was like he didn't say it. Kinda like a tree fallin' in the woods. If nobody hears it, it don't make a sound." Actually, Ham thought, you didn't say that.

"I don't give a rat's ass if he called you Jesus Efin' Christ, Trey! You got no business hittin' my son with a goddamned baseball bat." Thom Jeff was getting wound up now, and he hadn't even been drinking! Ham was impressed, especially since the last person Thom Jeff had argued with had pulled a gun on him.

42

Something on the shelf behind Coach Groves's desk caught Thom Jeff's eyes. It was part of the barrel and handle from the baseball paddle, posed like a kind of trophy. Thom Jeff reached up and pulled the pieces off the shelf. He turned the barrel fragment over in his hand.

"This the thing he hit you with Ham?"

"Yes sir, what's left of it."

"Jose Cardenal? Plays for the Cubs, don't he?"

Coach Groves tensed body slackened a bit. "That's right. Outfielder. The Cubs are my fav—"

"I oughta drag your ass before the school board or file criminal charges, but my wife says no. She's afraid that would come back to hurt Ham in some way. And she feels bad cause you and your missus is goin' through a bad patch. So, against my better judgment, I'm not goin' to go public, but dammit Trey, this better never happen again." Thom Jeff said it with such conviction Ham believed it to be true. Evidently, so did Coach Groves, who was probably equally relieved to learn Ham and his family were not going to pursue disciplinary action with the school board.

"All right, Thom Jeff, I hear you." Then Coach Groves said to Ham, "Ham, I'm sorry things got a little out of hand yesterday. I shouldn't have broke Jose over your butt." Ham thought Coach Groves sounded genuinely remorseful, but he thought it might be more for the loss of Jose than for any undue pain he had caused Ham.

"There are two conditions for me lettin' this go. First, you're gonna get an emergency room bill from us. I expect a certified check within a week of your gettin' it." Groves nodded.

"Second," he turned the bat handle over slowly in his hand, "you ever take a paddle or lay a hand on a single hair of my boy's head or any other student here, I will personally come up here and shove this handle and barrel so far up your ass you'll be readin' Jose's name with the back of your eyeballs."

Coach Groves's eyes widened.

"Let's go, Ham." Thom Jeff said and abruptly left the office. Ham started toward the exit where the Studebaker was parked. But Thom Jeff walked across the gym to where the baseball coach's office was. He found Coach Maynard leaning back in his chair, feet propped on the desk, reading the morning paper and eating a doughnut. Maynard jumped up when he saw Thom Jeff and his star pitcher.

"Mornin' Mr. MacPherson!" Coach Maynard beamed. "Ham." Coach nodded toward Ham. To Coach Maynard's knowledge, Thom Jeff had never been to see Ham pitch during his three years on varsity, but Coach Maynard knew who Thom Jeff was nonetheless.

"How can I help you?"

"Ham won't be playin' tonight, Coach." Ham was the regular Friday night pitcher; on Tuesdays he played first base.

"Why not, Mr. MacPherson?"

"He's injured."

"Why, how did he get injured?" Coach Maynard asked. It had rained yesterday so there was no practice, and Coach hadn't seen Ham at all yesterday.

"Why don't you ask Groves about that?" Thom Jeff turned to walk away. Then over his shoulder said, "He may not be able to pitch on Friday either."

Coach Maynard's mouth dropped open, but before he could say anything, Thom Jeff and Ham were headed out of the gym. Thom Jeff muttered, "That oughta take care of *that*."

Out of the corner of his eye, Ham saw Coach Maynard, who outweighed Coach Groves by 100 pounds, stomping across the gym floor toward Coach Groves's office yelling, "Groves! Groves! What the hell have you done now?"

As they got into the Studebaker to go home, Ham realized he should not have had such unkind thoughts about his father, at least not this time. His father really did care about him, Ham decided, even if he had a hard time showing it.

CHAPTER 8

When Ham showed up late for poker night on the Sunday after the Coach Groves's incident, he discovered his little brother, Michael Allen, had taken his place.

"Ah Ham, I thought you warn't gonna come!" Michael Allen whined.

"Thanks for your concern little brother," Ham retorted. He sat on another chair on a pillow he had brought to sit on. Even though it had been nearly a week, he was still very sore.

Carl asked him right away, "What happened to you, Ham?"

"Oh, it's nothin' Uncle Carl."

"Sonuvabitch Trey Groves broke a baseball bat over his ass," Thom Jeff said, counting out his twenty-dollar entry fee.

"What?" Bill, Mack, and Carl said simultaneously. Dubya and Brother Bob already knew the story. Thom Jeff proceeded to tell the story, ending with his threat to Groves.

Having heard the story several times, Michael Allen was bored with it. "Grandpa, go on with your story!" Michael Allen pleaded.

"What are y'all talkin' 'bout?" Ham asked, anxious also to change the subject.

"Mike Al wants to know how I started the poker group." Dubya replied.

Ham knew that was a good story. "Go on then."

"Well, like I was sayin', I decided to 'semi-retire' 'bout seven years ago. My first project was to turn this ole' tobacco barn into a poker room. Always wanted one." Ham thought Grandpa Dubya was starting to sound like Uncle Carl. "We warn't raisin' as much tobacco anymore and didn't really need the barn. So I made two rooms—the one out there for my landscapin' business," he pointed toward the other room, "and this one for playin' poker."

"I brung a fridge and small freezer for ice cream and what nots. Your Grandma didn't say nothin'. But when I installed the window AC unit over there, she got suspicious. Then when I brung this felt covered table over from the Cherokee Injuns, she come runnin' down here. Says, 'Dubya, are you makin' a poker room?' 'Well, I do believe I am, Cornelia,' I says. 'I give up drinkin' and cigarettes when we married, I just can't give up seven card stud too!' I knew she wouldn't protest too much, 'cause Cornelia likes a good game of cards much as anybody." Dubya winked at Brother Bob. Everybody laughed.

Bill said, "Dubya ante up."

"Oh yeah, sorry," Dubya apologized and threw a blue chip in the pot. "Even bought these chips from the Cherokee chief. He got 'em from the ole' King's Crown Casino in Las Vegas, what closed down six months after it opened in 1964.

"I promised her no alcohol and no cigarettes in the poker room, a promise I've kept all these years, despite resistance on some parts." He looked at Uncle Carl and Thom Jeff. "And no cussin'." He looked at Brother Bob, who informed Dubya after his first profanity-laced outburst that one of the most important lessons he learned in seminary was to distinguish between whom the minister could cuss with and with whom he could not! Of course, no one broke the no swearing rule more than Dubya himself.

"Then it was a matter of choosin' the group. Handpicked ever' one of you. I decided to call it the 'Young Men's Christian Association,' case anybody got suspicious. Had a plaque engraved with that on it and the year it was founded 1969." Everyone knew that because the plaque was nailed to the door of the tobacco barn. "And I put those blinds up in case the sheriff was to drive by." Dubya pointed to the drawn blinds. He had an irrational paranoia about being arrested for illegal gambling. "Once Harold died, I replaced him with Ham here, who has turned into be a mighty fine poker player!"

"When do I get to join the group, Grandpa?" Michael Allen asked.

"We'll see, Mike Al. You're already my number one substitute."

"Your bet, Dubya," Bill reminded Dubya to keep the game moving along. Annoyed, Dubya pulled a folded sheet of legal sized paper from his overall pocket and studied it. He did that about twice a night. Nobody except Dubya and Ham knew what was on the sheet, though there were plenty of guesses. The most common conjecture was that Dubya kept a list of which hands beat which in seven card stud. He continued to study the sheet, holding it so no one could see.

"C'mon and play, Dubya," Carl said, who was also getting anxious, especially since he was holding a full house. What Dubya was looking at was a list of the regular poker players with their tendencies. In a small, neat handwriting, Dubya had written:

YMCA Poker Players

1. *Thom Jeff (known to play for locks; will fold early in the hand if he did not get at least a pair in the first three cards of seven card stud. The drunker he gets, the more conservative his card playing.)*

2. *Carl Robinette (an eternal optimist. rather go for the inside straight or some other poor percentage hand. Wins more times than he should and pisses off other players, especially Thom Jeff playing locks. The drunker Carl gets, the more reckless his card playing.)*

3. *Brother Bob (learned in college; plays by the book.)*

4. *Kenneth "Bill" Fagg Andrews (unpredictable poker player, and therefore dangerous. If it looks like he has a full house, he might have nothing; or, if his face cards show nothing he could be sitting on a full house. Talks all the time, tells bad jokes. Is distracting—maybe on purpose?)*

5. *Mack Smith (sawyer at mill. best player, next to me* [Dubya wrote]. *Plays percentages. wins more often than he lost.)*

6. *Harold—unknown tendencies.* After he died in 1972, Harold's name was scratched off, and *Ham* was added. Beside Ham's name, Dubya wrote simply, *"Promising."*

Once Dubya confided to Ham that he sometimes had to look at the sheet to remember the names of the players around the table. Getting old is a bitch, Ham thought.

"Make up your mind, Dubya," Bill said, "You been studyin' that card the way ole' Crum does down at UNC when he's tryin' to decide what to call on a third down with twenty yards to go. Never works out for him."

Dubya looked up and said, "I fold." Bill and Carl let out a sigh of exasperation.

Feeling stiffness in his buttocks despite the pillow, Ham stood and went over to the snack table and grabbed a moon pie and a Cheerwine from the fridge (he had heard "Yankees" would drive all night from the North-east buy cases of Cheerwine and then drive all the way back home—stupid Yankees!). Then Ham walked over to the Wurlitzer jukebox. Dubya kept the jukebox full of Country and Western records, mostly Patsy Cline and Jim Reeves, his favorite artists. Each player had his favorite tune. Brother Bob loved Patsy Cline's "She's Got You." Mack chose the only R & B song in the Wurlitzer, "Sittin' on the Dock of the Bay," by Otis Redding. Dubya loved "Danny Boy," by Jim Reeves. Carl's favorite was "Crazy" by Patsy Cline. Cornelia and Ham liked anything by Jim Reeves—she because she loved "Gentleman Jim's" rich baritone voice and thought he was handsome, he because Reeves had been a professional baseball player before pursuing his musical career fulltime. Patsy and Gentleman Jim had died in airplane crashes within a year of each other.

Ham pressed K-9, the last slot in the Wurlitzer. The list said it contained "La Bamba" by Ritchie Valens (another victim of a plane crash in 1959 that also claimed the life of Buddy Holly), but nobody ever played the song. Several weeks ago, he had secretly replaced "La Bamba" with another forty-five rpm single. It began to blare over the jukebox:

Young man, there's no need to feel down.
I said, young man, pick yourself off the ground.
I said, young man, 'cause you're in a new town
There's no need to be unhappy.

"What in tarnation is that, Ham?" Dubya asked.

"Listen, Grandpa." Ham pleaded. About that time, the Village People belted out:

It's fun to stay at the Y-M-C-A
It's fun to stay at the Y-M-C-A.

"See they're singin' about the YMCA. I thought it could kinda be our theme song. Maybe play it at the beginnin' and end of each Sunday night."

"I've heard this song," Brother Bob said. "It's new, right?"

"Yep," Ham said. "Just released a couple of months ago."

Bob continued, "I read an article about it in the *New York Times* recently. Seems a couple members of the Village People are gay, and the gay community is adopting the song as their anthem."

"Gay whats?" Dubya said.

"That's what homosexuals call themselves now, Dubya," Carl offered.

"Well, Ham, we can't have no homosexual anthem as our theme song! Take that record out of the Wurlitzer right now!" Dubya commanded, as if somehow the record was defiling the very essence of the jukebox.

"I'm sorry, Grandpa. I had no idea. I just like the song and all." Ham stammered and removed the record from the jukebox.

Brother Bob intervened. "Look, I wasn't making a judgment. Who cares what consenting adults do in the privacy of their bedrooms?"

"It's against the Bible." Thom Jeff spoke for the first time since telling the Coach Groves story.

"What do you care about what's in the Bible, Thom Jeff? You don't go to church!" Carl challenged.

"The Bible supports slavery, but Christians nowadays don't support that, certainly not at the church your family attends, Thom Jeff," Brother Bob said quietly. Mack nodded in agreement. "And we have women deacons at Second Little Rock Baptist Church, and the Bible seems to be against that too. The Bible requires *interpretation*. One day, gays will have the same rights as everybody else, maybe not in our lifetimes, but it *will* happen. One day they will even be allowed to marry legally."

"Well, I just don't think it's right. And you don't need no *inTERpretation* to see the Bible is agin' it!" Thom Jeff said.

"I'll have to agree with you on this one, Thom Jeff," Dubya pronounced, looking over at Brother Bob. "Let's talk about somethin' else." Brother Bob shrugged his shoulders and waved his hands.

"Wait, wait," Bill said. "This reminds me of a story I heard over at Big Mama's house."

Big Mama was a woman in Ashe County that Bill had been having an affair with for years. Nobody knew why. Bill's wife, Jeannette, was pretty and sweet, and Big Mama, at least according to Bill, was, well, big and not very pretty. But she was a willing partner, which was what mattered most to Bill. Bill was on thin ice; he knew Dubya didn't approve of him speaking of Big Mama in the poker room (and he wouldn't have done so if Cornelia had been present). But Bill plowed ahead:

"See, there was this woman named Mary Margaret who lived in South Georgia. She was rich and lived on a plantation. Her and her sister took a trip to New York City and when she got back she invited all her girlfriends to come over for Mint Juleps so she could tell them about her trip. 'Do tell us all about y'all's trip, Mary Margaret.' (Bill mimicked.)

'Oh, darlin', the trip was fantastic! I saw so many wonderful, wonderful things. The Empire State buildin'. Central Park. Park Avenue. The shoppin' was outta this world!' Mary Margaret stopped and looked around, leaned forward, and said real quiet like, 'But I did see some things, I never ever thought I'd see.'

'Oh pray tell, what did you see?'

'Well, did you know in New York City, there are women who kiss other women?'

'Oh my. No, no. What do you call them?'

'They call them, *lesbians*.' (Bill said the last word in his very best Southern accent, which being a native of North Carolina, was pretty good.)

'Oh dear, oh dear! Tell us what else you saw, Mary Margaret?'

'Well, did you know that in New York City, there are men who kiss other men?!'

'Oh dear me, dear me.'

'What do you call *them*, Mary Margaret?'

'They call them, *homo-sexuahls*!'

'Oh my! Oh my! Did you see anythin' else, Mary Margaret?'

'Well, now, yes I did. Yes, I did. Did you know that in New York City, there are men who kiss women in their *private parts*?'

'Oh. My. God. Mary Margaret, what do you call them?'

Mary Margaret laughed and said, 'Shuga', when I caught my breath, I called him, *Precious!*'"

The poker room erupted in laughter.

The conversation drifted to politics. It was an election year, and the North Carolina presidential primary had been held the previous Tuesday, the day of the Coach Groves incident. For that reason, Ham had not been able to participate in the first national vote for which he was eligible. All of the YMCA group were "yellow dog" Democrats. They would all rather vote for a yellow dog than vote for a Republican, though apparently Thom Jeff would also vote for a yellow dog before he voted for a black Democrat running for office. Thom Jeff had voted for George Wallace; everybody else had voted for the Georgia peanut farmer, Jimmy Carter. North Carolina's favorite son, former governor Terry Sanford, had dropped out of the race before the primary season even began.

"I like Carter," Mack said. "Most of the church members down at Second Little Rock Baptist Church like Carter, too. And everybody is purty concerned, since Wallace beat Carter in South Carolina last month."

"I think Wallace will be out of the race soon enough," Brother Bob predicted.

"Wallace is a racist, Thom Jeff. In his 'naugural address as governor, he said, 'Segregation, now segregation tomorrow, segregation forever.' How could you vote for him?" Carl asked.

"No he's not a racist. He's a segregationist—"

"What the hell is the difference?!" Carl demanded.

Thom Jeff ignored him. "And he's a States' rights man. He is also a martyr; I feel sorry for him gettin' shot and confined to that wheel chair and all. Besides, Carter don't have no experience."

"He's been a governor same as Wallace," Brother Bob pointed out. "And he's run a successful business."

"I like his brother, Billy." Bill added. "I heard him say he was patriotic, all red, white, and blue. He has a red neck, white socks, and a Blue Ribbon beer. Even plannin' on makin' a new beer, 'Billy Beer.' Carter got my vote because of his brother!"

Ham was silent, but he was fascinated by politics and soaked up everything everybody said, especially Brother Bob and Uncle Carl. He loved this group of men, even Thom Jeff in this setting. Sitting around the poker table talking about religion, politics, and yes, even sex, reminded him a little of what a church should be, sharing your deepest convictions without fear of rejection. Knowing whatever outlandish thing you said, you could still come back next week. He knew there was more to church than that, loving God, helping the poor, stuff like that. But this was real, too. Ham knew the communion table and the poker table were not the same, and yet they were more alike than anyone who had not experienced the fellowship of the YMCA poker group could possibly know. God was here, too, Ham thought. God was in the middle of this table—not the money of course, but the unseen web of laughter and tears that bound these people together. The poker table was no less holy than the communion table, Ham thought. It was a ludicrous thought, a ludicrous, but true thought. He hummed, "Blessed Be the Tie That Binds."

Grandma Cornelia came down around 11:00 p.m. Michael Allen was sent to bed, and Cornelia took his place for a round of Acey-Deucy. Carl loved to play Acey-Deucy, especially when he was considerably up in his winnings or down in his losses. He had to explain the game every time they played. Dubya could never keep the rules straight:

"Everybody ante-ups a dollar and gets two cards. The first player can bet any part of the pot he wants that the next card will fall between those two cards. So if a player had a king and a three of any suit and drew a seven, he would win whatever part of the pot he bet. An ace and deuce, of course, gives you the best odds of winning. If your card falls outside the two cards you're holdin', then you pay the pot what you had bet. Now here's where it gets real interestin'. If your third card is the same as one of your first two, then you pay the pot double."

"What do you mean?" Dubya asked.

"Well, if'n you had a king and a three and bet five dollars and drew a three, you would pay the pot ten dollars or double what you had bet. Everybody understand?"

Everybody nodded, but no one really understood Acey-Deucey. Pots in Acey-Deucey could grow much larger than the typical pot of eight or nine dollars in a hand of seven card stud. It was during this game that the rule against swearing was most often and most vociferously broken! The game continued until someone "bet the pot" and won. Cornelia loved a good hand of Acey-Deucey and was more successful at it than the rest.

First time around this night, everybody lost, no matter what their cards. Ham had never seen anything like it. The pot was sitting at a little more than fifty dollars, and Grandpa Dubya had a Queen and a deuce. He bet the pot. Ham was the official dealer because Cornelia was playing.

Ham turned over the card. A queen. Dubya swore, "Goddammit it all." He put $106 in the pot. There was now over $150 on the table, a mixture of cash and King's Crown chips. Better hope the sheriff doesn't come in right now, Ham thought. Things were getting out of hand fast. By now, everybody was standing around the poker table. Some were holding on to the backs of their chairs, white knuckled. Others were hopping around as though they had to go to the bathroom. Perhaps some did, but nobody was leaving the table at this moment.

It was Grandma Cornelia's turn. "Do you want a card, Grandma?" Ham asked. Cornelia had a jack and a five.

"Why yes, Ham, I do. Thank you. I bet the pot," Cornelia said quietly.

"You sure you got 'nough money to cover the bet?" Dubya asked.

Cornelia reached into her purse and pulled out a roll of twenty-dollar bills. "Rainy day money, Dubya. And this feels like a rainy day to me." She plopped the money down. It made no sound against the felt covering of the poker table.

"Cornelia, you saw that I had a queen and a deuce and what happened to me."

"Of course, I did Dubya. I got eyes, don't I? But I'm a Brookshire, and the Brookshires have always had a better nose for these things than the MacPhersons." Dubya sat and folded his arms across his overall bib.

Ham turned over a seven. Carl let out a yelp! "Way to go Cornelia!" And he ran over to the Big Mouth Billy animatronic hanging on the wall. He pushed the red button and the fish began to sing Al Green's "Take Me Down to the River!" Everybody clapped; even Thom Jeff smiled.

Dubya muttered under his breath, "goddammit!"

Cornelia gathered up her roll of twenties and cashed in her winnings with Mack—over $150, a new record for the Sunday night crowd. Cornelia stuffed her money into her purse and headed for the door. She put her hand on the door knob leading out to Dubya's office, paused and looked back over her shoulder, and said, "Bill, you and Mack help Dubya clean up tonight."

"Yes ma'am," they responded.

Then, she smiled at Dubya and drawled, "I'll see you back at the house, *Precious*."

She batted her eyes at Dubya, turned on her heels and skipped out of the tobacco barn like a schoolgirl on the last day of school. Everybody's jaw dropped. As soon as they heard the outer door slam shut behind Cornelia, they burst into laughter and began calling Dubya "*Precious*," a nickname that stuck for several weeks in the poker room.

The next Sunday night, Ham was running a little late; the poker game had already begun. He was coming up from behind the barn; he could see the dull light through the drawn shades. Curious about Grandma Cornelia's clairvoyance the week before, he paused under the window on the left hand side of the barn. He could hear muffled voices and laughter, but couldn't distinguish what was being said. He walked over to the opposite window, where the window AC unit was installed. Through a gap between the unit and window frame, he could hear Bill Fagg telling another joke, in response to what Ham knew not, "Do y'all know the difference between a prostitute, a mistress, and a wife? A prostitute says, 'faster, faster'; a mistress says 'slower, slower'; the wife says, 'Beige. I think I'll paint the ceilin' beige.'" Laughter.

Ham walked to the front of the barn. He noticed a piece of masking tape on the front door. It was on the plaque, which now read

~~Young~~ Old Men's Christian Association (PPO)

Founded 1969

When folk asked Dubya why he had changed the name of his poker group (for it was no secret in Wilkes County), he said it was because everybody in the group, except Ham, was over forty. But the members of the ~~Y~~OMCA knew the real reason . . . .

CHAPTER 9

In the immediate days following the "Groves incident," Wilkes Central lost back-to-back-to-back games for the first and only time and began their 1976 season 0-3. Tuesday, the Eagles' pitcher, Ignacio "Nacho" Gonzales, had a sub-par outing and Ashe County beat Wilkes Central, 5-1 to open district play. Coach Maynard comforted Nacho by telling him even major league pitchers don't have their "stuff" every outing. Nacho didn't know if that was true, but it made him feel better, at least a little. As promised by his father, Ham did not play. They lost Friday's non-district game to Mount Airy 2-1. Ham did try to pitch, but his wound was not fully healed, and the hour-long bus trip didn't help. Ham was uncomfortable on the mound, and his large gluteus maximus muscles were stiff and inflexible. Ham found it hard to take his natural stride toward home, and his fastball came in high and with slightly less velocity. Still, Mount Airy was not able catch up to his fastball and had to rely on walks to get base runners. Fortunately, Ham struck out more than he walked in the first three innings. Going to the bottom of the fourth, the game was knotted in a 0-0 tie. As Ham grabbed his glove to go out for the bottom of the fourth, Coach Maynard pulled him back.

"That's enough, Ham. You've given us all you can, and I'm afraid you're gonna hurt yourself more if you keep pitchin."

"I'm okay, Coach." Ham protested.

"You're already at seventy-five pitches Ham, and your motion don't look good. Rely on your teammates."

A relief pitcher headed to the mound. Ham hadn't even noticed him warming up in the bullpen. Ham threw down his glove on the dugout bench and took a seat. Mount Airy proceeded to get four hits in a row off the relief pitcher and put up two runs in the fourth. It proved to be all they needed. JC hit a solo home run in the sixth inning to cut the lead to 2–1, and that is how the game ended.

But the Eagles rolled off six district wins in a row and stood at 6–1 in district play (and 6–3 overall), tied for first with Ashe County. Ham had been brilliant. He hurled three shutouts and averaged sixteen strikeouts per game. His record was 3–1 with one no decision.

Ham had, of course, been keeping up with Sylva High and the accomplishments of one Bobby Skeeter. The Mustangs were 10–0, and, astonishingly, Bobby had pitched every game! He apparently had what baseball insiders called a "rubber arm." Ham had taken to going to the Wilkes County public library every Sunday afternoon before poker night to read the sports section of the Sylva News. There was always an article about Bobby. Last week, Coach Babe Howell had been asked about Skeeter pitching every game and whether that was good for Bobby's arm. "Well," Coach Howell replied, "every player has a position to play, and Bobby's position is pitcher."

Bobby Skeeter wasn't the only pitcher in Western North Carolina to gain notice. The *Wilkes-Journal Patriot* had dubbed Ham the "Wizard of Wilkes County." Home games at Wilkes Central always drew a good crowd even when the team was mediocre. Folk liked coming out to the games, eating hot dogs from the concession stands, swapping stories with neighbors, letting the kids run around in the grassy area outside the fences to the field, and watching a little baseball. But with Wilkes Central's success this season, the crowds began to swell. The stands were full, and the fences down both baselines were lined with lawn chairs. Most of them were coming to see the MacPherson "twins," Ham and JC.

JC had been as impressive at the plate as Ham had on the hill. Since striking out to end the game against Sylva, JC was batting nearly .575. He had twelve home runs. All but two of twenty-six hits had been for extra bases, and his slugging percentage was a phenomenal 1.733.

College scouts began showing up on a regular basis. Assistant and head coaches from most of the colleges in western North Carolina were there every time Ham took the mound, including UNC-Asheville and Western Carolina. Knowing Ham was a practicing Baptist, coaches from most of the Baptist colleges made the trek to the Wilkes Central field: Mars Hill College, Gardner-Webb College, Campbell College (alma mater of

MLB pitcher, Gaylord Perry), as well as the local Baptist college, Stearns and Marshall. Another regular observer was Marvin Crater, new head coach at Wake Forest University, if Wake still counted as a Baptist school; there seemed to be some debate about that. Walter Rabb of UNC-CH, who had seen Ham on Opening Day, had sent several different assistant coaches to see Ham—it seemed they still had no scholarship money to offer.

Out-of-state coaches also began to show up at Ham's games. The most prominent of those was Jim Brock, head coach of Arizona State University. Brock had shown up unannounced at Ham's last start in which Ham had thrown a one-hit shutout and struck out eighteen batters in seven innings. Ham knew about Arizona State from his Sunday afternoon reading in the public library. He knew, for example, that their ace pitcher, Floyd Bannister, had gone 15–4 with an ERA of 1.66 and had led his team to a third-place finish at the College World Series. He and Jerry Maddux had been chosen first team All Americans by *The Sporting News*. He had conveyed all this information to Coach Brock, who was impressed.

"Ham, we don't usually recruit on the East Coast. Most of our players come from California and Texas."

"And South Dakota." Ham added.

Brock laughed and said. "That's right. Floyd Bannister is from Pierre, South Dakota. You remind me a lot of Floyd. Big lefthander with a great fastball and a wicked curve."

"Thanks Coach. I know my change-up needs some work."

"It's hard to want to throw a change-up when you know most of the batters can't catch up to your fastball. Walter Johnson is the first pitcher Old-Timers believe threw 100 mph. 'Course they couldn't know for sure, since there were no radar guns back then."

"Didn't they use a motorcycle to try and measure Johnson's fastball?" Ham asked.

"Say you do know your baseball. That's right. In 1914, Johnson's fastball was measured at 99.7 miles per hour against a speeding motorcycle. But everybody was sure Johnson was well over 100 mph. How accurate can a motorcycle be in measuring a fastball? Anyhow, they say Ty Cobb used to take two strikes from Johnson so he'd throw him an off-speed curve. Cobb used to say 'Johnson's fastball looked and sounded like a hissing watermelon seed. Only way to hit him was to hope he'd throw that wrinkle of a curve.' So throwing off speed to hitters who can't catch up to your fastball is a little disingenuous." Ham had never heard a baseball coach use the word "disingenuous" before; he was impressed.

"Besides," Coach Brock continued, "we'll teach you how to throw a change-up same as we did for Bannister."

"That'd be great, Coach."

"Ham, you've come on the scene out of nowhere. When I heard about you from one of Coach Rabb's assistants who used to play for me, I contacted a couple of 'baseball men' I know in NC to come over and watch you. They raved so much about you, I had to come see for myself. We had an open date this weekend, so I came over. And you did not disappoint, son, you did not disappoint. Why don't you come out for a visit to ASU after your season is done? We'd love to show you our school and facilities. It's one of the best venues for college baseball in the country."

Ham didn't doubt that. "How long does it take to get there, Coach? I'm not sure my folks would let me be gone all that long."

"Oh, we'd fly you out to Phoenix at our expense, Ham. It's what we call an official college visit. Frankly, it's a little late in the year, but we think Floyd Bannister may leave school early for the draft. And it looks like one of our recruits, left-handed pitcher Pat Underwood, out of Kokomo, Indiana, may also go in the draft. So we need a left-handed pitcher to fill that spot. We don't normally do this, but we can offer you a full scholarship."

"Wow! That'd be great. So that'd be a trip in June?"

"Yes, after the draft. But our offer stands even if Floyd returns or Underwood enrolls—we just don't think we'll get 'em both. Besides, you can't have too many strong southpaw pitchers! You'll need to go ahead and apply to ASU for admission. Has anyone talked to you about the draft?"

"No sir." Ham replied, a true statement at the moment.

"Great, Ham! We'll stay in touch, and we look forward to seeing you in Phoenix!" Coach Brock smiled, shook Ham's hand and left.

Ham went to find John "Hoot" Johnson, head coach at Stearns and Marshall, who was mulling around the dugout watching Ham and Brock but trying not to be too conspicuous. He was failing. Coach Hoot had been watching Ham since he was a freshman. At its best, the Stearns and Marshall team was mediocre, comprised mostly of ball players from western North Carolina who were not quite good enough, or smart enough, for ACC baseball, which still had a mandatory minimum SAT score for athletes.

Ham liked to talk with Hoot Johnson because Hoot, unlike most college coaches he had met, liked to talk about things other than baseball.

Not that Ham didn't like to talk baseball; he was a student of the game, as was obvious from his conversation with Coach Brock. He had read every baseball book in the public library and had memorized most every statistic of every player in his rather sizeable baseball card collection. But Hoot was a sort of scholar-coach who liked to talk about literature and novels he had read, a growing interest of Ham's after two years in Miss Turnage's English class. He pointed out to Ham repeatedly that baseball was a tool to use to get an education, and education was the path to a better and more fulfilled life. Since his sophomore year, Hoot had told Ham he would give him a half scholarship to play baseball for Stearns and Marshall. And since his growth spurt over last summer and his improved fastball velocity, Hoot had been telling Ham he could go to a much better school on a much better scholarship. Ham told Hoot about his conversation with Coach Brock.

"That's wonderful, Ham! That's what I've been tellin' you. ASU is one of the best college programs around. They've won several national championships, and I bet they win several more in the next couple of years. They've assembled quite a collection of ball players out there."

"So you think I should visit?" Ham asked.

"Absolutely. Though I'm not sure Nora would be very happy 'bout you goin' to Arizona! Where is she, by the way?"

"Oh, it's her mama's birthday, and her and her family drove over to Asheville to go to dinner."

"Oh. Okay. Anyhow, I'd also let Coach Rabb know; that might help him find that scholarship money he's been lookin' for." Hoot hesitated. "You know, Ham, there's a chance you could be drafted in June, right along with Banister and Underwood."

"What are you talkin' about, Coach?" Ham was genuinely surprised. Coach Johnson had never mentioned that before.

"Well, if Brock is offerin' you a full scholarship and askin' you about the draft, it means he thinks you have the kind of talent the big leagues are lookin' for."

"But I'm in high school. Bannister is a college man." Ham protested.

"That doesn't matter to professional baseball scouts. Look at Underwood; he's in high school like you," Hoot said.

"But I've never even met a professional baseball scout," Ham said.

"Keep pitchin' like you did tonight, and that will change," Hoot responded.

"Actually, son, it's going to change right now." A man who had been standing just behind Ham stepped up.

"Stan Huffman, major league scout." He shook hands with both Ham and Hoot. Hoot excused himself and left the two of them to talk.

Huffman was a "baseball man": someone who had devoted his life to the game. And he was a talker. He explained to Ham that he worked for the Major League Baseball Scouting Bureau. Although independent from Major League Baseball and the Commissioner's Office, the Bureau had been formed in 1974 to cut costs for major league teams looking to scout players for the First-Year Player Draft. Huffman told Ham there were other scouts like him assigned to different regions of the country to scour high school and college baseball players who might, with proper development, have the tools to succeed as a major league player. These field scouts completed standardized evaluation forms that were shared with Directors of Player Personnel at all the major league teams. Ham, in Huffman's opinion, had those tools. The forms were rated on a twenty-eighty point scale; pitchers were rated on velocity, quality and kind of pitches, location, and mound presence, among other things. Any score above forty merited a second look. Ham had scored seventy on Huffman's card.

"You've got a fastball that consistently hits ninety-five to ninety-seven miles per hour on a radar gun, and you've got a wicked curve. Change-up needs work, but that's normal for high school fireballers. And you're left-handed. There's no such thing as a can't miss prospect, but, Ham, you're close!"

Ham was stunned. "Ninety-five to ninety-seven miles per hour? My cousin, Leo Jr., clocked me at ninety-two."

"What was he using? A patrolman's radar?"

Ham nodded.

Hoffman laughed and replied. "Those things are about as accurate as a motorcycle." Huffman reached into his black bag and pulled out his radar gun. "These JUG radar guns are accurate to 1/10 of one mile per hour. They were put on the market in 1974 by Danny Litwhiler; first radar specifically for baseball," Huffman said proudly. "And you were hitting ninety-five to ninety-seven regularly, and even hit ninety-eight in the last inning you pitched. Reached back for something a little special on that one, didn't you?"

Ham knew exactly which pitch Huffman was talking about. He nodded vigorously.

"Did you play professionally?" Ham asked.

"Yeah, kid. Ten years in the minors. I was a catcher. Made it to spring training in 1945 with the Yankees in my fifth year. Was the last one cut. Everybody's bag was piled up ready to go from Florida to New York on last day of spring training. Mine was there, too. Coach Joe McCarthy called me into his office and said, 'Stan, sorry. We're not going to carry you on the roster this spring. Good luck, son.' I had to go back out and pick out my bag from the pile and then watch the drivers load 'em up and drive the team away. Close as I ever got to the Show. But I've helped a lot of other guys get there."

Ham nodded, still in a daze.

"Look, Ham. I'll be back. Major league teams like multiple reports on players, especially high school players. But I tell you, if anybody from Player Development on a major league team shows up here; it's getting serious. That's what happens for the kids they're planning to draft. So good luck, keep throwing hard, and take care of that Moneymaker!" Huffman patted Ham on his left arm and wandered away.

Hoot came out of the shadows, beaming! "Ham, I heard it all. That's great!" Then he got serious. "But I have one piece of advice. If you're not goin' to be drafted in the first round, go to college. Without the signin' bonus money that comes to first round picks, professional baseball in the minor leagues is a losin' proposition. You might end up like that guy or me . . . a *baseball man.*" They both turned to watch Huffman limp away, strugglin' to balance a black duffel bag in one hand and a Super Gulp coke in the other.

That Sunday night in the poker room, Ham told the group about the conversation with Jim Brock and Stan Huffman. Dubya said the only fellow out of his high school class who went to college was a doctor in Arizona—Scottsdale he thought it was. Bill liked that Huffman had referred to Ham's pitching arm as a "moneymaker."

"We'll have to start callin' Ham's left arm, 'Howard Hughes'! He's the biggest moneymaker I know!" Bill pronounced.

Brother Bob said, "I saw where Howard Hughes died on a plane not long ago, April 5, I think it was."

"Well, that settles it!" Bill exclaimed. "Ham's pitchin' arm is the new Howard Hughes!" And it was. Anytime one of the Young Old Men's Christian Association saw Ham (really it was just Bill and Carl), they'd ask, "How's old Howard Hughes doing? Is he tired? Is he sore? Is he makin' you any money yet?!" And they would laugh. Anyone overhearing would look confused, so Ham would have to explain the inside joke. The nickname lasted a lot longer than Dubya's "Precious" did.

CHAPTER 10

Wilkes Central continued on its current winning over the next three games. Both Nacho and Ham dominated the opposition with their pitching, and JC continued his torrid pace in hitting. The Eagles were tied with Starmount High in Boonville for first place. Starmount was their opponent in the last game of the regular season. The winner advanced to the state playoffs, which began the next week. The loser's season was over. For most of the seniors on the losing team, their time playing organized baseball would come to an end. Few went on to play at the collegiate level, and fewer still made it to the professional ranks, even at the minor league level.

It was a home game for the Eagles. Ham was warming up on the mound for Wilkes Central. Jesse and Roy were in their usual spots behind home plate.

"Ham looks good tonight," Jesse observed.

"Yep, he's hummin' it in there," Roy replied. "Sixty feet, six inches between Ham and home plate ain't far when you're throwin' it that fast. Ham knows everything there is to know about that pitcher's mound, too. Gives him a real advantage."

"What do you mean?"

"Ham came in this week for a haircut, and we got to talkin' about the mound and stuff," Roy said.

"Where was I?"

"Your day off, Jesse. Ham said the pitcher's mound was his favorite place in the world. It felt like his natural habitat, and Ham knew all its dimensions, not just the distance to home plate, which everybody knows."

"What dimensions?" The game was about to start. Roy and Jesse stood with the rest of the sizeable crowd for the recorded playing of the National Anthem. They ignored the introduction of the players.

"Well, Ham said the diameter of the mound is eighteen feet; the circumference is fifty-six feet and six inches. The pitcher's rubber is eighteen inches long and placed toward the back end of the circle. He said home plate was sixty feet and six inches away from his mortal enemy, the batter. We had a very philosophical discussion."

"Sounds more geometrical than philosophical. How'd you remember all those dimensions?" Jesse asked.

"Well, I was so impressed that Ham had 'em memorized that I looked 'em up in my baseball almanac and proceeded to commit 'em to memory, too!"

By this time, Ham had retired the side in the first inning on three strikeouts.

"You know, Jesse, Ham is a real student of the game, like me. He talked about comin' to our shop after school to watch the 1968 World Series with us. Do you remember that?"

"Oh yeah. He was just a squirt then. Cardinals against the Tigers. How could I forget that?" Jesse mused.

"Well Ham remembered Bob Gibson and Mickey Lolich squaring off in Game 7. Said he was completely taken with Gibson, even though they lost the Series."

"Well, who wouldn't be? Gibson had quite a season and a Series."

"Yep," Roy replied. "Gibson had an ERA of 1.12 for the year, and he would have won the seventh game if Curt Flood hadn't of misjudged Northrup's fly ball in the seventh inning. Ham said Gibson was the reason they lowered the mound after that. Said that was when he decided he wanted to be a pitcher. He hadn't even turned eleven years old."

"Well, he's made a mighty fine pitcher."

"Mighty fine," Roy agreed. "Best we've ever seen in Wilkes County, I reckon. And we had somethin' to do with it, Jesse!"

Ham was spectacular against Starmount, throwing a one-hitter. Wilkes Central won 3–0. JC hit two home runs, bringing his season total to sixteen. Starmount's only hit was a bunt that died between Ham and JC. Otherwise, it was a stellar evening before a crowd of more than 500 who had gathered to root for the Eagles in their first playoff appearance in more than twenty years.

There were plenty of scouts in the stand. Stan Huffman waved to Ham after the game, held up his evaluation sheet, and gave Ham the thumb's up. But he didn't come over to talk. Coach Rabb was there, too, and he *did* want to talk.

"Spectacular, Ham! Just spectacular," Rabb babbled.

"Thanks, Coach Rabb."

"Listen, we just found out that Bill Paschall is going to declare for the Major League Baseball Draft in June. That frees up a full scholarship, and I want to offer that to you, Ham. With you and the boys we've got coming in and coming back, we think we can win the ACC and make a serious run to the College World Series!"

"Wow, that's fantastic Coach!" said Nora, who was standing beside Ham and squeezed his hand. She really didn't want him going all the way to Arizona to play baseball.

"Think about it, and we'll talk after your season is over. There's no hurry, the offer isn't going anywhere, and I don't want you distracted in the playoffs. Your coach wouldn't be too happy about that! Good luck!" Rabb turned and walked away.

"Ham, I'm so proud of you!" Nora beamed. She reached up and kissed him on the cheek. Nora and Ham had been together every Saturday night since prom. They had kissed and made out, but they hadn't gone parking again since their time together in the back of Mr. Ed. Ham picked Nora up off her feet and swung her around and around. He couldn't remember when he felt this happy. Everything he had worked for in baseball had aimed toward this moment. It felt really good.

"Let's go get a Slurpee and celebrate, Nora!" They headed off to the Studebaker, feet barely touching the ground. Ham didn't even bother to shower or to leave his uniform with the student manager for washing. He knew they didn't play again until next week.

The next morning, Thom Jeff called Ham from the kitchen at 7:00 a.m. Ham remembered he was supposed to work at the sawmill doing "catch-up." The glow from the night before melted away quickly as Ham slipped on jeans, a work shirt, and boots. He dragged a comb through his curly brown mop of hair, brushed his teeth, washed his face, and headed downstairs. He ate a bowl of cereal, and he and Thom Jeff headed to the mill.

Ham didn't really mind the sawmill work; in fact, he enjoyed it. It was how he paid for his Studebaker. He liked being outside, and he loved the smells of the sawmill—freshly cut lumber, saw dust, mulch, even the smell of diesel fuel and the sound of the loaders working the trucks weighed down with logs. But he would never tell his father that.

When they pulled into the sawmill, Ham saw that Mack and Bill were already there. The Saturday routine was always the same. Thom Jeff would load the twelve-foot long pine logs onto the conveyer belt. These logs had been set aside during the month because they were the perfect size for the bull edger, which Ham ran on those Saturdays. The conveyer belt led to the debarker, which Bill ran on Saturdays. De-barking pine logs didn't take long in comparison to some of the hardwood logs like oak that had thick bark. The trick with pine logs was not to let the teeth of the debarker chew too deeply into the log and destroy valuable wood that the mastery of Mack Smith would turn into boards.

Mack was the sawyer and, so far as Ham or anybody else knew, the only black sawyer in western North Carolina. Dubya had hired Mack years ago when Mack was a teenager and when the sawmill was still portable. Dubya and Mack would pull the sawmill with a truck from tract to tract. Two loggers would cut down the trees and cut them into lengths of eight-, ten-, twelve-, fourteen-, and sixteen-foot long logs, depending on the kind of tree. Then somebody with a lift would bring them to Dubya and Mack. Dubya would saw, and Mack would manually turn the logs after each cut with a cant hook. Four other workers were needed: one to run the edger, which took off the rough edges of the first couple of cuts of the log; one to tail the edger and remove the two strips of waste and put the remaining board back on the conveyer; and two to pack the lumber. At some point Dubya asked Mack if he would like to try sawing. He was a natural, and from that point on Dubya would allow no one else to saw. Dubya worked a team of eight or nine like this for years.

When Thom Jeff took over the mill, he investigated the possibility of establishing a permanent site for the sawmill and paying loggers to bring the logs to the mill. He found some property and set up MacPherson Sawmill, Inc. He also modernized the mill by buying a debarker, a saw with a hydraulic log turner, a chipper (to turn the slabs into wood chips for paper), and a bull edger. It was a huge investment and not a small amount of risk. Early on, Thom Jeff had a hard time paying all the bills, and in those early days under Thom Jeff's direction, Nina, who did the payroll every Thursday night, worried if they could pay all the sawmill hands. But the housing boom of the early seventies increased both the demand and cost of single-family housing. And the cost of and demand for building materials also increased. MacPherson Sawmill found itself making money and operating in the black. That didn't mean, of course, the MacPherson's were wealthy, but the stress of living week to week did significantly subside. And maybe Dubya was a little jealous that Thom Jeff's innovations seemed to be working so well.

At any rate, it was hard to keep up with the demand for building materials, especially pine 2 x 4s and 1 x 6s. That's where the bull edger and Ham came in. During the week, Thom Jeff, who now had two mills functioning, devoted one to sawing hardwood (ash, mahogany, fir, maple, walnut, and mostly oak) for furniture making and one mill for lumber for housing (mostly pine). Mack sawed hardwood during the week because that was more challenging, and Randy Motsinger sawed pine, focusing mostly on two-inch boards for building (2 x 4s, 2 x 6s, 2 x 8s, 2 x 10s, and a few 2 x 12s). Logs not big enough to produce two-inch boards were set aside for the bull edger.

A regular edger has two small circular saws, one stationary and one movable. The edger man adjusts the movable saw to take both sides off a rough-cut board, producing a uniformly cut board. A bull edger, on the other hand, has multiple circular saws designed to take something like a 6 x 8 inch cant and produce four (or five) 1 x 6 inch boards. Obviously for that purpose, the bull edger is much faster and more efficient than a regular edger.

Because of this efficiency, Ham actually loved running the bull edger. And he thought it reflected confidence from his father that he could handle the machinery. It was certainly a promotion up from his summer job of feeding the chipper or packing lumber, jobs he had done since he was twelve. The only problem with the bull edger was that occasionally—but frequently enough you always had to be alert—the edger saws would get into a bind and spit one of the boards back toward the edger man, in this case, Ham. Often the board sent flying back was one of the end pieces and had a sharp edge. Always the shooting board came as a surprise. Ham had only been hit once; fortunately for him it was a board with a blunt end. But he had dodged dozens of these shooting boards. Ham had never heard of any accidental fatalities associated with shooting boards from a bull edger, though during one of his Sunday reading sessions in the public library, he did read about a fellow manipulating a bull edger to cause the death of a fellow worker over in Yadkin County. The headline read, "Death by Bull

Edger." Surely there were easier ways to off somebody, Ham thought at the time.

Sure enough that morning the bull edger decided to sling a board back at Ham. He saw it coming but not soon enough. Ham turned his back to the wooden missile, which struck him on the shoulder blade. Fortunately, it struck him on the right shoulder and not the left, and even more fortunately, it was a blunt ended board and not a sharp-edged slab. Still, Ham knew it was going to bruise and ache. Thankfully, he would have until next Friday before he pitched again. Past experience suggested to him it would not affect his swing or playing his position of first base. If he was going to be a baseball player, Ham thought, he probably ought to stay away from a place as dangerous as a sawmill. He certainly didn't want to make a career out of it. Mack came over to check on Ham. Ham said he was fine; Thom Jeff didn't see it, and since it was nearly lunchtime, he didn't see any point in telling him. Ham looked with a certain amount of self-satisfaction at the large stack of pine 1 x 6s that he, Mack, Bill, and Thom Jeff had produced in just under five hours of work.

Thom Jeff raised his hands and let out a whistle. "Let's go home boys. We're not finished; we're just quitting for the day." He said that at the end of every Saturday session at the mill.

Ham and Thom Jeff went home. Ham showered and took a nap. That night, he and Nora saw "Jaws." It had been released in late 1975 but had only made its way to Wilkesboro in April. The movie scared Nora; she said she'd have nightmares for weeks. It scared Ham, too, but he didn't say anything. He was just glad he didn't live at the beach.

The next day after church, Ham again went to the public library to check on Bobby Skeeter. He knew if they kept winning they would meet Sylva in the third week of play-offs during the regional semi-final round. He also knew Sylva would have the home field advantage because they had the better record. But Ham didn't know how well they had been doing. He hadn't been to the library in a couple of weeks. What Bobby Skeeter had achieved so far in the 1976 season was remarkable, unbelievable really. The Sylva High School baseball team was 17–1. Their only loss had come in a non-district game against Richmond County High School in Rockingham down near the South Carolina border. Richmond was a 4-A powerhouse, who had won back-to-back state championships in '74 and '75. And, according to the paper, they had lost 2–1 on a throwing error in the bottom of the seventh. Even more astonishing was the fact Bobby Skeeter had continued to pitch *every* game for Sylva! His record going into the playoffs was the same as the team's, 17–1! If "Jaws" didn't give Ham nightmares, Bobby Skeeter certainly would!

CHAPTER 11

Wilkes Central won their first two rounds of play-off games rather handily. They beat the Owen High School War Horses over in Black Mountain 5–0. Ham threw a two-hit shutout, and JC had another home run and a double. In round two, Ham and the Eagles defeated Trinity High School from Randolph County between High Point and Thomasville. This game was even more lop-sided than the first. Everybody was hitting for Wilkes County, and Ham performed like everyone had come to expect. Another two-hit shutout; Wilkes Central won 7–0.

The Regional Semi-Final game was schedule for May 21 and promised to be a tighter contest. Saint Stephens High in Hickory had won three consecutive state titles at the 2-A level, from 1973–1975, which put them in a tie for most consecutive championships with Raleigh Ligon, Pleasant Garden, Winston-Salem Gray, and Clemmons. Only Gastonia in the 1950s had more titles (six), and no one had matched this hat trick since Raleigh Ligon in 1958–1960. A drop in student enrollment moved them down to 1-A for the 1976 season. They had several returning players from the last couple of years, including their ace pitcher, a big righty, Mike Oakes, who had a minuscule ERA of 0.57 for the season.

Roy and Jesse were in their accustomed seats behind home plate. Since the play-offs began, they had to close the barbershop early in order to get their good seats.

"My God, what a game, Jesse," Roy breathed out, releasing tension. "End of seven innings, and we got a scoreless game."

"Yep," Jesse replied. "Extra innings. Do you think Maynard will keep Ham in the game?"

"Well, hell yes, Jesse! Loser goes home. Who else is he gonna bring in? Nacho? Nice kid, but he ain't the pitcher Ham is, even after seven innings." Roy looked at his book while Ham warmed up for the top of the eighth. "Ham's got nineteen strikeouts. The Oakes kid has eighteen."

"That must be some kinduv record?" Jesses asked.

"Naw, not even if you add 'em together. Back in 1968, an ole' boy named E. V. Spell had thirty-three strike-outs in a fourteen inning game against Garland."

"I don't think there's been but one hit between both teams, has there? JC's double back in the fourth?"

"Jesse, shut your mouth. You wanna jinx Ham?" Roy hissed.

"Oh, sorry. I forgot. So many damned superstitions in baseball!" Jesse said. "All right, here we go. Ham's ready for the top of the eighth!"

As they moved into extra innings, a feeling of déjà vu came over Ham: this feels a lot like the first game of the season against Sylva, he thought. "A no-hitter but we could still lose," Ham muttered to himself as he peered over his glove to get the sign from JC. Distracted, Ham walked the lead-off batter on four pitches. The next batter hit a routine grounder to the shortstop in a hit-and-run play. With no chance to get the runner at second, the shortstop's throw to the first baseman pulled him off the base. The baserunner advanced to third. Now there were runners on first and third with no outs. Ham struck out the next batter on three pitches. With the infield pulled in, the next batter tapped a slow roller to the third baseman who checked the runner on third and threw the batter out at first. As soon as the ball left the third baseman's hand, the runner on the third took off for home. The ball and the runner arrived at the same time. The runner barreled into JC shoulder first and knocked the big man flat on his back. JC didn't move for a moment, then stuck his catcher's mitt straight up into the air. He hadn't dropped the ball.

Jesse and Roy and everybody else jumped to their feet. "He's out! He's out!" "Safe, safe!" Opposing opinions were voiced from both sides of the stands.

"Safe," the umpire shouted as he simultaneously made the safe sign with his hands. "Tie to the runner!"

Coach Maynard came barreling out of the dugout. He threw his cap on home plate. He danced around the umpire. He cursed. "Goddamit! Are you blind? How could you not see that?!" The home plate umpire gestured with his thumb and threw Coach Maynard out of the game. The run still stood. 1–0 St. Stephens.

The fans booed. "Get that bum outta here! You're as blind as a bat, Blue!"

There were still only two outs, and the runner on first had advanced to third. "Play ball!" the umpire commanded, and motioned to Ham to pitch.

The players in the St. Stephens dugout tried to rattle Ham. "Come on deviled Ham, serve up a fat one. Hey cured Ham. Boneless Ham. Throw it in there and let us smoke you, Ham!" Unfazed, Ham struck out the next batter on three pitches.

"Jesus, Roy, I don't know if my heart can take this!" Jesse exclaimed.

"Dang it. Down 1–0 and the Oakes kid still lookin' strong," Roy agreed.

Ham walked off the mound, shoulders slumped. He had completed another no-hit game for the Wilkes Central Eagles. And once again they trailed 1–0 on an unearned run. To further complicate matters, the opposing pitcher, Mike Oakes, had struck out eighteen and given up only one hit. He struck out the first two batters in the bottom of the eighth, also bringing his total to twenty. The next batter, Nacho Gonzalez, who was playing right field this game, settled into the batter's box. Oakes threw a curve ball on the first pitch that bounced very near Nacho. Nacho began hopping and jumping around as though he had been hit. The umpire motioned for him to take his base. As he trotted down the first base line, he winked into the St. Stephens dugout. The coach immediately sprang out of the dugout and headed for the home umpire.

"He winked at me! He winked at me!" the St. Stephens coach protested. He threw his cap on home plate. He danced around the umpire. He cursed. "Goddamit! Are you blind? How could you not see that?" The home plate umpire gestured with his thumb and threw the St. Stephens coach out of the game. He joined Coach Maynard who was standing outside the right field fence observing the game. "Sunavabitch." "Ain't he though?" the coaches said to one another.

Once order had been restored, JC stepped into the batter's box. Nacho took a short lead off first base.

"C'mon, JC. You can do it, big fella!" Jesse shouted.

With one foot in the batter's box, JC went through his batting ritual: he tugged at his uniform, pulled up his pants (which were always sliding down), and spit tobacco juice over his left shoe. He stepped into box and struck an imposing figure. Nor was it all looks. Ham, of course, had seen this before, too.

But this time JC was looking fastball on the first pitch, and Oakes served one up. JC turned on the pitch with all 265+ pounds of him. He sent the ball sailing high and deep toward the left field fence. The left fielder raced to the fence, looked up and watched the ball disappear into the beautiful western North Carolina night. Just like that, Wilkes Central won 2–1.

Pandemonium broke lose as JC MacPherson jumped on home plate as a human exclamation point to their season. People laughed. People wept. People sang. Jesse and Roy jumped up and embraced each other in a bear hug. "We did it! We did it! We did it!" they repeated over and over again.

Ham sat in the dugout for a long time in disbelief. His shock was interrupted when JC came over, swept him off his feet and gave him such a huge hug Ham thought he would suffocate.

"That one's for you, Ham!"

"Thank you, JC!" Ham kissed JC on the cheek. JC looked away, embarrassed.

"I'll see you later tonight, JC! I ain't forgot!"

"All right then, Ham. I'll see you in a bit."

Nora came over and gave both JC and Ham big hugs. "You boys are somethin' else, you MacPherson twins!" They grinned.

JC wandered off to find his parents and sister. He looked back over his shoulder at Ham, pointed to left field and grinned. He passed Nacho on the way to his parents and kissed him on the top of his head, then gave him a high five. Nacho was all grins.

While Ham was hugging Nora, over her shoulder he saw a man walking toward them, smiling. He looked out of place and disjointed. The middle of him looked very formal. He had on a black suit and tie. But on either end he looked very casual. He had on red converse tennis shoes and on top a blue baseball cap with a red bill and a white *A* in italics. Ham recognized it as the insignia of the Atlanta Braves. He walked with a cane in his right hand and had a slight limp. His left arm hung lifelessly by his side. He had a black bag over his left shoulder. It was similar to the one Stan Huffman carried, but Huffman's was canvas. This one was polished black leather.

"Hello, Ham. Ma'am." He nodded to Nora. "My name is Paul Snyder, and I'm with the Atlanta Braves." He leaned the cane against his leg and shook both their hands. "I wonder if there's somewhere we could talk where it's a bit more private?"

"Sure, Mr. Snyder. There's a Dairy Queen across from the high school. Would that be okay?" Ham asked.

"Of course,"

"Is it okay if Nora comes?"

"That's entirely up to you, Ham. Your parents might also be interested in what I have to say."

"That's okay, the booths at the Dairy Queen get pretty crowded with five people. Plus, my dad's not here anyhow."

"That's fine. Whatever you want. I think I met your father a few minutes ago, but perhaps I was mistaken." Snyder remarked.

Ham looked over Mr. Snyder's shoulder, and sure enough, there was his father standing with his mother talking to some other parents. "Well I'll be damned," he said without thinking. Nora elbowed him in the ribs. "Sorry Mr. Snyder," Ham apologized.

"Quite all right. I'll meet you at the Dairy Queen, shall I?"

"Yes sir. See you there in a few minutes." Paul Snyder limped away.

"What's my daddy doin' here?" Ham demanded, as though accusing Nora of having something to do with it.

"I have no idea, Ham. But I think it's wonderful. You need to go over and speak to your mom and dad."

Ham knew that was true, though he dreaded it.

"Hi Mama." He kissed Nina on the cheek. "Thanks for comin' Daddy." He shook his hand.

"Hammie, you were just wonderful! Everybody is so proud of you! JC too!" Nina gushed.

"That was a mighty fine game, son. Congratulations," his father said.

"Thanks. Thanks for coming. I gotta go meet a fellow over at the Dairy Queen. Then I'm goin' out with JC. I'll be home kinda late."

"What fellow, Hammie?" Nina asked as they were walking away. "Don't forget you and JC are supposed to take those kids plinkin' in the morning." Ham didn't turn around but raised his hand over his head and waved in acknowledgment.

When they got to the Dairy Queen, Mr. Snyder was standing at the counter waiting for them. "Would you like something to eat or drink?"

"No thank you," said Nora.

Ham said, "I'd love a chocolate milk shake."

"How about a burger to go with that?"

"Only if you're havin' somethin.'"

Snyder rubbed his midsection. "When you get middle-aged like me, you have to watch what you eat late at night." Snyder was a big man, at least 6'2" and over 200 lbs. But he still looked fit, except for his limp left arm.

"A large chocolate shake and a cheeseburger, please."

"Yes sir. We'll have that right out to you. Go ahead and find a table if you like," the young woman said from behind the cash register. She rang up the order, and Snyder paid. Ham was amazed how quickly he was able to whip a ten-dollar bill out of his wallet with one hand.

They sat at a booth. "First, let me tell you about this so we can get that out of the way." He held up his left hand with his right.

"I had a stroke a year ago. I was only forty, so it came as a big surprise. I couldn't walk for the first month. But slowly, through physical therapy, I've been able to walk with the help of this cane." He pointed to the cane leaning against the back of the booth. "I'm hopeful I'll regain the use of my left arm, but for now it just hangs there. I apologize if it makes you feel uncomfortable." Nora shook her head no.

"No, not at all," Ham lied.

"Ham, I've read Stan Huffman's reports on you very carefully and with a lot of interest. Stan's a good scout, and we take his evaluations very seriously. A month ago he submitted several reports on you to the Major League Scouting Bureau that were among the best he's ever sent. I decided I had to see you for myself. And I have. This is the third game I've seen you pitch. All in the playoffs, all under enormous pressure. And I've liked what I've seen very much!"

"Thank you, sir." Ham's mind raced. He had seen Snyder last week or the week before. At least he remembered seeing a fellow in a suit with a limp and a cane. Not the kind of thing you'd forget on a baseball diamond. "Why didn't you come over before now?" Ham wished he hadn't asked that before the words got out of his mouth.

"Well, until I saw you tonight, I didn't know what I wanted to say. I knew we were interested in you, but I needed to know where you might fit with the Atlanta Braves."

"Yes sir, I understand."

"Ham, the Braves have the third pick of the June draft behind the Astros and the Tigers. All three of us need left-handed pitching. We expect Floyd Bannister to go first in the draft to the Houston Astros. And we expect Pat Underwood to go second to the Tigers."

"The southpaw high schooler from Indiana?"

"That's right. And we plan to draft you with the third pick of the draft. We think you have tremendous potential to be a dominant major league pitcher. Stan clocked you at ninety-five to ninety-seven on your fastball. I had you throwing ninety-seven consistently and topping out at ninety-eight. And you have a devastating curve."

"My change-up needs work," Ham offered.

"We're not worried about the change. That will come in time. I also think you might be a bit bigger than the report says." Snyder reached into his black bag and pulled out a tape measure. "May I?"

"Sure," Ham said, a bit taken back.

"Take off your cleats and hold this at the top of your head. Nora if you could just pull it down to the floor. I'm not ready for that, I fear. That's right. Now put your finger on the spot where the tape hits the floor."

Nora did as requested and held the tape up for Paul Snyder to see. By now everyone in the Dairy Queen was watching intently.

"6'6,'" Snyder said in a self-congratulatory tone. "People are usually under, not over, their advertised height."

"Sorry, I guess I musta grown more this year," Ham said.

"No need to apologize Ham," Snyder said and then laughed. "Still weigh about 230, do you?"

"Yes sir, I think so."

"Don't you have a scale in that black bag, mister?" the man at the next booth asked.

"'Fraid not, friend. I'll have to rely on Ham's honesty for that."

They all sat back down. "Ham, Mr. Ted Turner bought the Atlanta Braves this past January."

"Yes sir, I know. I read about it." Then he added, "I'm a huge Braves' fan. I listen to almost all the games on the radio. Hank Aaron is my all-time favorite player!"

"Most pitchers don't like hitters," Snyder responded.

"I make an exception for 'Hammerin' Hank! I was listenin' on the radio when he broke Babe Ruth's record. April 8, 1974."

"It's not public yet, but this season may be Hank's last. We hope to keep him in the organization somehow. Listen, Ham, it's Mr. Turner's intention to bring a championship to Atlanta. He knows that won't come cheap. He just signed Andy Messersmith last month to a record deal."

"Yes sir. I read about that too."

Snyder leaned in across the table and lowered his voice, so the man in the next booth couldn't hear his next words. "Ham, the Atlanta Braves are prepared to pick you third in the June Major League Baseball Draft. And Mr. Turner is prepared to offer you a signing bonus of $65,000 if you sign."

"What did he say?!" the man in the next booth whispered to his wife. He was straining so far toward Ham's table he nearly fell out of his seat. His wife jabbed him with her elbow.

"Wow!" was all Ham could think to say. Nora squeezed his hand under the table and smiled.

CHAPTER 12

Mr. Paul Snyder promised to stay in touch with Ham, and he left the Dairy Queen. On the way to Nora's house, Ham rehearsed the conversation with her over and over. Sixty-five thousand dollars to play the game he loved! And a salary on top of that, though Hoot Johnson had warned him minor league salaries were very low. But that didn't matter, Ham explained to Nora, he wouldn't be in the minors for long.

When they got to Nora's house, he kissed her and said, "I've got to meet JC."

"I know," Nora said, "but could you swing back by here when you're done? I've got somethin' I need to talk with you about."

"Do you want to talk now?" Ham's curiosity was up.

Nora hesitated for a moment. "No, no. You go on to JC's. He's waitin' on you. It'll wait til you're done with him."

JC was sitting on his front porch when Ham arrived. He skipped down the steps and got into the passenger side of the car, still beaming.

Ham started singing, "Happy birthday to you, Happy birthday to you, Happy birthday, Jaaay Ceeee! Happy birthday to you!"

"My best birthday ever, Ham!"

"I 'spect so! Walk off home run in the bottom of the eighth in the third round of the state play-offs. It don't get any better than that."

"And I'm finally eighteen to boot!" JC added.

"That's right. And it's not over yet!" Ham promised.

Ever since JC's thirteenth birthday, JC and Ham had celebrated by drinking a beer down by the Yadkin River. For 364 days a year (or 365 in Leap Years, as was the case this year), Ham was a teetotaler. Not because of any biblical mandate or for any particular religious reason but because Ham had seen the demonic forces of alcoholism at work in his own family, and he feared he possessed that demon too. He was afraid to "test the spirits," so he just refrained altogether. But when JC, who was an avid beer drinker throughout his teen years, asked his best friend to share a celebratory beer on his birthday, Ham could not refuse. JC's older cousin provided the beer; they always drank Budweiser. Ham didn't know if that was because it was JC's favorite or because it was what his cousin provided. Anyhow, Ham had one beer, and one beer only, each May 21—the date of JC MacPherson's birth. This would be Ham's sixth beer with JC over six birthdays.

"Where's the beer?" Ham asked. "Did Jackie forget?"

"I'm eighteen now, Ham. I can buy my own beer! Let's go to the ABC store."

Ham headed toward the Alcoholic Beverage Control store on 297 Wilkesboro Road. He pulled into the parking spot in front of the store, and JC hopped out.

JC came out with a paper sack under his arm, got in the car, and pulled a Heineken out of the sack.

"What happened to the Buds?" Ham asked.

"This is a special night. You only turn eighteen once, and I've always wanted to try Heineken. Jackie's too much of a cheap ass to buy it for me, so tonight I bought it for myself."

Ham drove down a dirt road to their usual birthday celebration spot. They got out of the car and leaned against the torpedo shaped hood of the Studebaker. The weather was gorgeous. Ham could hear the Yadkin River gently lapping its banks. Here with his best friend. Play-off winners. About to be drafted by the Braves, he thought. It was the perfect night!

JC twisted the top of a Heineken and handed it to Ham. "Drink it slow, Ham. We've got a lot to talk about."

Ham took the green bottle of lager in his hand and took a small sip. "That's a lot better than Budweiser!" JC agreed. Ham told JC all about the conversation with Paul Snyder of the Atlanta Braves.

"That's fantastic, Ham! You'll make a great major league pitcher. I can't believe how much faster you got this year!"

Then they talked about the game that evening, recounting almost every one of Ham's pitches. It is one of the mysteries of the world how some baseball players can remember nearly every play of every game. They lingered on the walk-off home run, Ham describing the scene as he saw it from the dugout.

"You looked like a bigger version of 'Hammerin' Hank, JC! There was no doubt that ball was goin' out of the park as soon as it left your bat. Oakes sure 'nough knowed it was gone, too."

JC liked the comparison to Henry Aaron. "Oh, I heard Sylva won tonight," JC informed Ham. "No surprise there."

"Skeeter pitch?"

"Of course, who else? That gives him what, nineteen wins?"

"Twenty," said Ham, "with at least eleven shut-outs."

"Well, we just gotta go down there and whoop their ass next week," JC said definitively.

"Yep."

JC said, "Oh hey. Almost forgot. I've got somethin' for you, Ham." He reached a hand into each pocket and produced two baseballs, then promptly dropped them on the ground. "Danggit! Turn your head lights on, Ham." Ham did, and JC collected both balls.

"What'cha got there, JC?" Ham asked.

"Balls!" JC exclaimed. "The game ball from tonight for you—it's the last pitch you threw in the game. Coach Maynard had it for you after the game, but you run off with that Snyder fella', so Coach asked me to give it to you."

"What's the other ball?"

"My game winnin' walk off home run!" JC said proudly. "Nacho fetched it for me."

"Which is which?"

"What?"

"Which ball is the home run ball and which is mine?" Ham asked.

"The one in my left pocket was yours and the one in my right pocket was mine."

"And which is that now?" Ham persisted.

"Uh, hell's bells. I don't know Ham." They inspected both balls in the headlights. "Don't this one look like it's been hit hard?" JC said pointing to a scuff mark.

"Maybe, but this one's got a scuff too."

"Crap, I can't tell. You take this one Ham, and I'll keep the other." JC said, thrusting one of the balls toward Ham.

"All right," Ham said.

"Here. Sign it." JC handed Ham a pen.

"Why?"

"All the great ones sign the game ball. It'll be worth a lot of money someday."

Ham signed his name. "Here, you sign yours."

Each one turned the ball in his hand over and over, inspecting the signature and generally thinking about the game that night. There was a long silence between them, not one to make good friends uncomfortable, but the kind of silence that signals a change of topics. Ham was still nursing his bottle of Heineken; JC was on his third.

"I've got something I need to tell you, Ham."

"Well, go on then."

"I'm gay," JC said without warning.

"You're what!"

"I'm gay. I like boys."

"I know what the word means, JC," which was true. Ham had learned it a couple of weeks ago in the poker room. "But that's impossible. You're an athlete. Hell, you're a football player. You're not some flamin' fag—er, homosexual!"

"Not all gays act the same way, Ham, and plenty of them are athletes, even football players."

"Well, I just think you've made a mistake, JC. It's just not possible. How do you know?"

"Because I'm attracted to boys, same as you are attracted to girls."

"Have you been with any boys?" Ham demanded.

"No."

"Then how do you know you're homosexual?"

"I just know Ham. When you think about bein' with a boy, how does that make you feel?"

"I don't think of bein' with boys!"

"Why not?" JC asked.

"Because it's fuckin' disgustin', that's why not!" Ham cried out.

"That's pretty much how I feel about bein' with girls."

"But you went to Winter Waltz with Sallie Mae whatshername."

"We're just friends. Besides I couldn't have gone with a guy!"

Ham was silent for a moment. "Have you told anybody else? Your parents?"

"God no, Daddy would throw me out of the house. The only person I've told is Brother Bob. . . . And now, you."

"Why are you tellin' me this now, JC? On your birthday and after we won the biggest game of our lives? Why ruin all that?"

"I don't want to ruin it, Ham. I think it's important for our friendship."

"Where in the hell did you get that idea?"

"Brother Bob encouraged me to talk to you because you've been my best friend pretty much all my life. And because he thought you'd understand. And because I've liked you for a long time and for us to get past that, we need to talk about it."

"What do you mean 'liked me,' JC?" Ham's tone was now anxious and defensive.

"I mean I have feelin's for you that go deeper than just friendship. I know you don't feel that way about me, and I'm okay with that. But if we are goin' to be friends, you need to know who I really am."

"Shit, JC! I thought I did know who you really are. And now you tell me you have a crush on me? I never knew you had those kind of feelin's toward me. That's sick, JC."

"Maybe it is Ham. I'm not surprised you didn't know. I denied it to myself for years, but I've come to accept that's who I am. I was hopin' you could come to accept me for who and what I am, too. I've never had any intention of actin' on my feelin's—"

"Well, you damn well better not! I'll knock you from here to next week if you ever try to touch me!"

"I want us to keep bein' friends, Ham. I know you'll need some time to get used to this."

"Maybe you just need some time to come to your senses, and change back to the way you was!"

"It's not somethin' I can just change like my shirt or my socks. It's the way God made me."

"I don't believe God made you that way. You're choosin' it, and you just need to choose to go back to your old self, that's all."

"Look, Ham, there ain't much more to say at this point. You're my best friend, and I don't want to lose your friendship. Maybe you could talk to Brother Bob about it."

"Nah, you keep talkin' to Brother Bob. I ain't got no problems to sort out with Brother Bob."

Silence fell, now of the uncomfortable variety.

"Okay, well I guess that's that for now, Ham. I guess you won't be needin' my help with the plinkin' in the mornin'?"

"No, I definitely will not be needin' your help tomorrow." Ham poured out the remainder of his Heineken on the ground. "Let's go."

They got back into the car and drove to JC's house in silence. As he was getting out of the car, JC said, "I know this is a lot to take in and maybe you never will be able to take it all in. For now, I'm just askin' that you not say nothin' to nobody, Ham."

Ham, who had been fuming all the way to JC's house, blew up: "Tell everybody that my best friend is a queer? Don't worry, JC, your secret is safe with me!" JC had just shot to the top of Ham's shit list.

Ham sped away, turning up gravel in the driveway. JC watched sadly as his best friend left him behind. He sighed and walked up the stairs leading to the front door of his house. He thought: this was my worst birthday ever.

Ham made a beeline to Nora's house. She was sitting on his front porch when Ham arrived. She walked slowly down the steps and got into the passenger's side of the car. She was not beaming and neither was Ham.

Sensing his agitation, she asked, "Is everythin' okay, Ham?"

"Yeah, fine," Ham had made the decision not to discuss JC's "situation" with Nora just yet. "What did you want to talk about?"

"Well, I was hopin' to wait til after the baseball season was over, but time's arunning out."

"Well, go on then," Ham said.

"I'm pregnant," Nora said without warning.

"You're what?" Ham said.

"I'm pregnant. I'm going to have a baby—our baby."

"How did this happen?"

"I think you know how it happened, Ham," Nora said.

"But we only did it once."

"Apparently, for some people, that's all it takes," Nora said. "I guess we shoulduv used protection."

"You mean like a condom? But that would make it seem premeditated and a worser sin, wouldn't it?"

Nora understood Ham's logic. The promiscuous girls were on the "pill." They said it was to regulate their periods, but everybody knew it was to keep from getting pregnant. The good girls didn't take any precaution, lest it seem like they were preparing to have sex. Of course, they were the ones who were caught unprepared. Nora now knew what young people who followed the kind of logic Ham outlined were called—parents!

"Have you told anybody else? Your parents?" Ham asked.

"Oh dear me, no. Daddy would kick me out of the house if he knew. Just Brother Bob. And now you," Nora said.

Brother Bob has been a busy fellow, Ham thought. "How far along are you?"

"'Bout three months. I'll be showin' soon." Ham didn't say anything but he thought maybe she had gained a couple of pounds. Not that it was unattractive or anything, but the slightest weight change on Nora was more noticeable than on most people because she was so petite.

"What are we goin' to do?" Ham asked.

"Well, Brother Bob went over the options. I could give the baby up for adoption. Or keep the baby. Or you know, get rid of it—Brother Bob said he'd help me with that if that's what I wanted to do. But it's almost too late now to do that, and Ham, I don't want to get rid of the baby. I don't expect you to marry me. I know we're too young for that, and you've got your baseball career and everythin'. I don't know what to do." She began to cry. Ham put his arm around her shoulder.

"Well, of course we'll get married, Nora. You know that's what I've always wanted to do." That was true. Ham wanted to get married right after high school, and she had wanted to wait, hoping they would both go to the same college—if they went to college—and get married after that. And then start a family. "Besides, you heard Mr. Snyder tonight. I'll get a $65,000 signing bonus. You can stay home with the baby or get Grandma Cornelia and Mama to help with the baby and go to Stearns and Marshall. We'll make it work. I love you."

"I love you too, Ham, but we're so young. Do you think we'll make good parents?"

"I think we'll make great parents," Ham said with a confidence not bound by knowledge or experience.

"You don't want me to put the baby up for adoption?" Nora asked.

"Absolutely not. No child of mine is goin' into a foster home," Ham said definitively. His words reassured Nora even as they unnerved him. He was more hopeful than sure, but he did love Nora. Of that he *was* sure. They talked on for a couple of hours and made tentative plans about a life together with each other and with the new life they had created together. Ham got home about 3:00 a.m.

CHAPTER 13

Ham could barely sleep that night. Thoughts and images swirled through his head. Nora was pregnant! Mr. Snyder telling him the Braves wanted him. Sixty-five thousand dollars! A no-hitter in the play-offs! His best friend was a homosexual! Nora was pregnant! He tossed and turned, and when daylight finally put an end to his nocturnal anxieties, he was grateful. He would put it all out of his mind. Today, May 22, he had promised some boys in the church he would take them plinking.

Nina already had breakfast on the table. Thom Jeff had eaten an hour earlier and gone to survey timber tracts. Ham looked at the clock above the kitchen table, 8:00 a.m. Still plenty of time to meet the boys at 9:00 a.m. Ham told his mom about the conversation with the Braves' Paul Snyder (but not about the ones with JC and Nora). Nina was happy for Ham, but wondered about college. Ham reassured her he'd go to college "later." He finished his breakfast, thanked and kissed his mother, and went back upstairs. He brushed his hair and teeth and proceeded to pack up his arsenal. He picked up his Daisy Red Ryder BB gun, along with his almost new Browning SS (side by side) double barrel, twelve-gauge shotgun. He checked the chambers to make sure they were empty and threw a couple of number six shells into his pocket. In the summer of 1973, Ham had saved a month's salary (at two dollars an hour) from the sawmill to buy the Browning twelve-gauge. It was his pride and joy, good for bird and small game hunting. The shotgun was just for show and tell with the boys; he only planned to fire it twice, to show them how the side by side worked and to see the shells eject.

He and JC were supposed to meet the boys in the parking lot of the church. Plinking was not an official church event. Brother Bob didn't approve of guns, but nearly everyone in Wilkes county owned one (or two). The young boys Ham was meeting all had Daisy Red Ryder BB guns like Ham's. It was a rite of passage for boys of a certain age in the Brushy Mountains, though Ham had noticed that age was getting younger all the time. Ham got his first BB gun when he was ten. It wasn't unusual these days for boys to get BB guns at age six (or even five!) and their first .22 rifle by ten. Part of the unofficial church outing, of course, was to pass on knowledge about shooting and gun safety.

Ham was relieved to see only four boys in the parking lot of Second Baptist Little Rock Church. He wasn't sure he could take more than that in the Studebaker, and since their fight last night he was certain JC wouldn't be there with his truck.

"Mornin' boys. You fellas' ready to do some plinkin'?"

"You bet, Ham." They all chirped in unison.

Ham popped the trunk of the Studebaker and each boy put his Red Ryder in the back next to Ham's two guns.

"That your Brownin' SS, Ham."

"Sure 'nuff."

"That's a twelve-gauge right?"

"Yep."

"She got a kick to her?"

"Oh yeah, it's a pretty mean kick."

"We gonna get to shoot it?"

"Not today. I just want you boys to see what it can do." Ham turned to the waiting parents and said, "We'll be back by noon."

"All right Ham. Y'all be careful. Great game last night! Can't wait to see y'all boys pour it on Sylva next week."

"Appreciate it." Ham replied.

They all rolled into the car, and Ham took off for a spot at the back of Dubya's farm—not far from the poker barn, but far enough off the road no car was in danger of catching a stray BB that missed its mark.

Earlier in the week and in preparation for the day, Ham had set an old fifty-five-gallon oil drum in the middle of a field and placed five tin cans across the drum's diameter. There were no animals or buildings close by. Ham had marked the shooting area with twigs about ten yards from the drum.

That's about all the advanced planning required for plinking. Plinking was a form of target shooting popular in rural areas. It involved shooting found objects, usually tin cans. BB guns were the perfect weapons for plink-ing. In theory, plinking gave young shootists the opportunity to do target practice in a relatively safe environment.

Ham popped the car's trunk, and everybody took out their Red Ry-ders. Ham loaded the twelve-gauge with the two shells and left it broken down as he shut the trunk and walked toward the field with a Red Ryder BB gun in one hand and a Browning double barrel, twelve-gauge shotgun in the other.

They had to cross a barbed wire fence to reach the oil drum, and what happened next has never been exactly clear. Apparently, Ham put the BB gun on the ground, facing away from the boys. The boys did the same thing; Ham planned to hand the Red Ryders back to the boys over the fence when they were safely on the other side. He snapped the shotgun shut and flipped on the safety (or thought he did) and leaned the shotgun against the barbed wire fence. He should have known better, but he was still distracted by the events of the night before, in particular the revelations by Nora and JC.

Ham had pulled up the middle string of barbed wire to allow the boys to pass through the opening. He intended to step on the bottom wire to make the opening larger, but a boy eager to start plinking started to pass through the wire fence before Ham was ready. Ham had heard a twig snap in the woods just beyond the clearing and turned to catch glimpse of a black rabbit scurrying off to safety. "You don't see many black rabbits in these parts. Wonder if that one's meant for good luck or bad luck." That was Ham's last thought before the boy stumbled and his foot caught the bottom wire.

A barb on the wire caught the trigger of the shotgun. Ham heard the blast of the shotgun and felt the birdshot tear through his left arm, which was stretched out to hold up the upper string of wire. Later, Ham would de-scribe the moment in almost "Damascus Road" language. He saw a bright white light, heard (inaudible) voices, and was struck momentarily blind. Though not a "conversion" experience in a religious sense, Ham's life was radically re-oriented in a way St. Paul would have recognized.

Hysteria followed. Ham screamed. The boys screamed. Ham ran one way. The boys ran the other. Ham saw blood pouring down his arm, but strangely he felt no pain. But he was bleeding and bleeding a lot. He looked down at his arm and saw a tangle of tissue, bone, and blood and decided not to look again. He was scared. Really scared. He ran to the tobacco barn be-side Dubya's landscaping business and banged on the door. Nobody there.

Panicked he ran down to the road. He crossed down into a vegetated drainage ditch and sat on the edge of Highway 268, hoping someone would come by. Out of nowhere MackieP, his German Shepherd, ran up the road and sat beside Ham like a sentinel.

"My guardian angel," Ham whispered.

He waited like Jasper Wilson but nobody came. It seemed like three whole days he waited, but it was only a few minutes. Finally, a truck came around the curve and slowed down. It was JC's truck.

Ham couldn't believe his eyes. Before he passed out, he could have sworn he saw JC get out of the driver's side of the truck, and from the passenger's side emerged Bobby Skeeter. They came running toward Ham. That was the last thing he remembered before falling over into the ditch. MacPoochie MacPherson took off down the road.

CHAPTER 14

When Ham came to, he was in the back of JC's dual cab. He was leaning against JC, who had his shirt off. Ham was light-headed and
woozy. He realized JC was propping up Ham's left arm, and he had used his
t-shirt to make a tourniquet on his arm just above his elbow.

"I'm shot, JC."

"I know Ham. You're hurt pretty bad, but we're goin' to get you to the
hospital so they can help you."

"I've done bled all over your truck."

"Don't worry about it, Ham. It'll be all right. Does it hurt?"

"No, it's just kinda numb. I can't feel anythin'. I feel light-headed."

"You need to stay awake, Ham." Ham heard a voice coming from the
front seat.

Ham looked to the driver's side It really was Bobby Skeeter. He was
driving the truck and driving it real fast.

"Hey Bobby Skeeter," Ham said weakly.

"Hang on, Ham, almost there." Bobby turned on his left turn signal.
They were at the entrance for the Emergency Room at Wilkes General
Hospital.

Bobby pulled up to the very front of the double doors and got out.
"Gunshot wound victim!" He shouted. It was before noon, and things were
pretty quiet. It would be different that night in the "Moonshine Capital of
the World."

Two attendants came running out the front door with a gurney. They
opened the back door on the driver's side of the truck cab, and the next
thing Ham knew he was being wheeled down the hall of the Emergency

Room. "We'll take it from here!" one shouted over his shoulder as they sped away.

JC walked into the Emergency Room while Bobby parked the truck. JC looked like a victim himself. No shirt and covered in blood. A nurse came running over to him. "Are you all right, sir?"

"Oh yes, ma'am. This ain't my blood. It's from my friend they took down the hall over there."

"There's a bathroom just there on the left, if you want to clean up a little." She pointed.

"Thank you, ma'am." JC went into the bathroom. He agreed with the nurse; he did look a war victim! He took wet paper towels and began wiping off the blood as best he could. When he came out of the bathroom, he saw Bobby sitting on a plastic chair in the corner. He went over and sat beside him.

"Heard anythin' yet?" JC asked.

"No, but I just got here." They sat in silence. After a few minutes, Nina MacPherson entered the ER waiting area, eyes searching for a familiar face. She saw JC and rushed over to him.

"JC! Where's Hammie?"

"They took him to the back, Miss Nina. He was shot. I don't know what happened. Me and Bobby was just goin' down the road and seen Ham sittin' by the side of the road with MackieP."

"I thought you were going plinkin' too, JC. Warn't you with him?"

"No ma'am. Ham and I got in a disagreement last night, and we thought it best if I stayed away while we cooled off," JC said, feeling guilty.

"Well, I know what happened, mostly," Nina replied. "The boys who went plinkin' with Hammie showed up at Cornelia and Dubya's, all hysterical. Seems Ham set his shotgun against the fence and somebody stepped on the barbed wire, and it tripped the gun's trigger and shot him. But I don't know where it shot him."

"It shot him in the arm, Miss Nina. He was bleedin' a lot. I made a tourniquet with my shirt. It seemed to slow the bleedin' down. I sat with him in the back of the truck, and Bobby drove us here."

"Are you Bobby?" Nina asked.

"Yes, ma'am. Bobby Skeeter."

"Thank you for helpin' my son, Bobby."

"You're welcome ma'am. Just hope he's okay."

"Where's Mr. Thom Jeff, Miss Nina?" JC asked.

"Cornelia took the boys back to the church and went over to stay with Diane and Michael Allen. Dubya went out to try to find Thom Jeff."

A nurse walked over to where they were standing. "Is one of you here with the gunshot victim?"

"I'm his mother," Nina replied.

"Could you come over to the desk and fill out some paperwork so we can get him admitted?"

"Yes, of course. Do you know how he is?"

"No ma'am. He's in the back with the doctor," the nurse replied.

"Which doctor?"

"Dr. Walker," the nurse said.

"Oh good, he's the young one. He's really good," Nina said, mostly to herself. She stood at the admissions desk filling out paperwork. JC and Bobby sat back down.

"Bobby, why don't you take my truck back to my house? I know you got stuff to do. Somebody here will take me home later," JC said.

"I don't mind stayin', JC."

"Naw, it's okay, really. Thanks for your help. Woulduv been a whole lot worse if you warn't there to drive."

"Okay, JC, I'll leave the truck at your house and tell your folks what happened."

"Thanks, Bobby." Bobby Skeeter, the Sylva Streak, walked slowly out of the hospital.

JC sat in the corner watching Miss Nina. She was incredibly calm. He knew he needed to be calm too. Why didn't I go with Ham this morning? I could've kept this from happening, he berated himself.

After a little while, Nora and Brother Bob came through the ER doors. Nina turned and saw them. They ran over to her, and Nina embraced Nora and they both began to cry. Brother Bob put a hand on a shoulder of each.

"Is he okay, Mrs. MacPherson?" Nora pleaded.

"We don't know yet, Nora. The doctor hasn't come out. How did y'all hear?"

"Cornelia called each of us, Nina. Nora and I met each other in the parking lot and walked in together. Do you know what happened?" Brother Bob asked. Nina explained what happened as best as she understood. The paperwork was completed, so the three of them joined JC in the waiting area.

"JC made a tourniquet out of his shirt," Nina said to explain why JC was sitting there shirtless. Brother Bob took off his windbreaker and handed it to JC.

"I don't want to get blood on your jacket, Brother Bob."

"Don't worry about it; it'll clean." JC put on the windbreaker. It was too small, but at least JC didn't have to be self-conscious about being half-naked in the ER. JC and Nina filled in details for Nora and Brother Bob. Still no doctor.

After another half hour or so, Dubya and Thom Jeff walked through the ER double doors and came over to the waiting area.

At the same time, Dr. Walker came out of the revolving interior doors and said, "MacPherson family?"

"Right here. I'm his mother, and this is his father," Nina said pointing to Thom Jeff.

The doctor held out his hand and shook with both of them. "Dr. William Walker. Your son has suffered a wound from a shotgun fired at close range. The shot nicked his brachial artery and he has lost a lot of blood. The tourniquet most likely saved his life." Dr. Walker looked at JC. "Did you do that son?" JC nodded. "Good job," Dr. Walker said.

"We've stopped the bleeding, but there has been significant tissue damage to the left forearm area. It looks like a Type 3 gunshot wound, which means that your son was less than three yards from the blast, basically point blank. I'm guessing a twelve-gauge shotgun using number six shot."

Thom Jeff nodded. "Yeah, that's what he has. Is he goin' to be all right?"

"We are concerned about the extent of the nerve and muscle damage, and we are very concerned about contaminants that may have entered the wound and could cause infection," Dr. Walker replied.

"What do you mean, doctor?" Nina asked.

"With a point blank blast like this one, in addition to pellets, wadding from the gun shell, gunpowder, and casing debris can enter the body, leaving the person vulnerable to infection and wet gangrene. We started him on penicillin, but he had a violent reaction, so we had to switch over to another antibiotic, which isn't quite as strong."

Nina said, "I'm allergic to penicillin. Is that hereditary?"

"It can be," Dr. Walker replied. "But the science is inconclusive. What I really need to tell you is that there's a good chance we will have to amputate your son's arm to save his life."

"You can't do that, Doc! He's a baseball pitcher, and a damned good one! Gonna sign with the Braves!" Thom Jeff cried out and stepped forward.

Nina stepped between Thom Jeff and Dr. Walker. She looked the doctor straight into his eyes. "You do whatever it takes to save Hammie's life, Dr. Walker. Do you hear? Whatever it takes!"

"Yes, Mrs. MacPherson. Thank you. I've got to get back into your son. I'll come back out when I have something to report." Dr. Walker went back through the revolving doors marked, "Hospital Staff Only."

Nina edged Thom Jeff away from the others and spoke in a stern but hushed tone so the others could not hear. "How dare you, Thom Jeff?! You come to one baseball game in Hammie's life, and all of a sudden you're the expert on his pitchin' and whether he should lose his arm to save his life?"

"But the Braves' fellow says he can be a major league pitcher. I had no idea!"

"He can't pitch if he's dead, fool!" Nina snapped.

Thom Jeff backed up a step. "You're right, Nina. I'm sorry. I just din't know what to say. I know baseball is real important to Ham, is all."

"Hammie is eighteen years old. He doesn't know what things really matter to him yet or what things will. We've just gotta pray that he survives." Nina turned pleadingly to the group. "Brother Bob, would you lead us in prayer for Hammie?"

"Of course," Brother Bob said. The six of them stood in a circle and held hands. Brother Bob prayed for Ham's safety. He prayed for wisdom for the doctors and nurses attending Ham. He prayed that even at this moment Ham could feel he was bathed in the love of his family and that he could feel God's comforting presence with him in the operating room. He prayed for God's grace and mercy. He prayed for a sense of calm for the family. He prayed for a long time. Then he said, "Amen." And everybody else said "Amen," squeezed the hands they were holding, and wiped tears from their eyes.

They sat in the plastic chairs in the Emergency Room of Wilkes General, and they waited. And they waited several hours.

Finally, Dr. Walker came through the ER revolving doors. He looked tired. He came over and smiled. "Things went very well and the prognosis looks very good for your son."

"He's going to be okay?" Nora gasped.

"We want to watch him closely for any reactions to the medication he's on, but all of his vital signs are stable. He's resting now. You'll be able to see him when he gets out of recovery; it will be a couple of hours."

"Recovery? What about his arm, Doc?" Thom Jeff asked.

"We had to amputate the left arm just above the elbow. I'm sorry."

CHAPTER 15

D r. Walker invited the family into a side conference room to discuss Ham's post-operative protocols. Dubya left to call Cornelia. The rest crowded around the small table.

"As I told you, we were concerned about potential infection, particularly gangrene. The tissue around the wound was severely damaged and beginning to present signs of infection. We felt the best course of action to save Ham's life was to amputate. The amputation was about halfway between the shoulder and elbow, several inches above the entry wound to minimize the risk of infection. Ham will be in the hospital anywhere from ten to fourteen days—longer if needed—depending on how quickly he responds to treatment. The wound is bandaged now to prevent infection, and the staff will change it several times a day. The nurses will show him and you how to keep the arm clean after you go home. He will wear a protective covering over the arm, probably for the rest of his life. It looks like an oversized sock.

"He did not feel much pain in the immediate aftermath of the accident, but when he comes out from under the general anesthesia, he will have a great deal of pain, which we will manage through medication. Most likely he will also have phantom pain—where he feels discomfort in the part of the arm that is not there any longer. We don't fully understand that phenomenon, but it's associated with trauma to the remaining nerve endings in the area, which continue to send signals of distress to the brain. As soon as he is able, we will begin physical and occupational therapy. After he is discharged, we'll find a place for him to continue his PT, either here or in another facility. Is he right or left-handed?"

"Left-handed," Nina said.

"Then he will have to learn how to do most things all over again. Brushing his teeth, combing his hair, using a fork. He will need to learn how to write right-handed. He will be able to perform most of his daily routine unassisted, but there will be some things he'll need help with, especially at the beginning. We will remove the sutures in two to three weeks. In six to eight weeks we will fit him for a prosthesis. He will have a choice between a hand or a hook.

"One of his biggest challenges will be psychological. His body image will change. He will go through a series of emotions, including, perhaps, depression. We have chaplains and social workers who can help. It is important that he have someone—a psychologist maybe—to talk through these issues and good emotional support at home."

"He has a wonderful church family and a great pastor," Nina said and nodded toward Brother Bob.

"Good. There will be things that come up I have not mentioned. Feel free to contact me. Do you have any questions?"

"When can we see him, Dr. Walker?" Nina asked.

"It'll take a couple of hours for him to come out from under the general anesthesia. Then you can go in for a few minutes. But just immediate family for now."

"Thank you, doctor."

Dr. Walker got up to leave the room. "Could I have a word with you, Dr. Walker?" Thom Jeff asked.

"Certainly." They moved into the hall.

Dubya, who had been listening from the hall, came into the conference room. "I talked to Cornelia. Everything's okay with Diane and Mike Al."

Nina looked at JC and Nora. "Why don't you two go on home? There's nothing we can do now, and they won't let you in yet to see him. I'll call if we find out anything more."

"Thank you, Mrs. MacPherson. C'mon JC. I'll give you a ride home," Nora said. The two of them left.

"Brother Bob, I know you need to get ready for church services tomorrow, so you go on home if you need to. Thanks for bein' here."

"Of course, Nina. I'll stay for a little longer if that's okay."

"Thank you. I'd like that."

The three of them headed back into the waiting area. They found Thom Jeff there.

"Everythin' all right with the doctor?" Nina asked.

"Yeah, I just had another question about Ham's arm," Thom Jeff said.

"All right then." They sat and waited some more.

Outside, JC squeezed into the passenger side of Nora's Volkswagen bug. JC and Nora looked at each other.

"This is my fault, Nora," JC said.

"Oh, I don't think so, JC. I'm pretty sure it's my fault."

"Ham and I had a big fight last night when we were celebrating my birthday," JC began.

"What happened?"

JC held Nora's gaze for a long moment. "I told him I was gay."

"Oh!" Nora said. "I didn't know."

"Nobody does, except Ham, Brother Bob, and now you." JC hesitated. "He didn't take it very well."

"Well, it's a lot to take in," Nora admitted. She reached out and touched JC's hand. "But Ham will come around. You two have been best friends for most of your life."

JC squeezed Nora's hand. "He didn't want me at the plinkin' this morning. If I had been there, this wouldn't'tuv happened."

"You don't know that, JC. Maybe it would've been worse. Maybe both of you would have been shot or one of you hurt worse. Besides, I think I'm more responsible for Ham's injury than you."

"Why? What happened?"

"I asked Ham to come back over to my house after he celebrated your birthday. He did—and he didn't tell me anythin' about his talk with you—I told him I had somethin' to tell him. I told him I am pregnant."

"What?" JC's eyes widened.

"You can't tell anybody JC. 'Course, I'll start showin' pretty soon, already am if you look close enough. Then everybody will know. I want to keep the baby. Ham does too, or at least he did before this happened."

"Of course, he wants to keep the baby, Nora! He loves you!" JC reached over in the tiny VW and put his hand on Nora's shoulder.

"I am worried about how we will make it financially. Last night, there was goin' to be signing bonus money to help us get settled and on our feet. Today there's nothin'. I don't know what Ham will want to do. *I* don't know what to do." A tear ran down her cheek.

"Have you talked to anybody else about what to do?"

"I talked to Brother Bob and then Ham. I think my mom will be okay; she will be upset at first, but she's gonna be supportive; least I hope she will be happy about her first grandbaby. I don't know when I'll tell my father, or how."

They sat in silence, each taking in what the other had said. Neither knew what to say to the other. Nora started the Volkswagen. "I guess I should get you home. You're a mess, JC!"

"We're gonna figure all this out, Nora. And Ham is gonna be okay. We're all gonna be okay. Don't you worry none, okay?"

"I hope you're right, JC." Nora pulled out of the ER parking lot.

After a couple more hours in the ER waiting room, a nurse came through the swinging doors. "MacPherson family?"

"Over here." Nina was beginning to get a bit impatient. Of course, they were the MacPherson family. They were the only ones in the waiting room. The Saturday night shift of car wrecks, home accidents, and domestic disputes had not yet begun to pour into Wilkes General ER.

"Your son's awake. You can see him for a minute if you'd like. Immediate family only." The nurse looked at Thom Jeff and Brother Bob. "This is our son's minister," Nina explained.

"All right, then. You can go on back."

Nina, Thom Jeff, and Brother Bob followed the nurse through the swinging doors. It felt to Nina as though she were entering some forbidden zone. The nurse paused as the second door on the left, gestured, and said, "He's in here."

Nina was not quite prepared for the sight that met her eyes. Two nurses were busy attending to Ham and the machines surrounding him. The machines were beeping, humming, and buzzing. There was an IV drip running into one arm and a catheter running out from under the sheet. Nora saw Ham's arm, or what was left of it, before she saw Ham's face, which was hidden behind the back of one of the nurses. Ham's left arm was covered with bandages and a drainage tube was running out to a bag attached to the side of the bed. It looked very similar to the set-up of the catheter. They waited until the nurses were finished and stepped away. Ham was clearly still under the effects of the anesthesia, but he saw his parents and Brother Bob. He raised his right hand and the IV tube shifted and a buzzer went off. The nurse came over to adjust the tube. The buzzing stopped.

"Mama, they cut off my arm!"

CHAPTER 16

Nina rushed over to Ham and hugged him the best she could through the tubes and wires and machines. He was wide-eyed and frightened and looked very much like the little boy she comforted in the middle of the night after a particularly bad nightmare. This was the worst nightmare of Ham's life and not one he could wake from.

"I know, Hammie, I know. They had to amputate your arm to save your life. If they hadn't, you would have died."

Ham looked away. Nina continued. "The main thing is that you are alive. We'll get through this, Hammie, like we have everythin' else."

"We've never been through nothin' like this, Mama! What am I gonna do without my left arm. That is—was—my future. I'm gonna be a major league pitcher." He began to sob quietly.

Nina didn't know what to say. She looked from Thom Jeff to Brother Bob standing behind her. Brother Bob stepped forward and said gently, "Ham, nobody knows how you're feeling right now. It's a terrible, terrible thing, and we don't know what to say to help you. But we're here and we won't go away."

Ham stared at Brother Bob but said nothing. He wanted to believe his words but could not. "I'm tired, Mama. I want to go to sleep now."

"All right, Hammie. I'll be right here if you need anythin'." Ham closed his eyes.

Nina stood, and the three of them walked to the corner of the recovery room so as not to disturb Ham. "I don't know what to do," she said.

Thom Jeff spoke for the first time, "Me neither."

They both looked at Brother Bob. "I don't really know there's anything we can do or say right now. He's in shock. We all are. It will take time, a long time, to work through all this. But Ham is strong; he'll come through this."

Nina gathered herself. "You two go home. I'll stay here overnight. Thom Jeff, you come back in the mornin'. Ask Cornelia if she can stay with the children tomorrow. Brother Bob, thanks for stayin'. Come back by whenever you can. I know tomorrow is a busy day for you."

"Okay, Nina, call me if you need me." Brother Bob said.

"I'll be back in the mornin'," Thom Jeff said. Both left the room.

Nina sat in the chair beside Ham's bed. It was 9:00 p.m. The nurse came in and turned off the lights. The only sound was of the monitors keeping track of Ham's vitals. The only light came from those same machines, and they gave off an eerie, otherworldly glow. Nina dozed off. Just as she was about to fall into a deeper sleep, a nurse came into to check on Ham. It didn't really matter. Nina couldn't really sleep.

At 2:00 a.m. the door opened, and a nurse and two male attendants came in the room. "We're moving your son to Room 242, ma'am."

"Oh, all right," Nina said. She began gathering her belongings and those also of Ham's. The nurse disconnected the heart monitor but left the IV. All the commotion woke Ham. He tried to focus his eyes and found his mother.

"What's happenin', Mama?"

"They're takin' you to another room, Hammie."

"Are you comin' with me?"

"Of course, Hammie." She followed the gurney out the door and down the hall to the service elevator. One of the attendants punched the two on the elevator panel.

They took Ham to a semi-private room, which at the moment was empty except for Ham. The nurse on duty on the second floor came in, introduced herself, and reconnected Ham's monitors.

"I'm thirsty, Mama."

"Only ice chips for now, okay?" the nurse said sweetly. She left the room and returned with a cup of ice and a spoon. Ham instinctively raised his left arm to receive the cup. "Oh, it's good that you can move your arm! That will help your recovery!" the nurse said. She handed the cup of ice and spoon to Nina. Ham looked down at the stump of what was once his left arm and lowered it again. Nina fed him ice chips from the cup. Neither spoke.

Eventually, Ham went back to sleep, and Nina tried to do the same in the chair beside his bed. The routine for the rest of the night was the same as it had been earlier. Nurses checking on Ham, wresting Nina from fitful sleep.

Around seven, Ham woke up and said, "Mama, I need to go to the bathroom."

"I'll get the nurse, Hammie." Nina left the room and returned with a nurse and a quarterly.

"Need to pee?" the nurse smiled.

"Yes ma'am."

"That's good. That means the anesthesia is wearing off."

The nurse again disconnected all the tubes except the IV. She and the orderly lowered the side of the bed. "Ham, can you swing your legs around to the floor?"

"I think so." Ham slowly swung around. He steadied himself with his right hand, but he was out of balance, since he didn't have his left arm to help shift his weight. The orderly helped raise him from behind and steadied him with a hand in the small of his back.

"You're a load, Ham!" Now sitting on the side of the bed, Ham felt light-headed. "Just stay here for a minute before you try to stand."

After a couple of minutes, the nurse asked, "Ready?" Ham nodded. The orderly came to the other side of the bed and pulled Ham up by his right arm. Ham was unsteady and held on to the shoulder of the orderly, who was pulling Ham's IV with one hand and guiding him to the bathroom with the other. Once inside, the orderly pulled the door. After some seconds, Nina could hear urine hitting the water in the toilet. Ham and the orderly emerged from the bathroom.

"Feel better?" the nurse asked. Again, Ham nodded. The orderly helped Ham back into the bed.

At 8:00 a.m. a nurse came in to change Ham's bandage. Nina came to the side of the bed to watch. When Ham felt the nurse touch the wrapping, he winced. "Does that hurt?" the nurse said.

"A little, yes ma'am."

"All right. I'll get you some pain medicine after I change this." She finished unwrapping the bandage. Underneath the wrapping was a tan covering that looked like a large sock, just like Dr. Walker had said. A tube ran out from under the sock. "Would you like to see your arm?" the nurse asked.

"Yes ma'am." She took off the sock and removed the surgical adhesive that was holding the tube in place at the site of the sutures.

Ham and Nina stared in shock. The stump that stood in the place of Ham's left arm looked unworldly. Sutures held the puckered and discolored skin in place. "It looks really good!" the nurse said encouragingly. "The doctor did a really good job!" Neither Ham nor Nina responded.

The nurse replaced the old soiled surgical covering with a new one. Then she re-wrapped the arm with a clean bandage. "We'll check it again this afternoon," she said and left the room.

Ham stared at his bandaged arm for a long time. "They cut off my arm, Mama . . . . "

"I know, Hammie, but they had to, to save your life. You would've died." Nina repeated her earlier words, but with less conviction this time.

"I wish I had died. I'druther die than live like this."

"Don't say that Hammie!"

Thom Jeff came into the room. Nina looked pleadingly at him. "Everythin' okay?" he said.

"Not really, Daddy. I've lost my arm, and I wish I was dead."

Thom Jeff stared first at Ham and then at Nina. "You don't mean that, Ham."

"Yes, I do, Daddy." Ham turned away from both of his parents toward his "good" side. The tube from his left arm shifted on the sheets.

"I don't know what to do," Nina whispered. She looked exhausted, eyes red, hair matted.

"I don't either," Thom Jeff admitted. In a moment, they could hear Ham's rhythmic breathing. He had fallen back to sleep.

"Why don't you go home and get some rest, Nina? I'll stay here with Ham." At first, Nina resisted, but finally she agreed it'd be best if she went home and freshened up.

Ham and Thom Jeff spent the rest of the morning sleeping or pretending to. They did not talk. Ham had nothing to say, and Thom Jeff didn't know what to say. Their silence was interrupted only by the nurses who came in to check this or that monitor. Around noon, an orderly brought in a tray of juice and jello for Ham's lunch. "Thanks, but I'm not hungry."

"Oh but you gotta eat somethin', Mr. MacPherson. Don't want you wastin' away like me!" the orderly said jovially. He was as wide as he was tall. "I'll just leave it here in case you change your mind."

"Ham, you need to eat," Thom Jeff said.

"I ain't hungry." Ham repeated. The food sat on the tray for most of the afternoon.

Around 3:00 p.m. Ham tentatively reached for the juice. He couldn't open the top with one hand.

"Here, let me get that for you," his dad said and opened the juice. Ham looked at him resentfully but drank the now lukewarm juice.

The hospital room door opened and Ham's cousin, Pete, walked in. Pete was Aunt Edith's son. He was studying to be a preacher at Freedom University, THE fundamentalist school in Virginia. He was in his third year. Pete had come home for the summer to serve as the Youth Pastor of his home church. Pete was married and already had two children under the age of two.

"Hey Ham. Uncle Thom Jeff. How are y'all doin'?"

"Pete, how'd did you get in here? Visitation is for immediate family only," Thom Jeff said. He had always been a bit wary of his nephew's religious zeal.

"Oh, I'm an ordained minister, Uncle Thom Jeff. We can get in almost anywhere." Pete pointed proudly to the Clergy sign attached to his shirt pocket.

"Well, you can't stay long, okay? Ham needs to rest."

"Of course. Of course. I just came by to give spiritual support and offer a prayer," Pete said. He walked over to bedside, looked at Ham's bandaged left arm and took Ham's hand.

"Ham, humanly speaking, this must seem like a terrible, terrible thing. But God has a plan for everythin'. We just have to seek out his will."

Ham could feel every muscle in his body tighten. He and Pete had been close as children, but as Pete grew more conservative in his views, they drifted apart. Ham's membership at Second Little Rock Baptist had sealed the rift. They were still cordial, but Pete was not on the top of Ham's list to receive spiritual guidance from.

"Sometimes, God tests us with sufferin' to educate us. There is a spiritual lesson to learn from every predicament. Like a good father who sometimes punishes his son to teach him a lesson. Do you think you've learnt anything spiritually from your accident?"

Ham's blood pressure began to rise. "I just lost my arm, Pete. I really hadn't had much time to think about its spiritual meaning." He spit out the words.

"I understand. I understand. Well, in time, you may find that losin' your arm taught you to be more dependent on God or somethin' like that. Other times, Ham, things like this happen as punishment for unconfessed sin. I know that's hard to hear, but do you think you might have some un-confessed sin that could have been at the root of this?"

Ham shifted in his bed. He could feel his cheeks turning red. "You sound like one of Job's friends, Pete. With friends like that, who needs enemies?"

A bit startled, Pete responded, "Well, Job's friends warn't exactly wrong 'bout Job, were they? Besides you're not comparin' yourself to Job, are you Ham? The Good Book says Job was 'perfect and upright . . . feared God and eschewed evil.'"

Thom Jeff intervened. "Pete, I reckon that's enough for now. We appreciate you coming by, but you really need to be movin' on now, okay?" Thom Jeff took Pete by the elbow and guided him toward the door.

"Wait, Thom Jeff, I was goin' offer a prayer for healin' for Ham."

"That's all right. Why don't you do that when you get home? Thanks for comin' by Pete." Thom Jeff made sure Pete exited the room. After the door shut, Ham spoke.

"Please don't let him come back here, Daddy."

"I'll let the nurses know, Ham. Shit like that is one reason I stopped goin' to church." Thom Jeff said.

"I never heard Brother Bob talk like that!" Ham said.

"Nah, but plenty of church goers do. Anyhow, he's gone."

"Do you think he's right 'bout me doin' somethin' that caused me to lose my arm?"

"Hell no! Get some rest, now Ham."

Nina returned around 5:00 p.m. "How's everythin' goin'?"

"Fine," Ham said curtly. Thom Jeff just shrugged. Neither one of them mentioned Pete's visit.

"Nora is here and wants to see you, Hammie," Nina said hopefully.

"I don't want to see nobody, Mama!"

"Not even Nora?"

"Especially Nora. Not now, not like this."

"What do you mean, Hammie?"

"I don't want Nora to see me like this!" he said, exasperated. He gestured with his right hand toward his left and set the IV unit to beeping. "I don't want any visitors for a while, okay Mama?"

"Okay, I'll tell her now's not a good time." Nina left the room, passing a nurse on her way in to check the beeping monitor.

Thom Jeff went home around 6:00 p.m. He had to work tomorrow. Nina and Ham spent the rest of the evening as they had most of the afternoon. Ham spoke only when he needed to go to the bathroom or wanted something to drink. He still had eaten nothing. Nina watched this boy in a state of bewilderment. This despondent, rude boy was nothing like the boy she had raised. Actually, he was only rude to her and Thom Jeff. He was very polite to the hospital staff. But with her, it seemed it was barely able to hold back the resentment and hostility anytime they exchanged words. She thought, it can't get any worse than this.

After another fitful night of sleep, it did, in fact, get worse. Around 6:00 a.m. orderlies wheeled another patient into the semi-private room. They drew the curtain separating the two beds, but not before Nina could see a very elderly and emaciated man lying on the hospital bed. Through the curtain, she could hear him moaning and groaning deliriously. The noise woke up Ham. "What's that?" Ham said, alarmed.

"I reckon it's your new roommate, Hammie."

A nurse came in to check on the man. "Mr. Wilson? Can you hear me? Are you okay?"

When the nurse came out from behind the curtain, Nina asked, "What's wrong with Mr. Wilson?"

"Oh, he just had a second surgery for colon cancer. We're not sure he's going to come through this, this time." She said. "Everything okay with you, Mr. MacPherson?"

"Yes ma'am."

Around 7:00 a.m. Dr. Walker made his rounds. He smiled at Nina and said, "Good morning." He turned to Ham and said, "How are you feeling, Ham?"

"Not so great, Doctor."

"Well, let's take a look." Dr. Walker removed the bandages and surgical sock. He nodded approvingly. "Looks very good. Good job, Ham." As though Ham had anything to do with the healing of his arm. "You need to start moving around. Walk a lot. A physical therapist will be in later to begin your rehabilitation. It's important you start that as soon as possible to increase mobility of the arm. In a day or two, an occupational therapist will come to help you relearn some basics like brushing your teeth and dressing yourself. If you keep on this trajectory, I think we'll have you out of here in ten days or so. Any questions?"

"No doctor." Dr. Walker left the room. Nina followed him. "Dr. Walker?"

"Yes, Mrs. MacPherson?" Dr. Walker turned back toward Nina. They were standing in the hallway just outside Ham's door.

"I'm worried about Ham. He seems really down. Said he'd rather die than lose his arm."

"Depression is normal after a traumatic injury like this, Mrs. MacPherson. Someone from the hospital staff, a social worker or chaplain, will be round later today. Tell that person and encourage Ham to talk about his feelings with them. And continue to make yourself available too."

"I don't really know what to say to him, Dr. Walker."

"Just let him talk at this point. It's important to be there."

"He doesn't want to talk, and he doesn't want to have any visitors either."

"This will take time, Mrs. MacPherson. Perhaps there's a favorite friend or relative—aunt, uncle, sibling—that Ham might be more willing to talk with? If you think of someone, you might ask them to drop by. Is there anything else I can help you with?"

"No I guess not. Thank you doctor."

"I'll be back tomorrow," Dr. Walker said. Nina went back into Ham's room. He was sleeping again, or pretending to.

This dance went on for two days. They got more or less accustomed to Mr. Wilson's moaning and groaning and incoherent speech from the next bed. He had no visitors. The physical therapist came on Monday afternoon. She showed Ham exercises intended to help him regain mobility in his arm and to retard atrophy of the muscles. Ham went through the exercises half-heartedly, just enough to satisfy the physical therapist but not enough to do much good for his arm. The same happened with the occupational therapist who came on Tuesday to assist with Ham's rehabilitation in learning how to care for himself. They went through strategies and procedures from buttoning shirts to brushing teeth. Again, Ham's efforts were marginal, and to someone not familiar with the typical gusto with which the pre-accident Ham engaged challenges, it might appear he was doing the best he could. But Nina knew better.

Furthermore, he refused visitors—Nora, JC, Uncle Carl and other members of the YOMCA, not to mention coaches, classmates, and church members who came by to lend their support. Nina was forced to turn them all away. Ham even refused to talk with Brother Bob. And he certainly wasn't going to talk with any of the chaplains or social workers who dropped in those first couple of days.

Late Tuesday afternoon, Nina returned to the room after taking a bathroom break. As she opened the door to Room 242, she heard an object hit the wall next to her head. She looked down: it was a pencil. "Sorry, Mama. I didn't mean to throw that at you." Ham was sitting up in bed with a legal pad on his lap. "I've been tryin' to write my letters. They look like a five-year old's." He held the legal pad up for his mother to see. She would have to agree.

She pulled up a chair and said, "Here. Let me help you." She put the pencil back into his right hand and helped him trace out a primitive A, B, then C.

"Do you have any vinegar sandwiches?" he asked, making a joke for the first time in three days.

"Do you remember that, Hammie?"

"Course I do, Mama. It's how I learned to write my ABCs—the first time, I guess."

When Ham was five, Nina used to take him out into the backyard to practice writing, and later reading. She remembered how embarrassed she had been when she got to first grade and couldn't read or write or even spell her name. She determined if she ever had children, that would never happen to them. When Ham had just turned five, they moved into the house they lived in now. Thom Jeff had done a lot of the work himself and contracted out the rest. He managed to get running water in the house, but the plumbing was only roughed in and not functioning for the first few years. So he dug a pit and built an outhouse in the backyard. Nina didn't object all that much. She had grown up with an outhouse, and they weren't the only ones in the early sixties in Wilkes County who still had outdoor privies. So there in front of the outhouse, Nina taught Ham how to read and write the first time. As a reward, she fed him pieces of white bread sprinkled with vinegar. She couldn't remember now why she chose that specific concoction other than Ham really liked them, even though they weren't particularly agreeable to his system. On especially productive days, when Ham got lots of vinegar sandwich rewards for "doing his letters," the privy became something of a necessity.

Ham was much less receptive to Nina's instruction the second time around. After just a few minutes, he dropped the legal pad on the floor. "I can't do this, Mama. I'm tired. Maybe tomorrow." Nina could see Ham was sinking ever deeper into the Shadow. Desperate, and remembering Dr. Walker's advice, she made a bold move. She called Ham's Aunt Nora—Thom Jeff's older sister who lived in Chapel Hill—who immediately agreed to drive to Wilkes General and talk to Ham. If Aunt Nora couldn't get through to Ham, nobody could. Meanwhile, Mr. Wilson, in the next bed over, died.

CHAPTER 17

Aunt Nora arrived in her Cadillac Deville on Tuesday night and stayed with her parents, Dubya and Cornelia. She had dropped everything when Nina called and headed for North Wilkesboro. The next morning Aunt Nora invaded Wilkes General Hospital. She entered Ham's room at 9:00 a.m. Ham had his dressing changed and had eaten breakfast, such as it was.

"Hello, Nina! Hello, Honey Ham!" (Ham hated it when she called him that.) She breezed past Nina and went straight to Ham. "My goodness, Ham, what have you up and done now?"

"I guess I shot my arm off, Aunt Nora." Ham dared not tell his Aunt Nora he was not up to receiving visitors.

"Nina, why don't you give us a few minutes? And ask those nurses to give us a few minutes, too, will you? Nothing they need to do is of an immediate urgency, I don't think."

"Sure Nora," Nina was relieved Nora was there and taking charge. She left the room, and the two of them were alone.

Nora pulled the chair up next to the side of the bed. "Are you eating, Honey Ham?"

"Not really hungry, Aunt Nora."

"Well, if you don't eat, you won't get your strength back. And if you don't get your strength back, you won't get to go home. And if you don't go home, this place will depress the hell out of you. It's already depressing me." Aunt Nora sighed.

"It's a pretty depressing place," Ham agreed.

"Yes, and you've had a very depressing couple of days, I understand."

"Yes, ma'am."

"What's this I hear about you refusing to have any visitors?"

"I'm just not ready to see people, Aunt Nora."

"Not even your sweet little gal? What's her name?"

"Nora, Aunt Nora. Her name is Nora."

Aunt Nora laughed and said. "Oh that's right." Ham wondered if mountain people lacked imagination or just drew from a list more limited than everybody else when it came to names. Outside his little circle of family and friends, Nora wasn't all that common.

"You don't want to see your sweet little Nora?" Aunt Nora repeated.

"Especially Nora. I don't want her to see me like this."

"What—all depressed and feeling sorry for yourself?" Aunt Nora asked.

"No, *this*." He raised his left arm as high as he could, which was higher than he could three days ago. The physical therapy, even practiced half-heartedly, was working.

"Oh, I see you. You're afraid because you lost half your arm that Nora will think less of you or love you less?"

"Yes, that's exactly what I'm afraid of, Aunt Nora."

"Well, you're just being a baby, Ham. You need to get over yourself. Sure, what happened to you was horrible, and there's nothing you can do to change the past. But you can choose to embrace the future. And you have a wonderful future in front of you, Ham!"

"What future Aunt Nora? I can't play ball anymore."

"Oh good grief, Ham. Don't be so melodramatic. Best case scenario, how many years could you have been a profession baseball player?"

"Uh, I don't know." Ham had never thought of that before. "Maybe fifteen."

"Ok, sounds a little long, but let's say fifteen for argument's sake. How old will you be in fifteen years?"

"Thirty-three?"

"Exactly. Thirty-three. And how long do you expect to live?"

"I don't know, Aunt Nora. Maybe til I'm eighty, like Grandpa Dubya?"

"Ok fine. Let's say eighty. How many years is that?"

"Forty-seven!" Ham said instantly. He was really good at doing figures in his head.

"So what do you think you'd do for those forty-seven years after your baseball career was over?"

Again Ham said, "I dunno. I hadn't thought of it before."

"Well, it's time to start thinking about it, Ham. Because now you're gonna get a head start on the rest of your life, without the baseball thing as a detour."

Aunt Nora had a way of making you think of things in a way you wouldn't normally think. She left that topic and went on to another.

"Ham did I ever tell you I wanted to be a race car driver?"

Ham's eyes widened. "Well, no, Aunt Nora, I can't say I 'member you ever mentioning that."

"Wilson doesn't like for me to talk about it. But I know you'll be discreet with the information I'm about to tell you." She looked around the empty room and lowered her voice. "You know your mother's father used to make moonshine, don't you?"

"Yes, I've heard stories about that." Truth was nobody much wanted to talk about the MacPherson and Robinette participation in the Wilkes County moonshine industry except perhaps Aunt Nora. Ham was engrossed. For a moment, he forgot his current plight.

"Mr. Robinette also liked to sample the product, maybe a little too much. Maybe someday your mother will tell you about how the revenuers showed up one day when Mr. Robinette was trying out a batch of that 'good ole' mountain dew' as he used to call it. He smelled to the high heavens of the stuff, so your mother and her mama sat Mr. Robinette down in an easy chair and painted him up with hot mustard, the only thing they could think of that smelled stronger than moonshine. Then they told him to pretend he was asleep. Worked too! The revenuer couldn't stand the smell of hot mustard and left." Aunt Nora laughed at the image she had conjured in her mind's eye and then said. "Oh dear. I've distracted myself. Where was I?"

"Somethin' about you wantin' to be a race car driver?"

"Oh yes, but not just any ole' driver, a *NASCAR* driver. Most of the MacPherson boys, including your daddy, worked for Mr. Robinette at one time or another running moonshine. Truth is most of the young people in Wilkes County were moon runners. Most of the NASCAR drivers got their start that way. Junior Johnson, and lots of others ran moonshine for Wilkes County bootleggers. But, at the risk of sounding immodest, none of those boys was a better driver than I was. Almost all of them got caught by the revenuers at least once and spent at least one night in the county jail. But I was never caught runnin' 'shine to Winston and back. They called me 'Torrid Nora' back then."

"You ran moonshine, Aunt Nora?" This *was* news to Ham. "I thought Prohibition happened in the 1930s." Ham remembered that from history class. "Was Grandpa Robinette still making hooch in the 1940s?"

"1940s? Oh, heaven yes. In fact, moonshine had its heyday in Wilkes County in the 1950s. Why, as late as 1957, revenuers seized over 40,000 gallons of pure mash in Wilkes County, which would have made over 4,000 gallons of illegal whiskey. In 1957, Ham! Farmers around here couldn't ever make a living just farming, and that got a lot worse after the Great Flood of 1940, when the Yadkin River rose nearly forty feet above its normal level and ruined most everything in its path. So they either turned to lumber, like your Grandpa Dubya, or to white lightning, like your Grandpa Tom, Mr. Robinette. It was 1950, I think, when that Yankee journalist came down here and pronounced Wilkes county 'the Moonshine Capital of the World.' Moonshine was an economic necessity and pretty much a family business. Most people think North Carolina mountain folk are just backward hill-billies like Snuffy Smith in that horrible Sunday cartoon. But moonshine was a business, and your Grandpa Robinette was a superb businessman. He recognized the business was a simple matter of supply and demand. The religious folk had worked hard to ban the legal sale of alcohol, and Mr. Robinette encouraged their efforts to keep Wilkes and the surrounding counties dry because he knew the unintended consequence would be a boost to the illegal sale of moonshine! It was brilliant: the evangelical teetotalers with bootleggers as silent partners formed an unlikely alliance to keep Wilkes County dry and to extend the life of the moonshine industry until around 1960.

"Anyhow, there were plenty of girls and women involved in the moonshine business, though most of them didn't participate in the actual delivery end of the business. But I certainly wasn't the only girl who was a moon runner. I had a girlfriend who got caught when she was sixteen and had an article written about her in the *Wilkes-Journal Patriot*," Aunt Nora said proudly.

"Warn't it dangerous?"

"Well, my daddy thought so. But really it wasn't as dangerous as people have made it out to be. Especially during the 1940s when I was runnin' 'shine." Nora's Wilkes county accent—which she had worked hard to shed over the years—was returning, Ham noticed. "There was a kinda unwritten code between the moon runners and the revenuers that there wouldn't be any gunfire, just very exciting car chases. And most of the time, both sides kept to the code. I worked for Mr. Robinette several years. He provided us with some sweet rides. Souped up cars with the back seats and passenger seat removed to make room for the 200-gallon container for the product. I made a lot of money til your Grandpa Dubya found out and made me quit. But by then I had already registered to race in the first race at the North Wilkesboro Speedway on March 18, 1947," she said proudly. "They thought I was a boy, and the race had already started before old man Enoch Staley, the track owner, found out different. I would have won too if 'Red' Byron weren't such a dirty driver! NASCAR was just starting, and I wanted to be a racecar driver. As I said, I could outdrive most all of those boys. But I couldn't pursue my driving passion because I was a woman, Ham, so I had to find new dreams and new goals. Do you get my point, Honey Ham?" Ham nodded in the affirmative, though he was dumbfounded. His family had more secrets than a mangy dog has fleas. Before he could ask any questions, Nora continued on to another topic. She seemed to Ham to be picking subjects at random, though, of course, she wasn't.

"Have you ever met Mr. Lackey, Wilson's father?" Wilson was Aunt Nora's husband.

"Just once, I think."

"What do you remember about him?"

"Well, I think he was really well off. Was he a bootlegger, too?"

"No, no. Mr. Lackey was a very successful banker. What else do you remember?"

"Well, I recall he walked kinda funny."

"That's right, Ham. Mr. Lackey had an odd gait. Do you know why?"

"No ma'am."

"That's right. You don't Ham. Most people don't. Mr. Lackey was born with club feet and had more than ten operations as a child to correct the disability. But he had circulation problems that the doctors could not address. When he was eleven, doctors had to amputate both legs because of gangrene. He learned to walk using prosthetics. He became a successful banker and a generous benefactor. He later became chairman of the board of the hospital in Raleigh where he was a patient. President Dwight Eisenhower appointed him to the Consulate in Edinburgh, Scotland, and Mr. Lackey was the President's host when he vacationed at Culzean Castle. Mr. Lackey was a great success by anyone's calculations."

"Geez, I had no idea, Aunt Nora."

"Of course not. Mr. Lackey was a modest man, and Wilson doesn't like to brag about his dad. But my point is this, Ham: Mr. Lackey refused to let what others perceived as limitations hold him back. He loved life and all it offered more than anyone I know. Ham, there are a lot of people counting on you to come through this. Your sweet little Nora. Your mom and dad. Your brother and sister. Your friends. And it has to start with three things. First, you've got to eat to keep up your strength. Second, you've got to devote yourself to your rehab in the same way you devoted yourself to baseball. And third, you've got to open up and let these people who love you back into your life—and that starts by letting them into your room. Am I making myself clear?"

"Yes, Aunt Nora."

"Good, do you have any questions?"

"No, Aunt Nora, I don't think I do."

"Good. If you think of anything, let me know, okay Honey Ham?"

"Aw'right Aunt Nora." Somehow Aunt Nora's words in those few minutes penetrated Ham's psyche in a way nothing his mother had said up to that point.

Aunt Nora went out into the hall. "I think we're going to be okay, Nina. We just have to give Honey Ham some time. I'm going to go home and see Mom and Daddy now. I'll be back later."

"Thank you Nora." Nina wondered what Aunt Nora had said to Ham. Aunt Nora stayed two more days to keep Nina and Ham company during the day and to visit with her parents in the evening.

That same afternoon, Nina noticed Ham was working harder at his rehab tasks, and he scrunched his forehead as he concentrated on his PT exercises. "Way to go, Ham," the physical therapist said. "That's excellent."

Later that afternoon, a man in a three-piece suit with a cane and a Braves baseball cap knocked on the door of Room 242. Nina went to the door. "May I help you?"

"Hello, ma'am. I'm Paul Snyder of the Atlanta Braves. I'm here to see Ham, if he's available."

"Oh hello Mr. Snyder. I've heard a lot of wonderful things about you. Wait here just a moment. I'll let Ham know you're here."

Nora stepped back into the room. "Ham, there's a Mr. Paul Snyder from the Atlanta Braves here to see you."

"Mr. Snyder. Wow, okay Mama—let him in."

Paul Snyder shuffled into the room. It didn't look to Ham like Mr. Snyder had regained much use of his left arm yet. "Hello Ham." He reached out his right hand.

Ham took Mr. Snyder's right hand with his own. "Hello Mr. Snyder. This is a surprise."

"Well, I heard about your accident, and I wanted to come check on you."

"I really appreciate that."

"How are you doing?"

"Well, I've been better," Ham said. "But I guess I've been worse."

"How's your rehab going?"

"It's hard. Learnin' how to do everythin' right-handed when I was used to doin' everything left handed has been real hard."

"I can imagine," Mr. Snyder said, lifting his left arm with his right hand. "I was right-handed before, but I still find the smallest tasks a challenge with just one hand."

"Is your arm gettin' better?" Ham asked.

"Not as quickly as the doctors had hoped." Mr. Snyder replied. "I'm not sure now if I'll fully recover use of the arm. My walking is better though."

"That's good." Ham nodded. "Looks like I won't be joinin' the Braves any time soon." Ham said.

"I wanted to come by and tell you how sorry I am about your accident Ham. You are a special young man, and I'm proud to have gotten to know you a little. I also wanted to come and tell you that while this may be the end of one dream, you've got lots of reason to dream other dreams. I want you to know I'd like to be whatever help I can. If nothing else, I can empathize with some of the difficulties of rehab you'll face! Oh, and I almost forgot. I have something for you." He reached into the inside pocket of his jacket and pulled out a get well card signed by all the Atlanta Braves players.

"Wow, thanks, Mr. Snyder."

Ham and Mr. Snyder talked for two hours. About the Atlanta Braves—it still looked like this was Henry Aaron's final season. About physical therapy. About Ham's other interests and talents and how best to pursue them. Nina sat in the corner, fascinated at the range of topics they covered. Finally, Mr. Snyder looked at his watch and said, "I better hit the road, Ham. It's been great to visit with you. Let's stay in touch." He handed Nina a business card with his name, address, and phone numbers.

"Thank you for comin', Mr. Snyder. You have no idea what it means to me."

"Take care of yourself, Ham. And say hello to your Nora for me." Mr. Snyder left.

CHAPTER 18

H am asked his mother if she could arrange for Brother Bob to see him the next morning. Of course she was thrilled to oblige. Around 8:30 on Thursday morning, Robert "Bob" Sechrest met with Ham in Wilkes General Room 242. Nina had gone home earlier that morning to see Diane and Michael Allen off to school. Cornelia had been staying with them all week, so Nina wasn't worried about them. But she did miss them. Knowing Brother Bob was coming over in the morning gave her the opportunity to check in with them.

"Hello Ham," Brother Bob smiled. "How are you feeling?"

"A lot better, Brother Bob." Ham said. "Thanks for comin' to see me."

"Of course. How can I help?"

"Well, there are several things I want to get your advice about. I talked to the chaplain here yesterday, and that was pretty helpful. Aunt Nora was here and Paul Snyder from the Braves, and both of them helped me get a better perspective on things. But—"

"But you're still having moments when you feel frustrated or angry or depressed or all of the above?" Brother Bob finished Ham's sentence.

"Yes, exactly. When will I get over these bad feelin's?"

"Well, you may not ever get over them completely, Ham. That's the bad news. It's like losing a relative. There's a hole there that can't ever be filled. But over time, and with help, those feelings of grief and anger and despair come less and less frequently. And you find ways to cope with those emotions when they do come. That's the good news."

"Are you willin' to let me come see you and talk with you when I get out of the hospital? I feel like I can tell you how I feel without upsettin' you. Mama doesn't like to hear me when I get mad and frustrated."

"Of course, Ham. We can set up a weekly meeting, more frequently at the beginning if you want. And if I think you're dealing with things I can't help with, we'll find you a professional psychologist. Deal?"

"Yeah, that already makes me feel better. Thanks, Brother Bob." Ham continued. "Also, I know Nora has talked with you about our 'situation.'"

"Yes, that's right. And she told me you two had talked, too."

"I told her I wanted to get married and have the baby. And I still do. But when we talked I thought I was gonna be drafted and get a big bonus that would, you know, help get us started."

"Have you changed your mind?"

"About wanting to get married and having the baby? Of course not. But I'm worried about how we're gonna live. And, to be honest, Brother Bob, I don't even know if Nora is gonna want to marry a one-armed man."

"Have you talked to her?"

"No, I don't want her to see me like this."

"Well I can't speak for Nora, and I think you ought to talk to her as soon as you can, but I'm pretty sure Nora didn't fall in love with a two-armed man or a one-armed man, Ham. She fell in love with you. But like I told Nora, you're young. You're very young. And just because you've decided to keep the baby doesn't mean you have to get married. You can be responsible to and for the baby and Nora without necessarily marrying right away. Maybe that would come later. Maybe it wouldn't. The two of you still have a lot of growing up to do. You may be different people at twenty-two or twenty-five than you are at eighteen, and you may find you're not as compatible as you thought."

"Are you advisin' us not to get married and live in sin?" Ham asked.

"No of course not. First, I'm not sure what or where 'living in sin' would look like. I'm saying don't confuse your sense of responsibility for the baby with your love for Nora."

"Well, I love 'em both and want to do right by them."

"I know and I agree. I just think you and she need to talk about what that means. If you decide it means you don't want to get married just now, I will support that decision and help you make your family understand. If you decide you want to get married, of course, I'll support that decision as well. In either case, you are right to worry about how you will be able to make it financially. But I'm betting your family would be more than happy to help you all they can til you can get your feet under you."

"Yeah, I think Grandpa Dubya and Grandma Cornelia will give their basement to us. It's finished. I'll have to find a job a one-armed man can do. Mama mentioned they were looking for a clerk at Lowe's. I'm pretty good at math and I think I could do that even with just one arm. You probably know that's where Uncle Carl works."

"Yes, I remember. Those sound like good plans. Well, it sounds like you two have a lot to talk about. Let me know if I can help in any way."

"Thanks, Brother Bob." Ham hesitated.

"Is there something else, Ham?"

"Yes, I wanted to talk with you about JC. He told me about his bein' homosexual and all the night before my accident. We hadn't talked about it since. To be honest, I don't really understand why he can't just go back to the way he was, so we can go back to the way we was."

"I think JC probably thinks he's always been that way. There's a lot about human sexuality that we are only now learning. For millennia, people thought homosexual behavior was simply the result of a person's preference, a kind of perversion of what was considered 'normal.' Until just a couple of years ago, the American Psychiatric Association classified homosexuality as an 'emotional disorder.' But they changed their minds about that; and somewhere around 1973, they removed it from the list of disorders in the big manual that all psychiatrists consult. Since the 1950s, there have been some doctors and scientists who think homosexuality is genetic and that as much as 10 percent of the male population *of all species* may be gay."

"But the Bible is pretty clear on condemnin' homosexuality, isn't it?" Ham asked, genuinely struggling to understand.

"Well, yes, that's true as your daddy pointed out the other week in the poker room. But in the first century, no one was making the kind of distinctions being made today. Plus, remember, in Genesis, God told Adam and Eve to 'be fruitful and multiply.' Homosexual sex can't produce off-spring, and for a long time, as humans were trying to establish their place in the life cycle, reproduction was critical to the survival of the species. It was part of what we call, 'creation theology.' But as you know from your biology and sociology classes, we don't have a problem today with human under population. Our problem is with overpopulation. So once marriage was separated from reproduction as its sole or even primary goal, we were free to explore other dimensions that give Christian marriage its distinctive character. Being faithful in a covenant relationship comes to mind, as well as companionship. That's why churches don't object to elderly widows and widowers remarrying; even though they have no chance of procreation, we still bless those unions. I would think both heterosexuals and homosexuals are capable of permanent, loving, faithful covenant relationships. And both are capable also of failing at that."

"So we don't take everythin' in the Bible literally?" Ham asked.

Brother Bob laughed and said. "I think you've listened to me teach and preach enough to know how I'll answer that one! The trick is how do we take the Bible *faithfully* and *seriously* without falling into the idolatrous trap of having always to take it *literally*. You remember that Paul said in 1 Corinthians that if you're a slave stay a slave and if you are single stay single?"

"Yeah, I remember you preachin' on that."

"Do you remember what I said?" Brother Bob put Ham on the spot.

"I do. You said Paul expected the end to come right away, and that affected what he said about slavery and marriage. And that Jesus didn't return right away, so the church had to modify its understandin' of End times. So there was no real justification for slavery any more. And people didn't follow Paul's advice to stay single. I remember you said that if our parents had followed that advice, none of us would be in church that day. Everybody laughed!"

"You've got a very good memory, Ham. So we have to consider the cultural context in which the Bible was produced in order to understand its message for us today."

"But don't Paul say straight out that homosexuality is bad?"

"Yes, that's in Romans 1. Folk take those verses and verses in Leviticus chapters 18 and 20 as the end-all statement on homosexuality, especially Romans 1. But Romans 1 isn't *about* homosexuality. It's about how God and humans relate to each other. It's about how humans ever since Adam and Eve insist on making gods of themselves and denying the honor that rightly only belongs to the reality and power of God. So the behaviors identified in Romans 1, including homosexual acts, are symptomatic of human tendency toward idolatry. Homosexuality in Paul's view is a violation of God's intention for the created order. But that doesn't give heterosexuals the right to condemn homosexuals since they participate in many of the other sins Paul lists as part of the symptoms of creation rebelling against the Creator. Paul says earlier in Romans, 'if you pass judgment on another you condemn yourself, because you are doing the very same things.' Self-righteousness is no less a sin than rebellious behavior."

Ham liked it when Brother Bob talked like this. It was like getting a private sermon.

"The truth is, Ham, Romans 1 is very much like 1 Corinthians 7. We have to take into account Paul's first-century context in both. We don't follow his thinking about remaining single in Corinthians because we have a different view of how soon—or late—the End will be. We have a different view of the End times. We may want to rethink Paul's words about homosexuality, not because human idolatry—putting something or someone else in God's place—isn't wrong, but because we have a different understanding of human sexuality.

"But this issue will never be settled by Biblical interpretation alone. Just like slavery and women in ministry, the issues involve a whole host of factors and not just a few proof texts from the Bible. Especially for Baptists, for whom experience has always been an important source of authority. When the daughters of Christians started saying God had called them to ministry, our views began to change. We, or at least some of us, began accepting them into ministry leadership positions. Not because the Bible changed, but because our experiences had broadened."

"Do you think the church will ever accept homosexuals then?" Ham asked.

"Some are already talking about it. But the church is often slow to catch up to the 'new things' God is doing. Look at the Civil Rights movement. The church was among the last institutions to see the injustice of racism. Martin Luther King Jr. called 11:00 a.m. on a Sunday morning the 'the most segregated hour in America.' You know the Brushy Mountain Baptist Association has twice tried to throw us out because we are integrated and ordain female deacons. But once the sons and daughter of Christians come out as gays, things will begin to change."

"Or wives?" Ham asked tentatively. He had never asked about Brother Bob's wife before, but he had heard rumors since Aunt Nora brought it up with Brother Bob over Sunday lunch. That seemed like an eternity ago.

"Yes, or spouses." Brother Bob smiled. "My view on homosexuality certainly changed based on my experience when my wife, Betty, told me she was in love with another woman. She tried, I think, earnestly to make things work with me, perhaps out of expectations from family and the larger culture. And I think she really liked me as a person. But she just couldn't control who she was attracted to. She just wasn't in love with me. We spent hours on hours talking about these things."

So the rumors were true. "Do you still hear from her?"

"We exchange Christmas cards and occasionally talk on the phone."

"Is she still with her—?" Ham didn't know what to call Brother Bob's ex-wife's lover.

"Her partner? Yes, they're still together, and I think very happy."

Ham nodded. "So did you really mean it when you said at the poker room that someday homosexuals will be able to marry legally?"

"Yes. It may not happen in my lifetime, but I expect it to happen in yours. I imagine the day will come when people your age look at being homosexual or heterosexual the same as being right-handed or left-handed. Most people are one way more than the other, but either is okay," Brother Bob said. "What's different for you now, Ham, is what was different for the Apostle Peter in Acts 10. Before his experience with Cornelius, gentiles were just a group to be avoided. When he saw that they worshipped and loved the same God he did, he had a conversion no less radical than Cornelius and his household. Last week, homosexuals were just a group you avoided at best, or ridiculed at worst. Today, you are struggling with the reality that your best friend is gay. And to maintain that friendship that has meant so much to you over the years will require a reorientation on your part, no less radical than the Apostle Peter's."

Ham was silent. "I'm tryin' to understand that, Brother Bob. But what do I do with the fact that JC said he has 'feelings' for me?"

"That's just JC trying to clear out the underbrush of your relationship so it can grow. Has he ever acted inappropriately toward you?"

"No."

"And I am sure he never will. Did you ever like a girl who didn't like you back?"

"Well, yeah, of course."

"How did it make you feel?"

"Kinda sad. They wanted to be friends. I wanted more."

"What did you do?"

"Well it hurt so much to be around them, I stopped. Until I liked someone else. Then I could be friends. But that was a long time ago, before Nora."

"JC has experienced that same kind of pain in his relationship with you. I know it's hard to understand, but you have had those same feelings, with the opposite sex, as you've just described. But JC chose not to walk away because your friendship was more important to him than romantic feelings he knew would never be reciprocated. It was as important for him to tell you that as it was uncomfortable for you to hear it so he could get 'unstuck' in the friendship."

"I guess he's kinda lonely bein' the only homosexual at Wilkes Central and all."

"Oh, he's not the only gay person at your school, Ham. I can assure you of that," Brother Bob said.

Ham looked shocked. "Really. I didn't have no idea."

"But JC is the one who has been your best friend all these years," Brother Bob added.

"So what do I do?" Ham asked.

"Be JC's friend. He's the same person today that you've known, and loved as a friend, all your life. Right now, you and I are the only two who know, and it's important for him to have one or two people he can talk to. And he really needs someone his age, whom he knows and admires and whose opinion he trusts, to accept him for who he is. And now the two of you share more in common than you did a week ago. Our culture will assume neither of you is a 'real man'—JC because he's gay, and you because you've lost an arm. Together, maybe, you can help people redefine what 'being a man' means. At the least, you can do that for each other."

Again, Ham was silent, but thoughtful. "Well, I guess I've got a lot of learning to do."

"We all do, Ham. We all do."

CHAPTER 19

Nora visited first. She came to the hospital after school as she had every day since Ham was admitted. And every day, Nina had to tell Nora that Ham wasn't ready to see anyone. Nora said she understood and returned home. She was hurt but refused to let Nina or anyone else know. On the afternoon of Thursday, May 27, Nora repeated this ritual. She went to the nurse's station on the second floor and asked to speak with Mrs. MacPherson. While she was waiting, Nina and Aunt Nora walked up from the waiting area, and Brother Bob emerged from Ham's room. They converged at the nurse's station.

Aunt Nora was the first to speak. "Nora, honey, it's so good to see you! How are you?"

"Hi Mrs. Lackey. I'm okay, I guess, considerin' the circumstances," Nora said, though she wasn't sure herself which 'circumstances' she was referring to.

"Nora, Ham is ready to see you today!" Nina reported and smiled.

"Really?" Nora was surprised and not sure *she* was ready to see Ham.

"Nina is right, Nora. I was just with Ham, and I think he is eager to see you. He's a bit self-conscious about you seeing him with the tubes, bandages, and especially his arm," Brother Bob confirmed.

"Oh, that's wonderful! Then it's okay if I go in now?" Nora asked just to be sure.

"Yes, yes," Nina said.

Nora walked over and knocked on the door of Room 242. "Come in," she heard Ham's voice through the door. She walked in and saw Ham sitting up in bed. He was playing with the controls on the hospital bed, raising and lowering the elevation.

"Nora! I am so glad to see you!" Ham exclaimed.

Nora rushed over and gave Ham a kiss. "Ham, I've been so worried about you! Are you okay?"

"I guess I'm okay considerin' the circumstances," Ham wasn't sure himself which circumstances he was referring to.

"I've come to see you every day, Ham," Nora began.

"I know, Nora. I'm sorry I didn't let you come in. It was stupid of me. I just warn't—"

"If we we're gonna be together, Ham, you can't shut me out."

"I'm sorry, Nora," Ham apologized.

"I know you weren't ready to see anybody. You've had a lot happen to you. But we've gotta talk about these things, Ham, and there's so much to talk about."

"I just didn't feel like talkin' to anybody. But you're right, Nora. We've gotta talk to each other."

"I feel like the accident was mainly my fault," Nora began.

Ham interrupted. "Nora, this warn't your fault!"

"Let me finish, Ham. I should have told you sooner that I thought I was pregnant. But I kept puttin' off taking the pregnancy test. And when I did, I didn't know what to do. Then tellin' you on the night of the baseball game. I feel like it was my fault you had the accident."

"Like I was tryin' to say, Nora, it's not your fault. If anythin', it's my own stupidity. I should have never leaned that shotgun against the fence! I know better than that." He reached out and took her hand. "I didn't want you to see me like this. I don't want nobody to see me like this." He looked away.

Nora turned Ham's face toward her and brushed the hair from his eyes. "I love you, Ham. I'm sorry this happened to you, but it doesn't change how I feel about you."

"Thinkin' about you and the baby has kept me sane in here, Nora. I think we should get married as soon as I get out of the hospital."

"But Ham, we don't have any money and neither of us has a job."

"I'll find a job, Nora, and I'm sure Grandpa and Grandma will let us have their basement. Mama and Dad would let us stay there, but Grandma Cornelia has more room."

"Let's just take our time, Ham. We don't have to rush to anythin'."

"I know that, Nora, but it's what I want. I was hopin' it's what you want too."

"It is Ham, it is. I can't think of anything I want more than to spend the rest of my life with you." She leaned over and kissed him. Even in a hospital bed, Ham was slightly higher off the ground than Nora! "We just have to keep talkin' about it. Promise me?"

"I promise."

"Well, first things, first. We've got to get you better! How do you feel?"

Ham looked at Nora then looked at his amputated arm. "It hurts, Nora," Ham confessed. "Without the pain medication, I don't know what I'd do. I'm doing exercises. I have two therapists—physical and occ'pational. That's helped. But it's like learnin' everythin' all over again. The Physical Therapist says I'm 'painfully left-handed.' Not much I can do with my right hand without a lot of effort." Ham fell silent for a moment. "Mr. Snyder from the Braves came by!" Ham brightened. "He just wanted to check on me. You remember he had a stroke and lost partial use of his left leg and arm."

"I remember. Is he doin' better?" Nora asked.

"'Bout the same, or that's how he looked to me. He brought me a card signed by all the Braves." Ham pointed to a card sitting between two potted plants in the windowsill. Nora picked it up and read it. "Henry Aaron signed the card?!"

"Yep." Ham paused. "I guess that's as close as I'll ever get to the 'Show.'"

"The 'Show'?" Nora asked.

"That's what 'baseball men' call the major leagues," Ham explained. Ham's countenance clouded at the thought of not making the 'Show.' He thought of Stan Huffman's suitcase sitting on the curb all by itself. A tear ran down his cheek.

Nora understood. "Ham, we'll make new dreams. We'll make a wonderful life—together." She patted her tummy.

"I know, Nora, and I am happy about that. It's just a week ago, I was being recruited by college scouts and talked to by major league player personnel directors, and today . . . "

"And today, we've still got each other. I've still got you, Ham. I thought I had lost you!" Now a tear rolled down Nora's cheek. Ham reached over and brushed it away.

"My Aunt Nora reminded me that even if I played baseball, I'd still have a lifetime away from the game. She made a lot of sense. I do have a lot to be thankful for, and you're at the top of the list, Nora. But I still get down. Brother Bob said it's natural."

"I'm sure it is Ham. You've lost something very important to you, and it's okay to be sad about it. I'll be sad with you. But I don't want you being sad all by yourself; I don't want you to isolate yourself from me and other people who love you."

"I know Nora. I won't." Ham and Nora talked for another hour. About the baby. About how she felt. About what was going on at school. A nurse came in to check Ham's vitals. "I'll go now, Ham. I'll be back tomorrow, if that's okay."

"Of course it is, Nora! Thanks for comin' today, and thanks for comin' every day. I love you!"

"I love you too, Ham MacPherson!" She kissed him on the lips. There was a light rap on the door. Ham's mom peeked around the door and said, "I've got your supper, Hammie." She brought the tray of food in and placed it on the table beside the bed. She turned to go out of the room. Ham looked at Nora, who nodded.

"Mama?'

"Yes, Hammie." Nina replied.

"Me and Nora have somethin' to tell you."

"Go on then," Nina said.

"I'm pregnant, Mrs. MacPherson," Nora blurted out while Ham was trying to gather words together.

"Oh dear. When did this happen?" Nina asked.

"The night of the Winter Waltz," Ham said.

"What are you children going to do? No jobs, no money," Nina said, mostly to herself.

"We're going to get married, Mama." Ham announced.

"Have you told your parents, Nora?" Nina asked.

"Not yet. But I need to do that soon. I'm startin' to show."

Nina thought for a moment. "Hammie, did I ever tell you that my parents got pregnant with me before they were married?"

"No Mama, I think I would remember if you'duv tole' me that." Ham's maternal grandparents had died in a car crash when he was very young. He didn't remember them and his mother rarely spoke of them.

"Everybody told them they were too young to get married. But they were determined to do so and to keep me and raise me. And they did." She looked out the window as if trying to conjure up long lost memories.

"They did a fine job of that, Mrs. MacPherson," Nora offered.

"Not so good with my brother, I'm afraid," Nina replied. "Are you sure this is what you both want?"

They both nodded. "You have no idea what you're getting into." She paused. "All right, it's gonna' be all right. You'll be the talk of the town for a while—gossipmongers love to chatter. But eventually nobody will remember or care if your baby was made four months before you got married or four months after. It'll be old news. Look at me. You can live with us or Dubya and Cornelia—they've got more room—and you can both go to school. We've got plenty of family to help watch the baby. *My* grandbaby!"

"What about Daddy?"

"Don't worry about your daddy. I'll tell him. And Grandpa Dubya and Cornelia. You are choosin' a long and hard row to hoe, but it can be done. After all, here I am."

"Thank you, Mama," Ham said.

Nina said. "Nora, if you want, I'll go with you to tell your parents."

Nora nodded. "I'd like that a lot!"

"Well, there's no time like the present," Nina said. "Let's go."

Nora said goodbye to Aunt Nora. Brother Bob had already gone. Nora and Nina left the hospital together to go to the Culpeppers's. Nina would be Nora's Gabriel and help with the annunciation.

After supper, there was another knock on the door of Room 242. Aunt Nora opened the door. Ham could hear her say, "Well, hello there JC! How are you, honey?" Before he could answer, she said, "Come in. Come in. Ham will be glad to see you."

And Ham was indeed glad to see JC. Nora excused herself to go grab a bite to eat. JC sat in the chair beside Ham's bed.

"Miss Nina called me and said it'd be okay to come by?" JC said questioning.

"I'm glad you did, JC. I owe you an apology for what I said and the way I acted last Friday."

"Oh no, Ham. I'm the one who owes you an apology. I shouldn't'uv said anythin' last week. And I should'uv been there Saturday mornin'."

"You were there Saturday mornin', JC. When I needed you most. You saved my life."

"I should'uv been there earlier to keep this from happenin'."

"Nobody can stop the stupidity of MacPherson men, JC. But I can't tell you how grateful I am for what you and Bobby Skeeter did for me. You saved my life." Ham repeated.

"I'm just glad we were there. I wish I coulduv saved your arm, Ham. Does it hurt?"

Ham lifted his bandaged arm. "Like hell, JC. Like hell."

JC grimaced. "I'm sorry, Ham. Like I said, I wish I could have been there."

Ham looked JC in the eyes. "I'll get through it. Brother Bob, Mama, Nora, and Aunt Nora are convincin' me of that. But I'll need my friends. And you're my best friend, JC."

"You still think that after what I told you?"

"Yes, I'm not saying I understand everything you told me. But I do believe that you are the same person who's been my best friend since we were eight years old. I'm sure I'll say and do some stupid things, but I want to try to understand. I really do."

JC's eyes filled with tears, and he began to sob. "Thank you, Ham. You have no idea how much that means to me."

Ham said, "Well, I figure we just need to stick together like we always have, JC."

JC nodded, still sobbing. "I'd like that too, Ham. Remember when we was kids and we went to the picture show at Justice theater, and the black people had to enter down the alley way and sit in the balcony?"

"Oh yeah. And I refused to go in the front entrance 'cause we couldn't sit together, so's I went down the alley with you and sat in the balcony."

"Yep. And ole' man Justice came out of the film room, and told you that you couldn't sit up there. Remember what you said?"

"Mr. Justice, the sign says 'coloreds' can't sit downstairs. It don't say nothin' 'bout white folk sittin' in the balcony. Why should the coloreds get the best seats?" They laughed.

"Ole' man Justice didn't know what to say. I knew then we was gonna be good friends, Ham."

"Yep, and we've got to stick together like we did against ole' man Justice—what a name!" Ham looked at JC. "I do have one question, though."

"What's that?"

"What was Bobby Skeeter doin' in North Wilkesboro? Are the two of you . . . " Ham didn't know how to finish his question. But he didn't have to; JC did it for him.

"Are we what? Lovers? Hell no, Ham, you idiot! Bobby is datin' my sister, Debra. She caught his eye at the ball game on opening day, and they've been seeing each other ever since."

"Oh," Ham said. "Well, I told you I'd say some stupid things. Just didn't think it would start so soon."

"It's okay Ham. We'll both have to give each other a lot of room to make mistakes. Neither one of us have been down this particular road before." Ham nodded in agreement. They talked for another hour or so. About Ham's PT. About tomorrow's game against Sylva and Bobby Skeeter. Finally, JC got up to leave. "I best get home now. Big day tomorrow." As he put his hand on the knob to leave, Ham spoke.

"Hey JC."

"Yeah, Ham?"

"Hit one out for me tomorrow night, okay? Off Bobby Skeeter."

"You got it, Ham. No problem!"

The next morning, Coach Maynard, JC, and Nacho came into the hospital room.

"Hey Ham," Coach Maynard said. "We're on our way to Sylva for tonight's game. Boys wanted to come by and tell you we're thinkin' of you and pullin' for you."

"Thanks Coach. That means a lot. You got the whole team with you?"

"Yeah, they're out on the bus. We didn't think it was a good idea to try to get all of 'em into your room."

"That's good thinkin', Coach," Nina said from the corner, smiling.

"Anyhow, we just wanted to drop by. Are you doin' okay, Ham?"

"'Bout as well as can be expected, Coach."

"Good, good. That's good, Ham." Coach Maynard was very uncomfortable and grasping for words. "Well, like I said, we just wanted to come by and wish you all the best, Ham. Gotta shove off now. It's a long drive by bus."

"Thanks for comin' by, Coach. Tell the fellas I said good luck tonight! And JC, don't forget what I told you!" JC smiled, and they all left the room. Ham wished like hell he was going with them.

CHAPTER 20

Ham continued with physical and occupational therapy for the next few days. Some days were better than others. Dr. Walker said the wound was healing well, and on Tuesday he took out the sutures. The "stump," as Ham had come to call it, had a scar that ran across its middle and turned up slightly at either end. It looked like a slight smile. Don't smile at me, you bastard, Ham said to himself. The doctor said Ham could go home on Friday. Ham had lost track of time, but Friday was June 4. By then, Ham had been in the hospital fourteen days. The discharge nurse helped Ham and Nora gather Ham's things that had accumulated over the hospital stay. A few toiletries, get well cards, some flowers and potted plants. She placed them all on a cart. Despite his protests, Ham sat in a wheelchair. Hospital protocol the nurse said. They scheduled a time later in June to return for his prosthesis. After loading all the stuff into the station wagon, Ham went home. It was odd to be home in a way, but more of a relief. He started upstairs with his suitcase.

"Let me take that for you, son," his dad offered, reaching for the suitcase.

"I can get it, Daddy. Thanks." Ham carried the suitcase upstairs to his room. Thom Jeff had stayed home from the mill and was pacing around the kitchen.

"Sit down, Thom Jeff," Nina said. "You'll wear out the floor with all that walking."

Thom Jeff sat. When Ham appeared at the bottom of the steps, Thom Jeff stood. "Want to take a little ride with me, Ham?"

Ham was surprised. "Where we goin'?"

"You'll see," his daddy said. His mother nodded approvingly.

"All right then."

They got into Thom Jeff's truck and drove to the poker barn and parked. They walked behind the barn toward the fence where Ham had his accident.

"This where it happened?" Thom Jeff had been there several times since the accident trying to reconstruct the scene. He still wasn't exactly sure how the barbed wire tripped the trigger of the shotgun. Gun must have been falling, which meant Ham was even luckier than he thought to be alive.

"Yep. This is the place." Ham took a deep breath. "Worst day of my life, I reckon." He reached out and broke a piece of the decaying post that held the offending barbed wire and stuck it in his back pocket. All this took considerable effort as he was doing it with his off hand.

"I reckon that's right. C'mon." Thom Jeff separated the barbed wires for Ham to pass through. What a weird feeling, Ham thought.

They walked silently through the pasture to the line of trees on the other side, near where Ham had seen the black rabbit.

They walked down a partially covered path into the woods for several hundred yards until they came upon a clearing. Ham didn't think he'd ever been here before. He thought he'd been everywhere on Dubya's property.

Thom Jeff walked over to spot just under a large oak tree. Ham could see there was a plaque of some kind flush to the ground. Beside it was a freshly dug hole. Ham walked over.

The plaque was a grave marker. It read simply, "Alexander Hamilton MacPherson, 1951. RIP."

"Why didn't you tell me he was buried out here?"

"You never asked, and after you got so upset when your mother told you about him, she decided to wait and tell you about this place. And then one thing led to another, and we never got round to it.

"The doctor who delivered Alex thought it'd be a good idea to have a funeral. Might help give what he called 'closure.' I guess it helped. I did grieve over losing him. Took me and your mother nearly six years before we had the strength and courage to try again. I'm shore glad we did though." Thom Jeff looked Ham in the eyes. Ham had never heard his father talk like this. He wondered if he'd been drinking.

As though reading his mind, Thom Jeff continued, "I've always drank too much, but I'm not drinkin' today. I've been proud that I didn't drink during the week, but I always seem to make up for it on the weekends. You mother says I'm a weekday workaholic and a weekend alcoholic. I guess she's right." Ham had heard his mother say this, too, and he also agreed.

"Anyhow, when I thought we might lose you, Ham, it scared me real bad. I said some stupid things, but it was really because I was 'fraid I'd lose you before the two of us really knew each other."

Ham started to interrupt. "Let me finish, son. First, I want to apologize for never comin' to your games—football, basketball, but especially baseball. I made up a lot of excuses, but truth is I just didn't make the time for it. I regret it, and I'm powerful sorry."

Ham started to cry quietly.

"My dad, your Grandpa Dubya, and I have never really been close. I felt like I disappointed him growin' up, never livin' up to his expectations. I know he was disappointed in my drinkin'. He gave it up cold turkey, but it's got a vise grip on me, Ham, and I can't seem to shake it loose. When I went into the sawmill with him, we was always buttin' heads. I wanted to do things one way, and he would want to do them another. Then, I think he was jealous about the way I took the sawmill and made it bigger, and I think, better."

Now Thom Jeff was weeping. "I know losin' your arm is an awful thing, Ham. I can't even start to understand how you feel. I never had a gift like you had for pitchin' or nothin' else really. And then to have it taken away all sudden like, well that's gotta be a bitter pill. But I also am hopin' that out of this tragedy, we might be able, you know, to get a fresh start. And I think it'd be good for you and Nora. Your mama told me 'bout the baby. You're young, all right, but if'n anybody can make it work, you and Nora can, son." Thom Jeff reached out and took Ham's hand. "I want to start by helping you get through this and off in the right direction. So I figured if a burial could help us deal with little Alex's death, then maybe it would help you deal with the loss of your arm."

"What do you mean, Daddy?" Ham asked, puzzled.

"I mean we've planned a little service for your arm. We'll bury it right here next to Alex."

"A funeral for my arm?"

"More a memorial service, but only if you want it. Brother Bob has agreed to officiate, but only if you agreed to the whole thing beforehand. If not, we'll forget about it altogether, and I'll fill this hole back in."

Ham was stunned. "You've got my arm?"

"Well, not on me. But yeah, it's in the freezer in the poker room. Dr. Walker took some persuadin' to release it to me, but I promised to keep it on ice and wrapped in the Formaldehyde casing and to bury it within three weeks. What do you think?"

Ham looked again at the fresh hole. It was rectangular and about the size of a cooler, about four feet long and three feet wide and nearly six feet deep. For the first time, he noticed a second plaque parallel to Alexander's. It read, "HH May 22, 1976."

"What's HH, Daddy?"

"Why, Howard Hughes, 'course."

Ham laughed for one of the first times since his accident.

Thom Jeff went on. "The YMCA poker group will be pallbearers. I got the old boy who makes cabinets for John Brookshire Jr. to make a child-sized casket for it. All dependin' on your approval, 'course."

"When is the funeral gonna be?"

"Sunday afternoon at 2:30, most likely. Or we can wait a bit if you'druther."

Ham thought a moment. "Yes, Daddy. I think it's a great idea." He squeezed his father's hand. They stood there, hand in hand, for a long time, looking first at one grave and then the other.

"Can I see the arm, Daddy?"

"You want to see the arm?" Thom Jeff repeated, startled. "We were kinda thinking it would be a closed casket affair."

"I know. I know. But I think I'd like to see it. With the memorial service, maybe it'd help bring what did you call it—closure?"

Thom Jeff hesitated, then said, "All right then. Come on."

They walked back to the tobacco barn, and Thom Jeff collected the key from under the rock and opened the door. They went through Dubya's office and into the poker room. Thom Jeff walked over to the freezer in the corner and lifted the medical transporter out and set it on the poker table. He opened and lifted the Formaldehyde pack out and set it on the poker table. He stepped back, and he and Ham stared at it for a long time.

The pack was transparent, and Ham could see the arm through the packing. It simultaneously looked like an alien from outer space and something intimately familiar. It was bluish-gray. It was palm up, and the fingers were curved inward almost as though they were holding a baseball.

Ham played "Four Walls" by Jim Reeves on the jukebox. The rich baritone voice was soulful and sad:

Four walls to hear me
Four walls to see
Four walls too near me
Closing in on me.

Ham sat in the chair and rubbed his stump with his right hand. He began to weep uncontrollably.

Sometimes I ask why I'm waiting
But my walls have nothing to say
I'm made for love, not for hating
So here where you've left me, I'll stay

Four walls to hear me
Four walls to see
Four walls too near me
Closing in on me.

Thom Jeff didn't know what to do, so he went over and stood behind Ham and rubbed his shoulders. And Ham wept.

Finally, Ham reached out and touched his arm and said, "I'm sorry." Then he turned to his father, said, "Thank you, Daddy," and walked out of the barn. Thom Jeff put the package back in the transport carrier and replaced it inside the freezer. He locked up the barn, and he and Ham walked to the car hand in hand.

CHAPTER 21

The next day, Sunday, Ham skipped church services. He wasn't ready to face everybody at once. The memorial service was set for 2:30 p.m. Thom Jeff went on ahead to get things ready. When Ham arrived with Nina, Diane, and Michael Allen, there were several familiar cars and trucks parked around the poker barn. They could hear commotion in the barn, pallbearers apparently retrieving the arm for the service. They walked behind the barn to the fence. Dubya had cut the barbed wire to make it easier for folk to get back to the burial site. It made sense, Ham thought, since Dubya hadn't kept livestock in that pasture for a long time. Wish he had done that before.

When they came to the clearing in the woods, they saw a small crowd gathered around three sides of the hole Thom Jeff had dug. Grandma Cornelia and Grandpa Dubya, Nora, JC, Coach "Hoot" Johnson, Coach Maynard, the four boys Ham had taken plinking and their parents, and a couple of others Ham couldn't make out. Ham was surprised to see Paul Snyder of the Atlanta Braves there in red converse shoes, a three-piece suit, a cane, and an Atlanta Braves baseball hat.

At the head of the gravesite stood Brother Bob. He had on the liturgical vestments he always wore for church services, weddings, and funerals. He smiled at Ham and his family and motioned for them to come stand by him. They took their places on either side. Ham looked down into the neatly dug grave. Brother Bob stood in front of the mound of excavated dirt, which was covered with a tan tarp. Brother Matthew, also in liturgical garb, handed each of them a mimeographed sheet with the order of service:

Memorial Service for Ham MacPherson's Arm

Processional

Welcome

Old Testament Lesson

New Testament Lesson

Eulogy

Hymn

Prayer

Recessional

Brother Bob motioned to someone in the distance, and everyone turned toward the direction of the tobacco barn, which was out of sight behind the trees. In a minute or two, a strange sight appeared. Four members of the ~~Y~~OMCA poker group appeared in the clearing carrying a miniature coffin between them. Uncle Carl, Thom Jeff, Bill, and Mack each had a handhold on the coffin. Leading them was MackieP, walking with a slow dignified gait. They approached the gathering. MackieP took a place between Nina and Ham. You would have thought he had rehearsed this time and again. Legend has it that until the day he died, MackieP returned to the gravesite around 3:00 p.m. every day and stood watch over Ham's arm for an hour or so before returning home. The pallbearers gently placed the coffin on the side of the gravesite.

Ham could see it was a beautiful coffin, made of walnut with gold-plated handles. Four green and gold ropes hung from each corner; Thom Jeff slowly and carefully folded them on to the top of the casket. The four pallbearers stood back and took their places in the congregation. The whole scene was surreal and bordered on ludicrous, but no one was laughing.

Brother Bob began.

"Friends and Family. On behalf of Ham MacPherson and his family, thank you for being here. We have gathered to grieve, to celebrate, and to worship God. Let us begin with a reading from Scripture."

Brother Matthew read from Exodus 13:19 and Joshua 24:32:

"And Moses took the bones of Joseph with him: for he had straitly sworn the children of Israel, saying, God will surely visit you; and ye shall carry up my bones away hence with you.

And the bones of Joseph, which the children of Israel brought up out of Egypt, buried they in Shechem, in a parcel of ground which Jacob bought of the sons of Hamor the father of Shechem for an hundred pieces of silver: and it became the inheritance of the children of Joseph."

Then Brother Bob opened his Bible and read from the King James Version of Romans 8 (both Brother Matthew and Brother Bob preached from the Revised Standard Version, but they used the KJV for funerals because they said congregants found the eloquence and familiarity of the KJV comforting):

"For we know that the whole creation groaneth and travaileth in pain together until now. And not only they, but ourselves also, which have the firstfruits of the Spirit, even we ourselves groan ourselves, waiting for the adoption, to wit, the redemption of our body. For we are saved by hope: but hope that is seen is not hope: for what a man seeth, why doth he yet hope for? But if we hope for that we see not, then do we with patience wait for it. . . . If God be for us, who can be against us? He that spared not his own Son, but delivered him up for us all, how shall he not with him also freely give us all things? Who shall lay anything to the charge of God's elect? It is God that justifieth. Who is he that condemneth? It is Christ that died, yea rather, that is risen again, who is even at the right hand of God, who also maketh intercession for us. Who shall separate us from the love of Christ? Shall tribulation, or distress, or persecution, or famine, or nakedness, or peril, or sword? As it is written, For thy sake we are killed all the day long; we are accounted as sheep for the slaughter. Nay, in all these things we are more than conquerors through him that loved us. For I am persuaded, that neither death, nor life, nor angels, nor principalities, nor powers, nor things present, nor things to come, nor height, nor depth, nor any other creature, shall be able to separate us from the love of God, which is in Christ Jesus our Lord."

"The word of the Lord," Brother Bob pronounced.
"Thanks be to God," everyone replied.
Brother Bob closed his Bible and began his eulogy.

"Let me get something out of the way, right off the bat. I know most of you have gotten accustomed to me doing 'innovative' things in church, and you've accepted it because I'm a crazy liberal, educated in the Northeast. And I appreciate your tolerance. But this service was not my idea. It was Thom Jeff MacPherson's.

"When Thom Jeff came to me with the idea, I was very skeptical. I'd never heard of conducting a memorial service for a body part. First, I asked how he got the arm out of the hospital, since usually such body parts are incinerated as 'bio hazardous' waste materials. Thom Jeff said he explained the situation to the doctor and had to promise keep the arm 'on ice' and isolated and to bury it within a couple of weeks. Thom Jeff told me how much it had meant to have a burial service for their beloved Alexander Hamilton, who died at birth and is buried here at this spot. He said it helped him and Nina deal with the devastating loss, and he thought a service like this might help Ham and the family express their grief. I pointed out there was a big difference between burying an infant child, no matter how little time he had spent on this earth, and burying a part of one's body.

"But Thom Jeff was persistent and he was prepared. He said the Catholic Church had an annual service, based on the teaching and practice of St. Francis, of blessing animals, and he reminded me that Second Little Rock Baptist Church, under my initiative, had instituted a similar blessing of the animals. And he stated that most of the residents of Wilkes County had buried beloved pets on their property. Then he quoted Scripture to me: 'Behold the fowls of the air: for they sow not, neither do they reap, nor gather into barns; yet your heavenly Father feedeth them. Are ye not much better than they?' Preachers don't like it much when parishioners quote Scripture to them and they have no comeback. So score a point for Thom Jeff, I thought. How many of you have buried a pet on your place?" Nearly every hand raised. "And how many of them had grave markers?" Again, nearly every hand raised.

"Then Thom Jeff gave an historical precedent. It seems Andrew 'Stonewall' Jackson, one of the leaders of the Confederate army in the Civil War, was accidentally shot by his own soldiers and had his left arm amputated in order to save his life. The surgeons wrapped Jackson's arm in a sackcloth and put it in a pile of other amputated arms and legs to be buried in a mass grave. Apparently there were a lot of amputations in the Civil War. When Jackson's personal military chaplain, Rev. Beverly Tucker Lacy, learned the arm was destined for a mass burial, he retrieved the arm and gave it a 'proper burial' on his brother's farm, complete with a twenty-one-gun salute according to some sources. There is a grave marker that reads, 'The Arm of Andrew Jackson, March 2, 1863.' When Jackson died, the rest of his remains were buried elsewhere. Apparently, every year thousands of pilgrims visit the gravesite of Jackson's arm over in Virginia.

"Now all of you know I am no fan of Stonewall Jackson or Robert E. Lee. However valiantly and bravely they may have fought, they were fighting on the wrong side. They were fighting for the right to enslave other human beings because of their skin color. That goes against everything I believe, and it fundamentally contradicts the Gospel of Jesus Christ. Still, I saw the point Rev. Lacy—and Thom Jeff—were making. If every human being is special in God's sight, then every part of that person must be special, too. As St. Paul said, 'the creation is awaiting the redemption of the body'—that must include our limbs too. The only fault I can find in Rev. Lacy's logic was that he thought Jackson was more special than the others and singled out Jackson's arm from that pile of amputated body parts for special treatment.

"So I told Thom Jeff he had me treading in deep waters I'd never been in before, and I'd need to do a little research. So I did. Other than the burial of Jackson's arm, I cannot find any record of similar burials in the Christian tradition. But I have to believe, given the number of amputees the atrocities of war have produced from the Civil War through two World Wars and the Vietnam War, some other chaplain somewhere performed a memorial service to help a serviceman deal with the loss of a limb. I also was reminded of how the early and medieval church venerated the body parts of saints as holy relics, believing they were instruments of divine healing and grace. Take St. Catherine, for example. Her head and a single finger are kept in reliquaries in San Domenico, Siena Italy. Since her death in the fourteenth century, countless miracles of healing have been attributed to these relics. Now, you can dismiss these accounts as medieval superstition, but they point to the fact Judaism and Christianity have always been embodied religions. It's why Moses brought Joseph's bones with him out of Egypt and why there were not forgotten but re-interred when Israel reached the Holy Land. It's why Christianity is based on the belief that the eternal and infinite God condescended to become a flesh and blood human being, Jesus of Nazareth, who cried when his friend died and bled and suffered when brutalized and tortured. I'd like to think the YMCA group gave Ham's arm the nickname 'Howard Hughes' not just as a joke because a scout called it a 'moneymaker' but also because the nickname is an imperfect recognition that every part of our body's was made to glorify God." A few snickers went up from the crowd at the mention of "Howard Hughes."

"All analogies are imperfect. St. Catherine's head and finger were removed posthumously because she was recognized as a saint who performed miracles during her lifetime. Ham is a good boy, but he's no saint and not likely to be canonized anytime soon. Plus, to my knowledge, he has not performed any miracles, although baseball fans who saw him pitch this season might disagree. He is, after all, known as the 'Wizard of Wilkes County.'

"So after prayer and deliberation I agreed to officiate this memorial service. More importantly, Ham agreed to it as well. After all, it's his arm. So we gather today to do two things. First, to grieve the loss Ham and his family have experienced. And make no mistake: it is a terrible and deep loss. Ham's body has been irrevocably changed. He is not a lesser man today because of his accident, but he is a different man. He is having to re-learn everything he had come to take for granted—from brushing his teeth to tying his shoes. And he will have to find a way to come to terms with the fact he will no longer be able to pitch a baseball. And pitch he did, like few others in these parts have ever done. Some will want to focus on the potential financial loss. In sports nothing is certain, but it looked as though Ham had a much better than average shot at making baseball his career. And he would have been compensated handsomely for that." Paul Snyder nodded slowly in agreement.

"But even more important, Ham lost the ability to participate in the thing in life that, outside of relationships with family and friends, gave him the most joy. Many will say Ham's ability to throw a baseball was a God-given talent. Which raises the question of 'Why?' Why, of all the folk who live in our county or in our state, did Ham have to be one to lose his left arm, when his left arm was able to do what few others are able to do. His loss, frankly, is greater than what anybody else gathered here would have lost had it happened to one of us.

"It raises theological questions for which there are really no satisfactory answers. Atheists will say if there were a God, God would grow back Ham's arm, yet we have no evidence they say, of God ever restoring the missing limb of an amputee. But, of course, their objection is not sincere; they are simply looking for ways to discredit religion. There are laws of nature that God created and that God chooses not to violate lest we find ourselves in an unstable and unpredictable world.

"The Hyper-Calvinist would say this event was predestined to happen as part of God's Divine Design. In this Design that none of us can comprehend it was planned from the beginning that at 9:35 a.m. on May 22, 1976, Ham was predestined to be shot and subsequently lose his arm. I don't know about you, but I find that entirely unsatisfying. Who wants to love and serve a God like that?

"Others will say this accident happened to teach Ham a lesson, maybe something about gun safety. Or perhaps God wanted to humble Ham; perhaps he had become too proud of his gift. We hear this a lot when folk lose loved ones, especially infants. But there are some 'lessons' the price of which—loss of life, loss of limb, loss of dignity—is simply too high to pay for the lesson learned. And again, who wants to serve a God who chooses to teach us lessons in this way?

"Some will think Ham committed some secret, terrible crime and that his loss is somehow deserved. It is no longer fashionable to articulate this view, but I have no doubt it still runs through folk's mind because it gives them a way, or so they think, to make sense of what is otherwise senseless. And it allows us to explain why it happened to Ham but not to us. Self-interest does not die easily, but we are right to silence such interpretations as sub-Christian in their logic.

"Others will argue such events are the result more generally of human Sin or Cosmic Evil. That it was not some particular sin of Ham that caused the accident but it was nonetheless an outcome of our sinful condition. I'm generally more sympathetic to this view than some of the others. I do believe humans have done unimaginably terrible things to other human beings and that this is a result of our tendency toward disobedience to our Creator and disregard of his Creation. I also think we moderns underestimate the demonic activities of Cosmic Anti-God Powers who seek to wreak Chaos in God's world. But I don't find human sinfulness or Cosmic Anti-God Powers a satisfying explanation for the direct cause of what happened to Ham. That's not to say we couldn't trace the invention of guns and other weapons of destruction ultimately to humanity's sinful and blind nationalism or self-interest—but I know that's a contested claim and a memorial service is not the place for that discussion. And at any rate, it doesn't explain the particulars of this specific situation.

"So if you are here today looking for an explanation as to why this happened, and why it happened to Ham, I'm afraid you will leave disappointed. I simply don't know. I've studied religion for most of my life, and this question lies at the heart of the conundrum that is the mystery not only of Christian faith but most of the world's religious traditions. I've continued to learn even after my formal education was completed. Most of you know I serve as 'chaplain' to the YMCA poker group." Dubya winced at the name. "Most of my theology has been reformed and reshaped through the profound discussions that occur there on Sunday evenings." Dubya looked around to make sure no law enforcement officials were present.

"The best answer I've heard to this question, 'why do these things happen?' Came from one of the theologians I hold in highest regard, one of the YMCA, Kenneth Bill Andrews Fagg." Bill stiffened a bit at the mention of his name. "Now, I know Bill doesn't go to church on a regular basis like the rest of us, but he has a keen theological mind that he expresses in plain and forceful language. When we discussed the problem of theodicy, the problem of why a good God apparently allows bad things to happen like Ham's accident, Bill said, '*Shit happens!*'"

Most congregations might have been shocked by that language in a church service, but Brother Bob had used profanity enough in the past—always strategically and in an appropriate context—that no one was offended or even surprised. Turns out when you don't take any salary for your services, a minister can cuss in front of most anybody he wants to. Another lesson learned in the crucible of parish ministry that went beyond the hallowed halls of Divinity School.

"The Greek for that expression is '*skubala ginetai.*' Simply put, it means in a world constantly in flux and process, bad things can happen and often do. And there is no ready-made explanation. They are not part of some hidden cosmic Design; they are not intended to teach us a lesson, even if we sometimes do grow from the adversity—it is an outcome of not a reason for the event; they are not the direct result of human Sin or Cosmic Anti-God Powers. They take no particular aim at the Unrighteous or detours around the Righteous; they come, rather, as the random convulsions of a world out of sync with its Creator. It does not mean God does not care for us or that God does not suffer with us when we suffer. But it does mean those of you who have come to this service burdened with guilt, thinking the accident was your fault, need to leave here relieved of this burden. It was not your fault!"

Brother Bob scanned the crowd pausing at Ham, Nora, JC, and the plinking boys. Bill meanwhile was beaming. From that day forward, people called him the Resident Theologian of Wilkes County. He didn't know it, but in addition to the agile theological mind he shared with theological giants like Karl Barth, Paul Tillich, and John Howard Yoder, he also shared with them a proclivity toward sexual indiscretions—or worse.

"We need to shift from why to how. How can we help Ham and his family deal with this loss? The answer is easy; it's practice that's much harder. Be there for them. Listen. Listen even when the grief is raw and unfiltered. And to the family and to you especially, Ham, grieve this loss. It is real and it is painful. But as you grieve remember this. Paul did not say that nothing could separate us from one of our limbs—an arm or a leg or a finger or a toe—but he did say that nothing could separate us from the love of God which is in Christ Jesus our Lord. Feel God's love and grace and mercy surrounding you.

"So we have come to grieve.

"But we have also come to celebrate. We often talk at funeral services about celebrating the life of the one deceased. Certainly Ham has accomplished much in his eighteen short years to celebrate. But we are not celebrating those accomplishments. Nor are we celebrating the accomplishments of Ham's arm, which again are many. We are celebrating the simple fact that Ham is still here with us. That is no small thing. Ham could have easily died on May 22. Had the gun blast been a few inches to the right, the entry wound would have been in the chest. Were it not for the quick thinking of his friend JC MacPherson and the able and competent work of doctors and nurses in Wilkes General Emergency Room, we could easily be conducting a full funeral service for Thomas Hamilton MacPherson. Thank God we are not." A few scattered "Amens" rose up from the crowd.

"Instead, we are celebrating the life that still lies ahead of Ham MacPherson. We don't know exactly where that path will lead, but it is strewn with hope and promise. He has met the love of his life, Nora. He has extraordinary gifts beyond the baseball diamond. He has a loving and supportive family and church. There is much to celebrate about Ham's future!

"Finally, some of you have expressed questions about the future. What will happen to Ham's arm in the End? Should it be reunited with Ham when he is buried? Will it be reunited with him in Heaven if it's not buried with him? There are different schools of thought on this issue. Orthodox Jews believe the old physical body would be reconstituted in the New Age. It's one of the reasons incineration of Jews during the Holocaust was such an especially heinous and reprehensible act. Others have argued our transformed bodies will be in continuity with our old physical selves but our resurrection bodies will be constituted out of 'new cosmic stuff' (that seemed to be an early response by church fathers to the hypothetical scenario of 'what happens to a Christian eaten by a cannibal'!). Others think the resurrection will be a 'spiritual body' that is immaterial in its essence. So, in this view, it doesn't matter what happens to the physical body. From dust we have come, and to dust we return—but our spirits live forever.

"I, for one, favor the new, resurrection body, but in any case I don't think we need to worry about Ham's eternal separation from his arm. Most of us will be dead, hopefully, when that question has to be addressed by Ham's children or grandchildren. I just want to go on record as saying there are other, more important things to worry about it. Reunite them in a future grave if you wish, but don't worry about it if you can't. God will take care of the rest.

"Another interesting issue is posed by our Pentecostal friends, whom I have heard assert that an amputee in the resurrection will raise not one but two arms in Alleluia praise to God. It's a beautiful image, and there is much in Pentecostal experience I affirm. Of course, I've never seen Ham raise one hand in worship, so short of a conversion to Pentecostalism, I can't really see him doing that in Heaven either." People chuckled.

"More serious is the question of what constitutes our core identity. Some disabled persons I know think their disability—whether blindness or deafness or loss of limb—is so much a part of who they are that they can't imagine being different in Heaven. And they point to the fact that the glorified, resurrected Lord Jesus still retained the wounds from the crucifixion in his transformed body. Again, I don't know the answer to this question, and it's too early to know what constitutes Ham's 'core identity.' There may be a difference between one who was born with a certain disability, such as congenital blindness, and another whose disability is the result of traumatic injury. One may experience loss in a way the other does not. But I do believe we will have the identity in Heaven that God intends for us and that our essential selves, whatever that consists of, will be able to love and worship God and each other in ways we cannot today imagine. That is our Resurrection Hope. That in Eternity we will find our true selves in the arms of an Infinite and Infinitely Merciful God. So may it be and so do we pray. Amen."

Those gathered said "Amen." Brother Matthew asked everyone to turn their sheet over, and they sang, "Leaning on the Everlasting Arms."

What a fellowship, what a joy divine,
Leaning on the everlasting arms;
What a blessedness, what a peace is mine,
Leaning on the everlasting arms.
Leaning, leaning,
Safe and secure from all alarms;
Leaning, leaning,
Leaning on the everlasting arms.

As they sang, Uncle Carl, Thom Jeff, Bill, and Mack came forward. Each took a green and gold cord, lifted the casket, carefully lowered it into the grave, and stepped back.

When they finished singing, Brother Matthew said, "Let us pray:

Christ go before you,
To prepare a way of service,
Christ go behind you,
To gather up your efforts for his glory;
Christ go beside you,
As Leader and Guide;
Christ go within you,
As comfort and stay;
Christ go beneath you,
To uphold with everlasting arms;
Christ go above you,
To reign as Lord and King eternal. Amen."

Then Brother Bob motioned to the family to lead the recessional. Sporadic sobbing could be heard from the crowd. MackieP, almost as if on cue, stood and turned and began walking away from the clearing. The rest of the MacPherson clan followed. Nina threw in a rose she had carried to the service. Diane and Michael Allen each threw in a handful of dirt from underneath the tarp. As Ham approached the grave, he stopped, reached into his pocket, and pulled out a baseball enclosed in a freezer bag. It was (he hoped) the game ball from the no-hitter he pitched in the play-offs—the last game he would ever pitch. He dropped it into the grave; it landed with a plunk on the coffin. More sobs. Everyone then joined the recessional past the open grave. When JC reached the grave, he reached into his pocket and pulled out a baseball. This was the one he had hit for the walk-off two-run, and he had carried it with him every day since the game. The freezer bag indicated Ham's act had been premeditated. JC's, on the other hand, was a spontaneous, impulsive act. But both acts were sincere, and each, in its own way, a gesture intended to bid farewell to the arm.

CHAPTER 22

The day after the memorial service for Ham's arm, a man stopped at Thom Jeff and Nina's house. Thom Jeff had gone to work, so he explained to Nina he was a "vintage car collector" and was interested in purchasing the Studebaker. They were standing in the yard looking at the car when Ham came outside to see what was going on. Nina explained the man wanted to buy the Studebaker.

"How much?" Ham asked.

"Seven hundred dollars," the man said. That was two hundred dollars more than Ham had spent on the car. This man did not know the fine art of dickering.

"What are you goin' to do with it?"

"Oh, I'm a collector. I'll restore it and use it for pleasure driving. I belong to a Studebaker Club. We ride in parades and special events," the man said.

"Oh, kinda like a Hearse Club?" Ham asked. The man looked puzzled. "I'll take eight hundred for her."

"Seven fifty, and that's my final offer."

"Sold," Ham said. With that the transaction was done. The man handed over a fifty and seven crisp, one hundred dollar bills and said he'd be back in an hour to get the car. Ham gave him the keys.

"You sure about this, Ham?" Nina asked. "You don't want to talk to your daddy?"

"No Mama. I need to sell the car. I love it, but I can't drive a manual transmission with the shift on the steerin' column." Nina hadn't thought about this, but Ham had.

"Oh, I see." Nina did, in fact, think this was a wise idea.

"Can you drive me down to Moore's garage, Mama? I wanna see if Glenn still has that Plymouth for sale."

"Sure, Ham. Let me get my keys." Nina went into the kitchen, took off her apron, and met Ham at the station wagon. At Ham's request, Nina stayed in the car while Ham went into Moore's auto shop. When he went through the door, he saw Scotty, the son of Glenn and Peggy Moore, sitting in his wheelchair in the middle of the room.

Scotty was singing his favorite song,

My Bonnie Lies Over the Ocean
My Bonnie Lies Over the Sea,
My Bonnie Lies Over the Ocean,
Oh Brrring Back My Bonnie to Me;
Brrring back, oh brrring back, oh brrring back my Bonnie to me, to me.
Brrring back, oh brrring back, oh brrring back my Bonnie to me.

He sang the "bring back" chorus with extra gusto, rolling his Rs with conviction. When Scotty finished singing, he said, "Who's there?" Those words signaled a game he loved to play with whomever entered the shop. They were not to speak, but rather "Who's there?" was an invitation for the visitor to come behind Scotty and place his or her hands over Scotty's eyes. Scotty would then smell the hands, sometimes pulling a wrist down to his nose. Most of the time, if it were somebody Scotty knew, he would correctly guess the person's identity. He had never failed to identify Ham.

So Ham put his hand on Scotty's eyes. Scotty sniffed and thought and then sniffed again.

"Ham, is that you?"

"Yep, you got me again, Scotty."

"Let me smell your other hand, Ham."

"I don't have it anymore, "

"Where'd it go?"

Before Ham could think of an answer, Scotty said, "Sing with me, Ham." And he started again on "My Bonnie." Ham sang with him, wondering if Scotty thought the plea to "bring back my Bonny to me to me" might now apply to Ham's arm. Before he could go too far down that path, Scotty's dad, Glenn, entered the room and said good naturedly, "Scotty, don't pester the customers! What can I do for you, Ham?"

"Hi Glenn, I was just wonderin' if that Plymouth Fury was still for sale."

"Sure is. Was fixin' to put a sign on it on Monday. You interested?"

"I believe I might be. How much?"

Glenn scuffed his boot along the linoleum floor of the shop. "I was thinkin' I'd ask five hundred dollars. I've re-worked her—new belts, tires, changed all the fluids."

"Oh, well, I just don't think I could come up with that much money, Glenn. I was thinkin' more along the lines of four hundred dollars."

"Well, I sure would like to see you have the car, Ham. I know you can't drive that manual transmission on the Studebaker. I guess I could come down to four seventy-five. But anythin' less than that and I'd be losin' money, don't you know."

"I understand, I understand. Really do. I guess I could stretch it up to four twenty-five."

By now both of them were scuffing boots on the floor and looking out the front glass window. Scotty sat perfectly still, listening to it all. After a moment's silence, Glenn spoke.

"So four fifty is it?"

"Yep!" Ham exclaimed. Scotty laughed and clapped his hands with glee. They shook hands and Ham pulled out exactly $450 from his right pocket. The rest of the money was in his left pocket, in case the dickering had gone sideways. Ham headed out to get his new purchase.

"See you Ham," Scotty said. "I hope you find your arm!"

Ham said, "Thanks, Scotty. See you later." He could hear Scotty singing under his breath, "Bring back, bring back, oh bring back my Bonny to me to me . . . . "

Ham drove away with a new car for $450. The most important thing to Ham was that it was an automatic transmission. He drove straight to Lowe's Hardware Store (where he would begin working the next week) and bought a knob for the steering wheel to make it easier to turn corners. Uncle Carl mounted the knob for him, and Ham was set. When Thom Jeff heard what Ham had done, and especially the prices he sold and bought the cars for, he expressed his approval. Coming from Thom Jeff, who was the consummate wheeler/dealer, that was high praise indeed.

Ham spent the next couple of days catching up on homework and preparing for final exams. Nina really wanted him to graduate with his class. The winter of 1975–1976 had been exceptionally harsh; some weathermen

said it was the coldest winter in 200 years. It had been brutal, especially following four mild winters. Between the cold and the snow, Wilkes Central
had cancelled five days of classes, all of which had to be made up at the end
of the year. That pushed graduation from the first to the second Saturday in
June. What that meant for Ham was that he could take his exams and could
graduate with his class. Neither prospect particularly warmed Ham's heart.
He could not, of course, take written exams, so the principal, Mr. Sigmund,
arranged oral exams in each of his classes on Thursday and Friday. Much
to Nina's delight (and Ham's disappointment), Ham was approved to attend
graduation ceremonies on Saturday morning, June 12.

Nina had ordered Ham's academic apparel months before his accident, and the gown had been hanging in his closet for several weeks. On
Saturday morning, Ham went down for breakfast. The whole family was
there—Thom Jeff, Nina, Diane, and Michael Allen—a fairly rare occur-
rence in the MacPherson household. Ham had to eat slowly, and he needed
help slicing open his biscuit. Diane and Michael Allen stole furtive glances
to see how Ham would negotiate certain food items with just one hand.
He did okay; the occupational therapist had taught him a few tricks about
getting food to his mouth in the most efficient way possible. And also a few
tricks about dressing, which Ham was eager to put into play after breakfast.
For example, he knew now it was easier to dress sitting down and to use his
"good" hand to dress the affected side first. He put his dress shirt face down
with the neck furthest away and the sleeves hanging down the sides. He
lifted the shirt up and slipped the sleeve onto his stump as far as he could.
Then he put his right arm into the sleeve and put his head down and lifted
the shirt up and over his head. Voila! He could button the sleeve dangling
down from his amputation but he'd need help later with the other sleeve.
He wondered if he could manage cuff links better? Next came his socks. His
mother had bought some that had loose elastic and he popped both socks
into place. Next his pants. He put his pants on, also sitting down, and then
stood to pull them up over his rump. He could latch the top and pull up the
zipper. He could also thread the belt through the loops, but he would need
help buckling it. He hoped soon to be able to buckle it himself. He rarely
wore ties before his accident, and even then when he did they were of the
pre-tied snap-on variety. So he put the tie on. Since he was wearing a gown
he wouldn't need a coat. He slipped his feet into loafers—he wasn't sure if
he'd ever wear lace-up shoes again.

He grabbed his gown and tam with his right hand and went downstairs. His belt was flapping across his waist. His mother smiled and said, "Good job, Hammie," and she buckled his belt for him.

He got behind the wheel of the Plymouth, and Thom Jeff got into the passenger side. Nina and the two kids piled into the back. They headed off to the Wilkes Central gym where the ceremony was to take place. Ham dreaded it.

Everyone was nice enough. Some people gawked at the empty shirtsleeve that used to contain Ham's "money-making" left arm. Ham tried not to be self-conscious. Nora and JC were very protective. Nora's belly protruded slightly under her gown. People had begun to whisper about it the last few days of school, but she ignored them. Since they were lined up alphabetically, Nora had to go on to the front to join the other "Cs," but JC stayed with Ham. He would cross the stage just ahead of Ham.

JC's sister, Debra MacPherson, sang "You'll Never Walk Alone." It was mesmerizing. She did have a beautiful voice, and she was beautiful. Ham clearly saw why Bobby Skeeter was head over heels for her. The valedictorian of the class, Bill Owens, gave a brief charge to the graduating class of 1976 and introduced the graduation speaker, Billy Packer. Billy Packer was a basketball analyst, best known to Ham and his friends for doing color commentary for ACC basketball games. He had been thrust into the national limelight the year before when he was the TV commentator for the 1975 Final Four. Packer told a lot of humorous stories. Ham wasn't sure what the theme was—maybe about how our success depends on our relationships with other people. He talked about his coach at Wake Forest, "Bones" McKinney. McKinney was a colorful coach known for his on-court antics and off-court quips. In order to cut down on the number of technical fouls, he had Piedmont Airlines install a seatbelt on the Wake Forest bench so he could restrain himself. Packer said he used to drive "Bones," an ordained Baptist minister, around to different churches and campuses for speaking engagements. Sometimes McKinney would spend the rides studying Greek verb tenses for the class he was taking with Dr. Cronje Earp of the Classics department. He said Len Chappell was one of the best players ever to play in the ACC. At 6'8" and 240 lbs., Chappell had quick hands and a sure jump shot and was so strong, Packer said, that when he got the ball near the basket he was sure to put it "and whoever was guarding him" through the hoop. Chappell led Wake Forest to the NCAA semi-finals at

Madison Square Garden where they lost to Ohio State, who was led by Jerry Lucas and John Havlicek.

Finally, Packer talked about his relationship with Cleo Hill, the gifted African American basketball player who played for the legendary Clarence "Bighouse" Gaines, who coached at Winston-Salem State University (then known as Winston-Salem Teachers College). Packer and Hill arranged for their two teams to scrimmage against each other several times. Since such integrated competitions were illegal, there were no coaches, referees, or fans involved, though Packer hinted strongly that both McKinney and Gaines were aware of, and approved, these pick-up games.

After Packer's address, it was time for diplomas to be awarded. Several of his classmates with last names closer to the beginning of the alphabet received wildly enthusiastic responses from members of the audience when their names were called and they crossed the stage.

JC leaned over to Ham and whispered, "Some folk graduate cum laude. Some folk graduate magna cum laude. Some folk graduate summa cum laude. These folk right here, with family and friends hollerin' their heads off, are graduating thank the laude!" They both laughed. It helped ease Ham's nervousness about walking across the stage.

Mostly he was worried about holding his diploma and shaking Mr., Sigmund's hand. It went better than expected however. When his name was read, the crowd applauded loudly, embarrassing Ham (though JC had received a loud ovation as well). It soon led to a standing ovation. Most people there had not seen Ham since the district playoffs, and this out-burst of applause was as much as anything a show of appreciation for the magic that the Wizard of Wilkes county had performed in the 1976 season, and especially in the playoff run in which he had pitched so brilliantly. He instinctively stuffed the diploma under his shortened left arm and shook Mr. Sigmund's hand. Billy Packer had come over to shake Ham's hand, too, which brought another round of approving applause from the crowd. JC was waiting for him at the bottom of the stage's stairs.

"That was awesome, Ham," JC exclaimed. Ham had to agree.

That evening, Nina and Cornelia had invited a few friends to join the family in a celebratory dinner for Ham and Nora's graduation. The din-ner was at Dubya and Cornelia's house because they had a larger dining room. The usual suspects were there. In addition to the immediate family, the ¥OMCA group, Brother Bob (who came in his role as minister and not ¥OMCA member), and JC. Aunt Nora and Uncle Wilson had come over from Chapel Hill. After a dinner of fried chicken, sliced ham, sweet potato casserole, green beans, corn, potato salad, pinto beans, and pecan pie, everybody moved into the family room.

Ham stood in front of the fireplace and said, "'Scuse me everybody. Could I have your attention? Thank you. First thanks for comin' to this dinner, and thanks especially to Mama and Grandma Cornelia for fixin' such a wonderful meal. Me and Nora thank you for being here to celebrate our graduation from high school. Nora, come up here too!" Nora stood beside Ham.

"While y'all are here, we wanted to announce that we're gettin' married!" Ham raised Nora's left hand with his right, so everybody could see the tiny engagement ring sparkling on her finger. The ring had been Nina's mother's. Everyone clapped.

"When's the big date?" Bill Fagg hollered from the back.

Ham looked at Nora, "July 1?"

"July 2!" Nora corrected.

Aunt Nora cupped her hands around her mouth and blurted from the back of the room, "And you're expecting a baby, aren't you Nora, dear?" Instinctively, Nora placed her hands on her tummy, and Ham turned red. Actually, almost everyone in the room knew they were pregnant. Still, it was an awkward moment, and in an effort to move past it, Uncle Carl made his way to the front.

"Do you wanna know if it's a boy or a girl?" He asked, fishing into his pocket for a piece of string, which he always carried in cases such as this.

"Uncle Carl—!" Ham began.

Nora cut him off, "Of course we would, Uncle Carl!"

Carl smiled. "Well, I'll need to borrow that there ring," he said, pointing to the engagement ring. Nora obliged and handed the ring to Carl.

He quickly tied the string to the ring and said, "Now it's real important that you don't move, Nora." Ham rolled his eyes. Carl let the ring dangle right in front of Nora's tummy, holding it as perfectly still as he could. In a minute, the ring began slowly moving in a clockwise circle round and round.

"You're doin' that Carl!" Bill exclaimed.

"Am not!"

"What does it mean?" Nora asked.

"It means you're goin' to have a girl," Cornelia pronounced solemnly.

"That's right," Uncle Carl agreed. "You and Ham are goin' to have a sweet li'l ole' girl." Carl coughed and reached for his inhaler.

Sadly, only one of the two making the prediction would live to see if it was fulfilled.

CHAPTER 23

The next day, Sunday, was Ham's last before he was scheduled to begin work at Lowe's Hardware Store. He decided not to go to the library that afternoon; he had gotten out of the routine in the two weeks since he had come home from the hospital. So after church and Sunday lunch, Ham was doing some exercises with his arm in his room. He heard a knock on the front door and knew immediately they had a visitor since family and friends all came to the screen door at the back of the house. He could hear his mother say in a surprised voice, "Well hello. We didn't expect to see you. How nice of you to come! Ham will be very pleased to see you!"

"Hammie," Nina yelled up the stairs. "You've got company!"

Ham wondered who it could be and hurried down the stairs. There standing in the hallway to his house was Bobby Skeeter!

"Hello, Bobby."

"Hi Ham," Bobby replied. "I thought I'd come by and check on you. I hope this is not a bad time for a visit." Bobby glanced at Ham's empty left sleeve.

"Not at all. Come on in." Ham motioned to the living room.

"Would you like some iced tea, Bobby?" Nina asked.

"Yes ma'am. That'd be real nice."

"What are you doin' back here, Bobby?" Ham asked. "I thought y'all would still be down at the state championship in Chapel Hill."

"We came back late last night. I came over here today to see Debra. I thought I'd drop by here first for a few minutes."

"Well I'm glad you did. How'd y'all do in the tourney?"

"Oh, we won it all, Ham. State champs!" Bobby replied.

"I knew y'all could do it. Who did you play?"

Hallsboro High, down around Wilmington. Beat 'em 2–0 Friday night and 2–1 yesterday afternoon."

"Did you pitch both games?"

"Yep. Couldn't really trust nobody else to do that. Neither could Coach Howell."

"You pitched every game you played this year?" Ham said, amazed.

"Yeah, I guess I did. We had a couple of relief pitchers come in if we was way ahead at the end of the game. So I didn't pitch every inning of every game, but I started 'em all."

"So you finished 23–1 as a pitcher?" Again Ham was amazed.

"I reckon that's right."

"Did your arm ever get sore?" Ham had wanted to ask Bobby that question since the first time he read Bobby was pitching every game earlier in the year.

"It's funny. My arm would get tired, but it never really hurt. Coach says I have a rubber arm. Since I'm gonna play football instead of baseball and because I was a senior, I didn't really care. In fact, I wanted to pitch all the games."

"So Coach Rabb hasn't been able to convince you to play baseball in Chapel Hill, too?"

"More accurate to say he hasn't convinced Coach Crum, the football coach! Since football is paying my scholarship, I'm gonna do what Coach Crum says."

"That makes sense," Ham nodded.

Nina brought in two glasses of sweet tea and set them on the table between Ham and Bobby and left the two alone to talk.

"How are you doin' Ham? I've tried to keep up with you through JC. You sure did give us a scare that day you got shot. I've never seen so much blood!"

Ham lifted his stump. "Well, I guess I'm lucky to be alive, Bobby. I've had a lot to deal with, but I've got good friends and family, and I think I've come a long way. I'm gettin' married in a couple of weeks!"

"I heard that from JC. Congratulations! What's your girlfriend's name?"

"Nora. Nora Culpepper."

"I think I saw y'all at the first game of the year."

"Yep. That was her. I'm surprised you noticed anybody at that game except Debra MacPherson." Ham winked and took a big gulp of tea, He loved his mother's sweet tea.

"Well, yeah, when I saw Debra everythin' and everybody else kinda faded into the background." Bobby admitted. "And then when I heard her sing, I was 100 percent slain."

Ham laughed and said. "Debra does have a beautiful voice. And she is a looker, if I can say so myself."

Bobby changed the subject back to Ham. "Where are you and Nora goin' to live?"

"Probably here, or over at my Grandpa and Grandma's house. They have a finished room in the basement. We're gonna have a baby in November!"

"Wow! Congratulations! Are you goin' to school?"

"Not really sure about that. I hope to eventually. I'm startin' to work over at Lowe's tomorrow. Hopefully I can save up some money and enroll here at Stearns and Marshall. Or maybe go over to UNC-Asheville."

"I hear Lowe's is a good place to work," Bobby sipped on his tea.

"Yeah, my Uncle Carl has worked there for a long time, back when they just had the one store. Bobby, I haven't had a chance to thank you properly for what you did for me that day. You and JC saved my life. I'm sure I would have died there in that ditch if the two of you hadn't come by."

"Well, I don't know about that, Ham, but I'm glad we were there to help. I know JC thinks the world of you. And I think the world of JC, so I know you must be good people."

"You might not think as much of JC if you knew he was braggin' about tappin' a home run off you in the regional finals!"

"Ah, I just let him hit that one 'cause I'm datin' his sister!"

"That's what I told JC. 'Course he was havin' none of that."

"Speakin' of JC, do you happen to know what 'JC' stands for anyhow?" Bobby asked.

"I think it's just his name—Jay Cee. I don't think it stands for nothin'. What did he tell you?"

"He told me it stood for Jesus Christ."

"That's what he told me." They both laughed.

"He said he was gonna be the Messiah for the State University football program."

"What'd you say?" Ham asked.

"I told him no offensive lineman had ever been Savior of a football program. JC said, 'God works in mysterious ways. Jesus was born in Bethlehem, and nobody was expectin' that.'"

They laughed again. Ham thought for a moment. "You know, it's funny Bobby. I loved playin' sports, especially baseball, but one of the things I realize now is how little we know about the people we play. And the less we know about our opponents the easier it is to make them into some kind of devil or evil person. Brother Bob calls it 'demonizin'.'"

"That's interestin'. I know what you mean though. I've thought the same thing, especially after gettin' to know JC and his family." Ham wanted to tell Bobby his thoughts about him the Sunday Brother Martin England had preached on the Good Samaritan. About how Ham had put Bobby on his "shit list" as one he would least like to get help from. And, lo and behold, the person who turned the corner to help Ham when he was in the ditch was none other than Bobby Skeeter, the Sylva Streak.

Instead, Ham said, "I think coaches think we won't play as hard against people if we know them. But that can't be true. Think about Tommie and Hank Aaron. They were brothers who played several years against each other, even though they were teammates most of their careers."

"Or Joe and Dom DiMaggio back in the fifties," Bobby offered.

"That's an even better example," Ham admitted. "Joe played for the Yankees and Dom played for the Red Sox, the team the Yankees hated the most."

"But I bet they both enjoyed their mama's home cooked meals together at Christmas. And drank their mama's sweet tea, if Italians drink sweet tea." Both laughed.

"I'm real sorry this happened to you Ham. Does it hurt?" Bobby said, pointing to Ham's arm.

"It's the damnedest thing, Bobby. Most of the time it don't hurt, but every now and then when I wake up in the mornin', it hurts right here." Ham pointed to the missing part of his arm. "Kinda hurts like it did after I pitched a game. But there ain't no arm there. Doc called it phantom pain."

"That's really weird." Bobby said. Ham agreed. "Kinda hard to figure why things like this happen." Ham agreed with that, too.

"Brother Bob says there are some things we just can't understand in this life. I'm trying to accept that and be happy for the good things in my life. Like Nora and the baby. But it's hard sometimes, Bobby," Ham admitted. "Thinkin' I won't ever get to pitch again. Thinkin' what people must think when they see this. I get pretty down sometimes." He lifted his left arm.

"Screw them, Ham MacPherson! You show 'em what you're made of! You did it on the field; now you gotta do it off the field."

Ham nodded slowly. "Thanks Bobby."

"I guess I better be goin', Ham. Debra will start to wondering where I am." Bobby drained the remaining tea from his glass.

"You don't want to keep that girl waitin'! Thanks for comin', Bobby. It means more than you can know. And thanks again for savin' my life."

Ham walked Bobby to the door. Ham stuck out his hand to shake, but Bobby grabbed him in a bear hug and held him tight for a long time. "Let's stay in touch, Ham. Thanks for the tea, Mrs. MacPherson."

"You're welcome, Bobby," Nina appeared in the doorway to the kitchen. "Thank you for comin'. You feel free to drop by anytime you're in this neck of the woods."

"I will," Bobby said and left.

CHAPTER 24

O n Monday, Ham reported to Lowe's Hardware Store for his first day of work. Ham pulled the Plymouth Fury into the parking lot of the Lowe's at 8:45 a.m. He was to meet the store manager, Bob Tillman, at 9:00 a.m. in his office. Ham walked into the front doors of the store. This was the original location of Lowe's and had retained its homey, small-town feel. The hardwood floors were worn with years of service since Mr. L. S. Lowe had opened the store fifty-five years ago.

"Good morning. Welcome to Lowe's," said a greeter who met him at the door.

"Good morning," Ham said. "I'm lookin' for Mr. Tillman."

"Follow me," the greeter said, taking a furtive glance at Ham's sleeve. He was not scheduled to get his prosthesis for another couple of weeks.

Ham was led to an office with glass on all sides. Mr. Tillman came out from behind his desk. He smiled and shook Ham's hand. He was a tall, thin, middle-aged man with a receding hairline. "You're Ham MacPherson?"

"Yes sir," Ham replied.

"Come in, come in. Let me tell you about Lowe's." Mr. Tillman showed Ham to a chair beside his desk and proceeded to give Ham a brief history of the successes of Lowe's Hardware Store.

"As a native of North Wilkesboro, you may know, Ham, that Lowe's is a local 'rags-to-riches' story. In 1921, Mr. L. S. Lowe opened a builder's supply store under the name 'Mr. L. S. Lowe North Wilkesboro Hardware Store.' His son, James, took over the store following old man Lowe's death in 1940, and in 1943, he took on his brother-in-law Carl Buchan as a partner. In 1949, Lowe and Buchan opened a second store in Sparta, North Carolina.

"In 1952, Buchan traded his interest in a cattle farm and car dealership he co-owned with James for full ownership of the hardware store. He kept the name 'Lowe's' to preserve the slogan, 'Lowe's low prices' and opened a third store in Asheville. The business continued to expand and grow, and by the time he died in 1960, Buchan owned fifteen stores. Lowe's bought directly from manufacturers and was able to keep customer prices 'low,' as a result and as promised.

"Board members Robert Strickland, fresh from Harvard Business School, and Leonard Herring took the company public in 1961 and incorporated as 'Lowe's Companies.' Riding the crest of the 'do-it-yourself home improvement' wave, Lowe's increased sales from 4.1 million dollars in 1952 when it was still a mom and pop store to more than 700 million dollars with nearly 200 chains nationwide."

The history seemed rehearsed and a bit canned. While Tillman talked, Ham saw Uncle Carl walk behind Mr. Tillman and wave from behind the glass wall. Ham smiled.

"So Ham, your Uncle Carl tells me you're good at math."

"Yes sir, I made really good marks in math at school."

"Good, good. We want to train you as a checkout clerk. Do you have any experience with a cash register?"

"No sir, but I've worked a lot on my mother's addin' machine, helpin' her do Daddy's payroll for the sawmill."

"Good. That's good. We're still using the original National Cash Register Series 300 in this store that Mr. Lowe purchased when he opened the store in 1921. They're reliable but a little slow. We're scheduled to modernize to electronic cash registers, though some of the folk in the corporate offices down the street," Mr. Tillman nodded toward the left, "would like to preserve the nostalgic feel of the 'mother store.' I've no objections to that so long as it doesn't slow business." Mr. Tillman was obviously an ambitious man. Ham had no way of knowing at the time, but even from that initial encounter, he would not be surprised when he heard Mr. Tillman had been promoted to Vice-President of the Southeastern Region of Lowe's in 1985.

"Today, you'll shadow Christie Phelan, our senior checkout clerk." Mr. Tillman led Ham out of the office and introduced him to Christie. She was a courteous, heavy set, middle-aged woman who took an immediate liking to Ham. When she saw how quickly he caught on, she liked him even more.

Business was slow that morning, so Christie was able to show Ham the intricacies of the NRC 300 series cash register. Ham immediately fell in love with NRC. The Lowe's employees kept the brass finely polished. The cash register itself had a simple elegance in its function. To make a sale of fifty cents, one simply pushed down the key marked "fifty cents." It was manual and had to be pushed all the way down. Removing the finger from the key caused the key to return to its original position, the bell to ring, and the cash drawer to open. The indicator showed the amount of the purchase, added it to the counter, and printed it on the detail strip. Items that required two keys to be pushed down simultaneously, such as the $1 key and the fifty cent key for a purchase of $1.50 were more challenging to Ham, but luckily he had a large hand and was able to reach most all the keys. Christie told him if he couldn't press two keys together, just to call another clerk over to help. That rarely happened.

After lunch, Ham was ready to try the cash register by himself. He checked out three customers, all carpenters who had come in for various supplies. At first it was awkward; Ham had a hard time coordinating the keys, and he made several mistakes. He was sure he could have been much better if he had use of his left hand. His left hand. Ham looked at the empty sleeve hanging on his left side. He was determined to master this machine. Mr. Tillman watched from his office with open curiosity. At 5:00 p.m. Christie showed Ham how to get a statement of the day's business, count out the money for the day, enter it into the account book, and put the money in a plastic bag in Mr. Tillman's office. Mr. Tillman then put the bag into a large cast iron safe behind his desk. He made bank deposits each morning.

"He done real good, Mr. Tillman," Christie complimented Ham.

"I can see that, Christie." Mr. Tillman replied.

"Good work, Ham. We'll see you back here in the morning. Come at 7:30 so you can have the register up and running when the doors open at 8:00 a.m. Sharp."

"Yes sir, thank you Mr. Tillman. I promise I'll get better with the register," Ham apologized.

"Oh you should have seen me my first day. You did just fine, Ham," Christie reassured him.

"Thank you Christie."

"See you tomorrow, Ham."

Ham walked out into the parking lot. Uncle Carl was standing beside the Plymouth Fury. "How'd you like your first day on the job, Ham?"

"Hi Uncle Carl. I liked it a lot. I warn't real good on the register, but think I can get the hang of it."

"That's great, Ham! Glad to have you on the team. See you tomorrow." Uncle Carl got into Mr. Ed and sped away. Ham could hear Jimmy Buffett's "Come Monday" coming through the hearse's speakers.

By Wednesday, Ham had improved his skills on the NRC 300 series. He still had trouble reaching certain keys, but he knew how to unjam the keys and change the paper and ribbon for the receipt printer. There were only a few things Ham couldn't do with one hand, and his co-workers were eager to help when that happened.

On Thursday afternoon, Mr. Tillman asked Christie to take over Ham's register so he could talk to Ham. Ham walked into Mr. Tillman's office, alarmed. "Is everythin' all right, Mr. Tillman?" Ham asked nervously.

"Oh yes, Ham, everything is quite all right. You are doing a marvelous job, just marvelous. I have a question though."

"Yes, Mr. Tillman?"

"Did you tell me you helped you mother do a payroll for your dad's business?"

"Yes sir, I did."

"How many workers does your dad employ?"

"Generally eight to ten. Why Mr. Tillman?"

"Well, the woman who does our books and cuts payroll checks had a baby this week, and I was wondering if you could stay late tonight and help me get those checks out. We'll pay overtime. Christie says you are indeed a whiz at math. She says you check the machine's math by adding the numbers in your head as you go. She swears you don't need a cash register to keep up with the totals."

Ham blushed. "Well, like I told you, I do real good with figurin' numbers, and I like workin' that stuff out in my head. Plus I took a course in accountin' in high school—double entries, that sort of thing."

"Wonderful Ham," Mr. Tillman said. "Workers don't like to miss a paycheck. I don't expect you want to miss your first one either. So if you think you could lend me a hand, I'd be grateful." Ham smiled to himself; good thing I only need one hand. Ham couldn't provide two. Brother Bob would be proud. In their last weekly counseling session, he said humor was a sign of healing and acceptance. It wasn't too funny, but at least Ham was making an attempt.

"Oh, no sir, we wouldn't want that. Do you mind if I call my mother and let her know I'll be late for supper?"

"No, of course. That'd be fine. And Ham, did I hear you were getting married this weekend?"

"No, it's in a couple of weeks, on the evenin' of July 2." Ham added, "After work."

"I don't remember you asking for time off for your honeymoon?" Mr. Tillman had a hint of worry in his voice; he was obviously thinking about the payroll in a couple of weeks hence.

"Oh no sir. Me and Nora aren't takin' a honeymoon just yet. My folks are goin' to Carolina Beach for the week of the Fourth. Our honeymoon will be havin' the house to ourselves for the week. I'll be here every day next week, Mr. Tillman. I do need to go next Friday afternoon to be fitted for a prosthesis, if that's okay?"

"Oh sure. Of course. All right, let's get to work on those payroll checks, Ham."

CHAPTER 25

O n Sunday afternoon, Ham decided to go the public library and catch up on his reading. He hadn't been there since the accident. He thumbed through the *Wilkes-Patriot Journal* for the past week. Thumbing was much more difficult with one hand, but Ham managed. Then he wandered over to the rack that held the *Sylva Herald*. There on the front page was a full-length picture of Bobby Skeeter with a headline that read, "Sylva Streak National High School Player of the Year." Ham lifted the paper off the rack and sat down in an overstuffed chair to read. Sure enough, Bobby had been named the 1976 National High School Baseball Player of the Year. The paper reported Bobby's stats for the season. They were beyond impressive; they were incredible. A pitching record of 23–1, as Ham knew. Ham didn't know that set the record for the most wins of any pitcher in the history of high school baseball in America. It made sense, of course, since surely no one else had pitched every single game of his team's season, or certainly no one had been as successful at it as Bobby Skeeter. Ham didn't know that Bobby had pitched twelve shutouts and three no-hitters, as the paper reported. In the state championship series against Hallsboro, Bobby pitched the first game on Friday night and won the game 2–0. The paper reported that some of the Hallsboro players had been heard to say after the game that they sure wish they'd have another shot at Skeeter, which they got the next afternoon! And, as Bobby had reported to Ham, Sylva won that game also, 2–1, behind Skeeter's three-hit effort. Ham felt both pride and jealousy reading the article: pride for knowing Bobby and now counting him as a friend, jealousy because Ham would never have the opportunity to compete on a baseball diamond again. He replaced the paper and went home.

That week at work, Ham continued to learn about the NRC register specifically and the business of Lowe's more generally. Mr. Tillman certainly seemed pleased. He remembered on Friday morning that Ham had to leave right after lunch for his doctor's appointment.

"Thanks for another good week of work, Ham, and thanks especially for helping with the payroll again."

"You're welcome, Mr. Tillman. I've enjoyed the work."

"So I remember that you're off to a doctor's appointment about your arm?"

"Yes sir, I'm supposed to get a prosthesis today." Mr. Tillman looked puzzled. "An artificial arm."

"Oh yes. Well I hope that all goes smoothly for you."

"Thanks Mr. Tillman." Ham left the store and drove to the hospital. There was a small medical supply store located just across the street from the hospital that shared its parking lot. It wasn't actually a doctor's appointment, but Ham thought it'd be easier just to call it a "doctor's appointment" since it was, after all, medically related.

He walked into the supply store. A bell rang serving notice of his presence. Ham looked around. The front room was crowded with a variety of medical supplies, as advertised. Canes, walkers, toilet seats, catheter packages, all lined up on the floors and shelves. There was not much more room for any additional inventory. A short, stocky bald man in black pants and a white shirt came out of the back room and stood behind a cluttered desk.

"May I help you?"

"Yes, I'm Ham MacPherson, here to be fitted for a prosthesis? I have an appointment."

The man pushed aside papers and stuff on the desk to reveal a calendar. "MacPherson? Oh yes, I see it here. Wait right here, please." The man waddled to the back room. In a minute he appeared with what Ham assumed was his prosthesis.

"Here it is. Ever worn one of these before?"

"No sir."

"Well, they're pretty simple. Why don't you take yer shirt off? Got a t-shirt under there?"

"Yes sir." Ham began unbuttoning his shirt with his right hand. The man continued to talk.

"It's easier than it looks really. Just got this one in yesterday. They make 'em over in Asheville." He waited patiently for Ham to remove his shirt and pointed to an empty chair beside the desk. Ham dutifully draped his shirt over the chair.

The man saw the surgical sleeve protruding out from under Ham's t-shirt. "You're wearing your sleeve. That's good. Lot of folks forget." Ham didn't realize the sock was optional. It didn't really matter; he had become accustomed to it, and in fact gave him the sense—illusion perhaps—of his arm being slightly more protected by the sleeve.

The prosthesis was attached to a shoulder harness. First the man showed Ham the inside of the prosthesis. "They took a temporary fitting of your arm at the hospital. It's called an immediate postsurgical prosthetic fitting. Do you remember that?"

"Not really."

"Well, the inside here should fit snugly against your arm. When was your surgery?"

"May 22," Ham replied.

"Any problem with blistering around the suture scar?"

"No sir. I mean, it hurts a lot still."

"Phantom pain?"

"Well, yes. But not just that. The arm itself hurts."

"Yes, that's normal. The prosthesis won't reduce the pain, but it shouldn't add to it either. Okay, put your surgical sleeve in here." The man pointed to the opening at the top of the artificial arm. "And lift the shoulder strap up over your head with your other arm. This is a figure-eight ring-type harness."

Ham did as he was instructed. The additional weight felt weird.

"How does it feel?"

"Weird," Ham confessed.

"Yeah, that's normal, too. This is an elbow disarticulation arm. It has a coil spring and cable that allow you to flex your arm and control the prosthesis. It comes standard with a Model 10X aluminum alloy, two ounce, 3¼ inch APRL Sierra Hook. If you prefer, we can replace the hook with a cosmetic mechanical hand. They do basically the same thing. Both have the seal of approval of the American Board for Certification in Orthotics and Prosthetics. Both are covered by your family's insurance." He lifted a mechanical hand off the desk for Ham to examine. As strange as the hook looked, Ham was convinced he liked the hook better.

"I'll just stay with the hook. How does it work?" Ham asked.

The man showed Ham how flexing his arm caused tension on the control cable and opened the hook. Releasing the tension caused the spring-loaded hook to close. "This is a voluntary-opening terminal device, good for grabbing onto things," the man said. They make a voluntary-closing device, but most people prefer this model."

Ham tried flexing. Nothing happened. This would take a while. Ham started to take off the harness, but the man strongly advised that he keep it on to "begin the adjustment process." He helped Ham put his shirt on, and Ham signed the necessary paperwork. He drove home with his new appendage. He wasn't sure what to think; he had just gotten more or less used to the feeling of an empty sleeve hanging down from his left side. Now there was a prosthesis. He just knew the poker group would start calling him, "Captain Hook." For that reason, he stayed away from the poker room that Sunday evening.

Ham's family was curious about his new "arm." He tried to show them how it worked; he was better by the end of the weekend at opening and closing the hook than he had been at its beginning. Co-workers at Lowe's complimented the prosthesis. Even though he hadn't mastered the "voluntary-opening terminal device," he was able to use enough force to push the hook down on the hard-to-reach keys on the NRC register.

On Wednesday afternoon, two days before Ham and Nora's wedding, an important-looking man came into Lowe's. He was wearing a three-piece dark suit and had slicked-back black hair. He nodded in the direction of the checkout clerks and headed into Mr. Tillman's office. A couple of minutes later. Mr. Tillman and the stranger came out of the office and walked over to Ham's register.

"Ham, this is Mr. Robert Strickland, Chairman of the Board for Lowe's Companies, Inc. His office is over at Corporate Headquarters," Mr. Tillman proudly stated.

Mr. Strickland held out his hand to shake. "Hello Ham. It's a pleasure to meet you. I've heard a lot of good things about you." Mr. Tillman smiled. "I wonder if we could chat for a moment in the office over here." Mr. Strickland was more giving a directive than asking a question. Mr. Tillman motioned for another clerk to take over Ham's register.

"Of course, Mr. Strickland. It's very nice to meet you." Panic coursed through Ham's veins. What had Ham done wrong? He knew Mr. Strickland had said nice things, but nobody comes over from Corporate Headquarters.

Despite the fact it was just across the street from the "mother Lowe's," it was in reality a world away from what went on in the little store.

"Ham, I think Mr. Tillman told you that Corporate Headquarters plans to replace the old NRC registers with new, electronic ones."

"Yes sir." That wasn't exactly what Ham had heard, but he guessed it was close enough.

"We'd like to keep one of the old classic NRC registers for nostalgic reasons. A kind of tribute to Mr. L. S. Lowe who bought them new and Carl Buchan who kept them running."

"That makes sense to me, Mr. Strickland." Ham wondered why Robert Strickland was consulting him about this.

"We'd like you to be the primary clerk in charge of the NRC. You know, keep it oiled, polished, in perfect working order, and run the register when you're on duty."

"Why, sure, Mr. Strickland, I'd like that." Ham was relieved. He wasn't being fired, and he really did like the old register, though he had nothing to compare it with.

"Folk have been intrigued by how you handle the machine with your, er—," Strickland struggled for the right word, "handicap, I guess."

Ham felt the hair on the back of his arm stiffen, a kind of involuntary action that happened to him whenever he felt threatened, like when a runner reaches third base with no outs. "I see, Mr. Strickland, kinda like a sideshow?" Ham's words came out more sharply than he intended. Later, he would say he meant what he said, he just didn't mean to say it!

"Wait now, Ham, just wait a minute. I'm not insinuating that we want to set up a circus here. Don't get me wrong. I don't mean to insult you. It's just that people admire the way you don't let your handicap inhibit your work."

"Sorry, Mr. Strickland. I don't mean to be so forward. It's just that this is all so new to me, and I guess I get defensive pretty easily. I'm still tryin' to wrap my mind around the fact that I'm not just Ham, the baseball pitcher anymore. I'm Ham the one-armed boy. Brother Bob says there's a fine line between acceptin' my new identity, whatever it is, and lettin' others define my identity."

"Brother Bob is Bob Sechrest, the preacher?" Mr. Strickland asked.

"Yes sir, do you know him?"

"We've met, but I can't say I know him well. Do you go to his church?"

"Yes sir."

"I hear he's turned that Baptist church into more of an Episcopalian church than the Episcopalian church in Moravian Falls!" Strickland exclaimed.

"I wouldn't really know about that Mr. Strickland," Ham said.

"Real wine at communion? Minister wears a robe? Preaches from the lectionary? Sounds like an Episcopalian to me. I should know—I am an Episcopalian!" Strickland exclaimed. "Let me tell you the real difference between a Baptist preacher and an Episcopalian priest." Ham thought Mr. Strickland was starting to sound like Bill Fagg. Was a joke about to be told?

"There was a Baptist preacher who was asked to perform a wedding for a Baptist and Episcopalian. Though he had serious misgivings on participating in an 'inter-faith' wedding (which is what any marriage not between two Baptists was to him), he agreed to conduct a wedding together with an Episcopalian priest. The bride was Baptist and a member of Brother Baptist's church, and the groom was a member of the priest's parish. The service went fine, and after the service both ministers attended the reception at the swanky country club of the groom's family. A waiter came by with champagne, and the Episcopalian priest took a flute off the tray. The Baptist preacher looked at the priest with an expression of disgust and contempt. 'I'd rather lie down in a harem of prostitutes than let that devil's brew pass over my lips!' he thundered. With that, the Episcopalian priest politely replaced the flute on the tray and said, 'Oh, I didn't know we had a choice!'" Strickland laughed at his own joke. Ham joined him.

"That Brother Bob of yours is making half-ass Episcopalians out of a flock of Baptists. But the biggest problem I have with your church, Ham," Strickland said in mock seriousness, "is that you have a minister with clearly inferior academic training." Later Brother Bob explained the rivalry between Ivy League foes and that the "Harvard man" did not want to miss an opportunity to "give it" to a Yalee.

"Thanks for your good work, Ham," Mr. Strickland said and left the building to go back to Corporate Headquarters across the street.

The next day, all but one of the old mechanical cash registers were replaced with new, electronic ones. As requested, Ham continued to operate the brass NRC register that had been left in registry #1, just in front of the main entrance, and, as anticipated (by both Ham and Mr. Strickland), folk did marvel at Ham's one-handed dexterity with the old machine. Sometimes Ham's line would be four and five deep while the other registers remained empty. The contractors and carpenters who were regular customers began referring to Ham as the "one-armed bandit," first behind his back and later to his face. "Watch out for that one-armed bandit," they'd say, "he'll rob you blind!" Ham would always chuckle as if that was the first time he'd ever heard that line. Deep down though, Ham harbored resentment. The long lines dissipated long before the nickname—and resentment—did.

At the end of that first day as sole operator of the last NRC, a cute little preschooler with blond curls was with her mother in line, obviously to see Ham at work, since three other checkers were open. When the little girl saw Ham's hook dangling from the end of his prosthesis, she buried her head into her mother's skirt.

"What's wrong, dearie?"

The little girl peeked around her mother's skirt and pointed at the prosthesis. "What's that *thing*, Mama?"

"Don't point dear," her mother replied, pushing her daughter's hand down and forcing a smile at Ham.

Ham pretended not to hear. Later that evening, Ham sat down beside between the graves of the brother he never knew and the arm he would never see again. He rubbed his stump and wept.

CHAPTER 26

By the time Friday, July 2 rolled around, Ham had worked two whole weeks at Lowe's and had brought home his first paycheck. More importantly, that evening, Ham and Nora would be joined in Holy Matrimony. The service was to be held at the church. Nora had to be convinced that having a church service was okay. She and Ham had met with Brother Bob for premarital counseling several evenings since Ham had been released from the hospital. Ham indicated to Brother Bob that he'd like to get married in the church on a Saturday afternoon. Nora objected that it would be inappropriate since she was in a "family way" and that she wouldn't be wearing a traditional white wedding dress because she wasn't worthy. Brother Bob then told Nora he didn't want to speak untowardly, but he was quite sure she'd had less sex than most of the young women who were married with a full service, complete with white gown, veil, and ten-foot long train! Nora finally relented on marrying in the church, but she decided to wear an off white, knee-length dress. She also insisted the service be on a Friday night and that only family and close friends should be invited.

Everyone was more or less satisfied with those arrangements, except for Nora's father, Mr. Culpepper. Roger Culpepper was a proud man and a conservative man. And when he first found out that Nora was pregnant, he was furious. He told Nora she would not get married in the church and if she chose to defy him, he would pay for nothing. Eventually, under the influence of Mrs. Culpepper, he gave in. Part of his resistance was rooted in the pride he took in his family name. Some would say he was simply arrogant. He loved to quote Katherine Howard, wife of King Henry VIII, who had carried on an affair with one Thomas Culpepper before—and during—her marriage to Henry. Legend, which Mr. Culpepper quoted as Gospel truth, had it that on the scaffold, Katherine had said, "I would rather die the mistress of a Culpepper than the wife of a King." In Mr. Culpepper's eyes, Nora's pregnancy had besmirched the good name of Culpepper. Imagine the family's surprise when they discovered years later, at Mr. Culpepper's funeral no less, that Mr. Culpepper had a mistress of his own, and a daughter just a year younger than Nora. None of this was known at the time of the wedding ceremony.

JC was Ham's best man, and he, Ham, and Brother Bob were standing in the back of the church listening for their cue to come into the sanctuary. Debra MacPherson, JC's sister, finished singing "What a Difference You've Made in My Life," made popular that year by Ronnie Milsap. Nora really liked the song. Ham liked the fact Millsap was raised in the Smoky Mountains by his grandparents after his mother abandoned him and the fact he was legally blind. Ham felt like somehow they shared something in common. Additionally, he and Nora had heard him live in concert on the Stearns and Marshall campus last year.

Through the door they could hear Debra's sweet voice,

> What a difference you've made in my life
> What a difference you've made in my life
> You're my sunshine day and night
> Oh, what a difference you've made
> What a difference you've made in my life.

JC whispered, "Is that our cue? That's the chorus, ain't it?"

Ham realized maybe the song wasn't such a good "cue" song since the chorus was repeated four or five times. "I'm not sure," Ham confessed.

Thankfully, Brother Bob had been counting. "That's the fourth repetition of the refrain; we go out on five. Let's go!"

And out they marched, taking their place as the pianist shifted to the "Wedding March."

Nora's maid of honor was her best friend, Marie Dwiggins. Ham's sister Diane and Nora's cousin Ginger were bridesmaids. Each one came down in a champagne colored dress (at least that's what Nora called it) and smiled at Ham as she crossed in front of Brother Bob. Marie was last and took her position opposite JC. Now Nora headed down the aisle on the arm of her father, who looked very uncomfortable in his suit; really he looked very uncomfortable to be there at all. Everyone stood as she walked slowly to the beat of the music. "Everyone" meant Ham's parents, grandparents, and siblings, along with Aunt Nora and Uncle Wilson Lackey. Uncle Carl, Mack, and Bill Fagg were there representing the ~~Y~~OMCA. Nora looked beautiful, Ham thought, and the slight bunching of material over her expanding midsection made her even more beautiful to Ham.

The service went off without much of a hitch. Later everyone said it was beautiful. Brother Bob talked about marriage and its meaning. He quoted a German fellow named Bonhoeffer who had been killed by the Nazis. Although Bonhoeffer never married, Brother Bob said, he thought deeply about marriage and, while in prison, wrote a wedding sermon for his niece who married his best friend. Brother Bob quoted from it:

> "Marriage is more than your love for each other. It has a higher dignity and power, for it is God's holy ordinance. . . . In your love you see only your two selves in the world, but in marriage you are a link in the chain of the generations, which God causes to come and to pass away to His glory, and calls into His kingdom. In your love, you see only the heaven of your own happiness, but in marriage you are placed at a post of responsibility towards the world and mankind. Your love is your own private possession, but marriage is more than something personal—it is a status, an office. Just as it is the crown, and not merely the will to rule, that makes the king, so it is marriage, and not merely your love for each other, that joins you together in the sight of God and man."

They made their vows, and Ham's voice cracked only once. The one hitch came in the exchange of the rings. JC pulled Nora's ring from his pocket and proceeded to drop it as he did the baseball on the night after the regional semifinals. At least he didn't say "Shit" loud enough for anyone not on the stage to hear. Ham wondered how in the hell JC was ever a baseball catcher. Brother Bob pronounced them husband and wife, they kissed, and Brother Bob presented "Thomas Hamilton and Nora Culpepper MacPherson."

Everyone went back to Dubya and Cornelia's house for wedding cake and punch. Nora and Ham opened presents. They got typical gifts: a set of dishes from Aunt Nora, glasses from Uncle Carl, a gift card from Nora's parents to Sears for appliances and bed sheets, and cash from the poker group. Thom Jeff and Nina gave them $500 in a card, marked for college tuition. With his profit from the sale of the Studebaker, that would just about cover the first semester's tuition and fees at Stearns and Marshall, and he could live at home. Or it would cover the entire year at UNC-Asheville, but they'd have to find a place to live. Evidently, Thom Jeff had come around to the idea of college for Ham—probably because he realized Ham wouldn't be much good for the sawmill or any other kind of hard manual labor. Or so Ham thought. Grandpa Dubya and Grandma Cornelia gave their gift: an official offer of their finished basement as a place to live and unlimited babysitting services, especially during the day when Ham and Nora would be in school. That was the best present Nora could ever get. She really wanted to go to college and study nursing.

Uncle Carl had booked Nora and Ham a room at the Inn at the Biltmore House over in Asheville for Friday and Saturday nights, July 2 and 3. No one was quite sure how Carl had pulled that off, since it was the Fourth of July weekend. They were to return to Nina and Thom Jeff's house for the rest of their "honeymoon" since Thom Jeff, Nina, Diane, and Michael Allen were leaving for their annual week vacation at Carolina Beach on Saturday morning. Nora and Ham would have the house to themselves for a week, or at least that was the plan.

It was about a two-hour drive to Asheville, and Ham and Nora were both tired when they arrived. It was hard to see the grounds of the Biltmore house at night, but both of them had visited the privately owned mansion before. The Vanderbilts had completed the house in 1895 or '96, Ham couldn't remember exactly; he had other things on his mind! Ham and Nora's room was small but elegantly appointed. Both were nervous. They hadn't really been with each other alone much in the past few weeks. Nora came out of the bathroom in a black, sheer negligee.

"Wow, you look beautiful, Nora!" Ham said sincerely. He was under the sheets in his boxers and t-shirt. The artificial arm, which he had worn at the wedding and the reception, was hanging by its figure eight harness on a chair next to the bed. Nora slipped under the covers and snuggled up to Ham. They kissed. Ham slipped the negligee over Nora's head. "Whole lot easier than taking off a bra that fastens in the front!" he quipped.

"You have on too many clothes now!" Nora whispered. Ham quickly shed himself of his boxers.

"The t-shirt too, Ham!"

Ham resisted. "I don't know, Nora. Maybe later." Before he could pull away, Nora had Ham's t-shirt up over his head. He reluctantly let her remove it the rest of the way. He instinctively pulled his left arm closer to his body and tensed up. Nora gently touched the stump, tracing her fingers across the end of it. It was very sensuous. Then she leaned over and kissed it, and smiled at Ham. He relaxed. She gently kissed his shoulder and then his neck and finally her lips found his. Her kisses, soft and wet, made him shiver. Their legs entwined, and they melted into each other. They made love like they were in love, and Ham knew then everything would be okay.

The next morning, Ham was awakened by a warm and soft sensation. Nora was kissing his neck.

"Good mornin," he said.

She did not respond. She was a woman on mission. She kissed his chest and flicked his nipples with her tongue. She worked her way down Ham's torso past his stomach. Then she took him into her mouth. Ham's whole body tensed up. Ham and Nora had touched each other in their "private" areas before; that's what it meant to reach third base. But she had never done anything like *this* before. Ham moaned and grabbed the sheet with his hand. The more he moaned the faster she worked. He tried to think about a baseball analogy for what was happening to keep from exploding. He failed. He finished. Nora snuggled up beside him.

"Where'd you learn to do that, Nora?"

Nora giggled. "After the bridesmaid's luncheon last week, my cousin Ginger from Raleigh grabbed two bananas from the fruit bowl and then led me into a back bedroom. She said she was gonna teach me how to give 'mind-blowin' oral sex.' She said it was a secret tradition."

"Kinda like Colonel Sanders's secret recipe for Kentucky Fried Chicken?"

"Yeah, kinda like that, only different. This recipe is passed down from one generation of Culpepper women to the next, mostly older cousin to younger cousin. Mother to daughter would be too weird. Was your mind blown?"

"Well, yeah, among other things!" Ham declared. He thought he would have to learn to write again so he could send cousin Ginger a proper thank-you note. He couldn't imagine his cousin Pete or Leo Jr. sharing anything quite so useful as that, but that may simply have been a lack of imagination on Ham's part. Of course, there was that time when Grandma Cornelia called Grandpa Dubya "*Precious*" . . . .

"You're softer than a banana," Nora observed.

Ham's eyes widened.

"But harder, of course," Nora hastened to add. "Softer *and* harder. And bigger. Much bigger!"

Ham laughed.

Nora flipped over onto her back. "Okay, it's your turn."

"My turn for what?"

"You know," Nora said and pulled Ham's head toward her breasts.

"I'm not sure I have the recipe," Ham whispered.

"We can figure it out together," Nora whispered back. They stayed in the room past noon adding ingredients to their own secret formula.

Later that day, they wandered around the grounds and rooms of the Biltmore House, but they spent most of their time in Asheville in their room making love. Fireworks came a day and a night early in the Inn at the Biltmore House that year. A visitor in the hall who listened closely enough might have heard singing coming from that room, "Let's do it again. . . . "

Mid-morning on Sunday, they headed back to North Wilkesboro. They were surprised to see the station wagon sitting in the driveway. Ham went in through the back screen door and shouted, "Mama?"

"In here Ham," came a voice from the living room. Ham and Nora walked into the front room and found Nina lying on the couch with her arm covering her eyes.

"Is everythin' okay, Mama?"

"Your daddy pulled another drunk at the beach, Ham, and I had enough. We got into the car about midnight and drove home." That was a three hundred mile trip and could take up to six hours, depending on traffic, Ham calculated.

"Where's Daddy?" Ham asked.

"We left him there," Nina replied.

"You left Daddy at the beach, without a car," Ham repeated.

"Yes, and served the bastard right." Nina almost never cursed. "He run off around 8:00 p.m. After supper. When he warn't back by 10:00, we went lookin' for him. We saw him through the window sittin' at the bar of a honky tonk. I sent your brother into get him, but Thom Jeff refused to come out." Ham knew this routine. He used to be the one sent into the bars trying to coax his drunk father to come out. Usually he was successful, but it was always a challenge. Especially at the beach, where Thom Jeff would have a roll of twenty dollar bills in his pocket that were intended for their meals and spending money while on vacation. But the money burned a hole in his pocket, and he loved taking the roll out and flashing his money around.

"Was he carryin' a lot of money?" Ham asked.

"Of course he was, like he always does on vacation. When Michael Allen said Daddy warn't comin' out, I sent him back in to say if he warn't out in five minutes, we were leavin' his ass at Carolina Beach." Ham imagined Michael Allen relished the opportunity to repeat that message verbatim since it would give him the excuse to curse.

"So . . . ?"

"So, when he didn't come out, we went back to the hotel, packed up all our stuff and drove home. And, don't you know, it rained for the first two or three hours on the road."

"Well, okay then. How do we think Daddy is goin' to get home?" Ham asked.

"I don't know, and frankly, I don't give a damn. I am sorry for one thing. I'm sorry I ruined your honeymoon."

Nora spoke for the first time. "Don't worry about that, Mrs. MacPherson."

"Call me Nina, please, Nora dear."

"All right. Don't worry about that Nina. We had a great time in Asheville." Ham blushed. "And we'll look forward to spendin' some time with you all, or most of y'all." Nora said uncertainly.

They spent the rest of the day unpacking and settling in as best they could. At the end of the week, they would move into Dubya and Cornelia's basement. Ham cooked hamburgers for the Fourth, and Cornelia and Dubya came over.

Lowe's was closed on Monday, so Ham went outside to shoot hoops with Michael Allen. It was odd trying to shoot with one arm, so Ham mostly got the rebounds and passed the ball to Michael, who shot. He was getting pretty good, Ham thought. At about 11:00 a.m., a strange sight came down the driveway. Stranger even than when Uncle Carl showed up in a hearse. A yellow cab was edging slowly up the gravel road. There were no cabs in North Wilkesboro. It stopped in front of the house, and Thom Jeff got out of the back. The cabbie rolled down his window, and Thom Jeff asked how much he owed. The driver muttered something Ham couldn't hear, and Thom Jeff reached in his pocket and pulled out his roll of twenties. At least he wasn't robbed, Ham thought. He peeled off a small stack of twenties and handed them to the cabbie, who counted them and, satisfied, wheeled back down the driveway back toward Carolina Beach.

Thom Jeff looked a mess. Hair disheveled, shirttail out. He headed toward the house, muttering to himself. He ignored Ham, but when he saw Michael Allen, he turned on him, "You left my ass in Carolina Beach! I had to take a goddam taxi all the way home!" Michael Allen opened his mouth to speak, but Thom Jeff just motioned him away in disgust. He headed to the house. Another kind of fireworks were about to go off.

CHAPTER 27

Usually conflict between Dubya and Nina was handled in a passive/ aggressive manner. For example, Nina did not allow alcohol in the house, so Thom Jeff would plant his whiskey bottles in strategic locations outside the house—in a flower pot, in the cavity of a tree, under a box. Nina would spend part of her day on Friday trying to locate the hidden bottles— mostly of Wild Turkey, which was Thom Jeff's favorite brand—in the hopes of reducing his alcohol consumption that weekend. But she was never able to locate all the bottles since Thom Jeff kept multiple hiding places going simultaneously.

Occasionally Thom Jeff would forget where he had hidden a bottle. A favorite hiding place was an old brick fire pit Thom Jeff had built for grilling. Since he rarely used the pit, it seemed a logical place to store a 1/5 of liquor. That is until Ham decided impulsively to grill some hamburgers for JC and a couple of friends. He built a mound with charcoal bricks and doused them with lighter fluid. Then he lit the fire and went back into the house to get the burgers while the bricks heated up. He was unaware his dad had placed a whiskey bottle in a crevice inside the fire pit. Evidently the top to the bottle was loose, and vapors had built up in the corner of the pit. When the heat and flame reached a certain intensity, the vapor ignited and blew a hole in the side of the fire pit just as Ham was coming out the back door of the house with the burgers. He watched in amazement as the flames leapt several feet into the air. The explosion was brief—but loud and intense.

Nina came running out of the house when she heard it and cried, "Ham, what have you done?"

"Looks like I've blown off the top of the fire pit, but I swear I don't know how it happened."

Nina watched the flames a moment, deep in thought. "Your daddy's whiskey," she concluded. She confronted Thom Jeff when he got home, and eventually he admitted that he may have hid a bottle there, though for the life of him he wasn't sure how long it had been there. No one knew which Thom Jeff lamented more, the loss of the fire pit or the bottle of Wild Turkey. The fire pit was never repaired and stood as a silent reminder of the dangers of alcohol abuse or at least of forgetting where the liquor is hidden.

Sometimes Nina's covert war against Thom Jeff's alcohol consumption escalated into a battle of words. This happened when Thom Jeff entered the house after his long cab ride from Carolina Beach. Before the back door slammed shut, Thom Jeff was yelling, "Nina, why the hell did you leave me at the beach?"

Nina was ready for him in the kitchen, "Because I'm tired of huntin' your sorry ass in every honky tonk at Carolina Beach!" Thom Jeff was taken aback. Nina never cursed, or rarely did so, and "sorry ass" was about as strong a phrase as he'd ever heard her use. Sensing she had him on his heels, she charged forward with a verbal barrage: "I can't believe you, Thomas Jefferson MacPherson. The Fourth of July. The two hundredth anniversary of this great country of ours. Instead of watchin' the fireworks with your family, you've got to go wander off drinkin' yourself into a stupor. And then when we do find you, you refuse to leave that hole in the wall and come back to the hotel with us! I had no other choice but to leave you there to keep our children safe!" Just as she was about to launch round two, they both heard the stairs creak and looked at each other.

Nora entered the room. Nina had forgotten she was there, and Thom Jeff didn't know.

"Is everythin' okay?" Nora asked. Ham had told her about his parents' sporadic fights, but she had never witnessed one first hand.

"Oh Nora, dear! I didn't mean for you to hear that. Thom Jeff and I are havin' a 'conversation.'"

"Is that what you call it?" Thom Jeff asked and slipped past Nora down the hallway. The "conversation" came to an end without resolution, but truthfully, this "conversation" could have no real resolution that satisfied both parties.

"Let me get you some breakfast, Nora! You must be starvin'," Nina said.

"Thanks, Mrs. MacPherson," said Nora, unsure as to what she had just witnessed or how she should respond.

"Call me Nina, honey." Nora watched as Mrs. MacPherson broke two eggs into the frying pan.

Ham and Nora spent the rest of the week at Thom Jeff and Nina's house as planned, although it wasn't much of a honeymoon. Thom Jeff was gone most of the day at work, and he took Michael Allen with him. Diane stayed home to help her mother with chores around the house. There was little privacy for Ham and Nora.

This was Michael's first summer to work full time at the sawmill. Ham could see the excitement in his eyes when he talked about the day's events at supper. Michael Allen was tailing the edger, throwing strips on to the conveyer belt that led to the chipper and the remaining board back on the conveyor belt to be stacked with the other lumber. Ham remembered how exhilarating those first days at the sawmill were, especially anticipating the first paycheck. There was an underlying tension in the house, however. Thom Jeff and Nina were decent enough to each other, but it was the kind of cordiality experienced between two persons who barely acknowledged each other's presence. By Sunday afternoon, both Nora and Ham were ready to move into their basement apartment at Dubya and Cornelia's house. On Monday morning, both went to work—Ham to Lowe's and Nora to the Second Little Rock Baptist Church Community Center where she served as office manager for the summer camp. They settled quickly into a routine, and both were much more comfortable at Ham's grandparents' house. Nora helped with supper each evening, and Ham and Grandpa Dubya did little chores as needed.

On Tuesday of the second week after the "honeymoon," Ham was back at work. Around 11:00 a.m. on July 22, Grandpa Dubya pulled into the parking lot of Lowe's. He stepped in the store, saw Ham, and motioned. "Ham, can you step out here for a minute?"

Mr. Tillman was watching from his office. Realizing something was wrong, he came out of his office. "Go on outside with Mr. MacPherson, Ham, I'll cover for you."

Ham followed Grandpa Dubya out the front door. Dubya stopped on the sidewalk and turned to face Ham. He was white as ash.

"There's no good way to say this, Ham. There's been an accident. Your daddy, he's—. The tractor turned over on your daddy."

"What?!" Ham exclaimed in disbelief. "Is he all right, Grandpa?"

"No, Ham, I'm afraid he's not. Your daddy is dead,"

Ham stared at his grandfather. Daddy? Dead? He was frozen. He didn't know what to do.

"We gotta go home, Ham. I'll tell Mr. Tillman." Dubya walked back into the store and spoke to Mr. Tillman, who followed Dubya back outside.

"I'm so sorry Ham. Go on home with your grandfather. We'll take care of things here."

Ham and Dubya got into the truck and headed toward the house.

"What happened Grandpa?"

"Like I said, the tractor turned over on your daddy, Ham," Dubya said simply.

"What was he doin'?"

"Well, best I can figure, it was too wet to run the mill this mornin', so your daddy went on the red belly out to the pasture to pull out that old tree stump at the top of the hill. He's been after me to do it all spring, but I hadn't got round to it. He must have been movin' pretty fast across the hill to get to the stump and hit a big rock about the same time the red belly slipped into a little depression. Whole thing turned over sideways on him. Your mama called me this mornin' worried. Said Thom Jeff had gone out to pull a stump early and should've been back by 8:30. That was around nine. I drove over to the pasture and saw the tractor from the bottom of the hill. I ran to the top quick as I could and found your daddy pinned under the red belly. He was already dead." Dubya looked out the driver's side window. "That damned Curse," he muttered under his breath.

To keep from thinking about his daddy, Ham thought about the tractor. The "red belly" was Dubya's old Ford 8N tractor. He had purchased it new in March, 1948. It was called a red belly because, while the engine cover was a light gray, the body and underside of the tractor was painted bright red. The 8N replaced the Ford 9N series, the first tractor to sport the three-point hitch (still used today) and the short-lived 2N series. Over 50,0000 8N tractors were made and sold during the years of production 1947–1954. They were priced between $1000 and $1500 during those years, and the Ford 8N red belly tractor was the most popular tractor ever made. It continued the three-point hitch of its 9N predecessor but went from a three to four speed transmission and included a "position-control" that allowed the operator to set and hold the depth of an attached implement. The red belly, however, was not equipped with a rollover protective structure.

So when they turned over, it could result in serious injury or, as in the case of Thom Jeff, death. Ham's thoughts returned to his father.

When they got home, there were cars all over the driveway. Ham and Dubya went in through the back door, and people were gathered in the kitchen. His mother was sitting at the kitchen table, staring into a cup of coffee. When she saw Ham, she leapt up and crossed over to throw her arms up around his neck. Ham leaned down to embrace his mother with his one arm. She was trembling and felt very small in his arm.

"Oh Ham, I can't believe it. I can't believe. Your daddy is dead!" She wept. He held her for a long time, until her hands dropped and she held his one large hand in her two small hands and looked him in the eyes. "What are we goin' to do? What are we goin' to do?" Before he could answer, Ham realized she was not directing her question to him specifically.

He stepped back and surveyed the room. There was Mack and Bill Fagg from the sawmill and Brother Bob. Diane and Michael Allen were huddled in the corner. Grandma Cornelia was making coffee and trying to serve everybody cold biscuits—anything to keep busy and not focus on the loss of this, her last living son. Aunt Nora and Aunt Edith were on their way to North Wilkesboro.

The EMT had already removed Thom Jeff's body and taken it to the Wilkes County Emergency Room, where he had been pronounced dead. Nina had just returned from the hospital where she had released the body to Pruitt's Funeral Home. The next three days were a blur to Ham. He went to the funeral home on Wednesday morning to meet with Mr. Pruitt and make arrangements for the visitation and the graveside. Brother Bob came back over on Wednesday afternoon to plan the funeral service, which Nina finally decided to hold in the church rather than the funeral home. People brought food, lots and lots of food, and Aunt Nora, who arrived on Tuesday night, took over the task of greeting people and collecting the food and making sure each person was properly thanked. Thank-you notes, of course, would follow later. Nina was like a zombie, moving to where she needed to be and answering questions when prompted.

Lots of people showed up for the visitation, more than Ham expected, and quite a few he did not know. Most of the loggers he knew, but some of the men from the lumber companies Thom Jeff dealt with Ham had never seen before. Ham stood with Diane and Michael Allen at the head of the coffin, which was closed. The damage to Thom Jeff's body and head was evidently too extensive for Mr. Pruitt to make him presentable. So people paused at the coffin to pay their last respects to Thom Jeff and to offer the children some words of consolation. People then gathered in small groups on the opposite side of the room from the coffin and engaged in small talk. Occasionally, muffled laughter would seep out of one group or another.

Brother Bob gave a touching eulogy for Thom Jeff at the funeral. Dubya, Ham, Mack, and Bill—the remaining members of the ¥OMCA—were the pallbearers. Despite the fact Thom Jeff had not been a regular attendee for years, Brother Bob knew him quite well and was able to relate some anecdotes that illustrated the essence of Thomas Jefferson MacPherson. At Nina's request, Brother Bob did not shy away from mentioning Thom Jeff's struggle with alcoholism. Nina hoped to spare others from the pain it caused by pulling back the curtain on something rarely discussed, at least in Wilkes County in those days. Then Brother Bob did something that surprised Ham. He turned the service over to two people who, he said, had come to him that week and "asked to share a story about Thom Jeff."

"When I heard their stories, I knew you would want to hear them too."

Ham looked over at his mother. She did not seem surprised or distressed, so he assumed Brother Bob had cleared this with her.

The first person to speak was somebody Ham had never seen before. He said, "Afternoon, folk, my name is Charlie Roberson. I'm from over in Stokes County. I don't know many of y'all here, but I did know Mr. Thom Jeff MacPherson. You see, I'm a dairy farmer over in Stokesdale. The farm has been in our family for four generations. In the winter I sometimes cut a few logs for extra money. That's how I know Mr. Thom Jeff. Anyhow, a couple of years ago, our dairy barn burnt down. We thought we was goin' lose the farm, but Mr. Thom Jeff showed up with three loads of lumber that he donated to us, and our neighbors helped us rebuild the barn. I tried to work out a way to pay Thom Jeff back, but he said he just wanted to give us the lumber. Said he knew if he was in a similar fix, someone would be there to help him out. I doubt he could really afford to give us that much lumber free of charge. So thanks to Thom Jeff and our neighbors, we were able to save the farm. I can't thank him and his family enough, and if there's anythin' I can to help the family now, I just want to let it be known that I'm here. Thank you." He sat, and a few scattered "Amens" went up from the congregation.

Mack Smith spoke next. A short wiry black man, Mack was a man of few words. Ham knew this both from his experience with Mack at the saw-mill and in the poker room. Mack came to the front and stood beside the closed casket. His relationship with the MacPhersons began with Dubya MacPherson, he explained. He had worked at the sawmill, first with Dubya and then with Thom Jeff for most all of his life. He started when he was sixteen years old.

"Thom Jeff MacPherson saved my life," Mack said. He paused. "Years ago, it was about 1955, 'fore you wuz born, Ham, I was takin' my mama to the grocery store. A car swerved at us and run me off the road, but the car didn't stop. I hit a tree on the driver's side. Mama was fine, but a branch went through the windshield on my side and I got cut up purty bad. Mama run up to the road and flagged down a truck. She said, 'Please, mister, my son is hurt bad. Can you take me to a phone?' The man in the truck took Mama to a gas station and she used a pay phone to call the ambulance and Mr. Dubya, who sent Thom Jeff to see about me. Thom Jeff, he stopped and picked up Mama from the gas station and still got to me same time as the ambulance did. I was layin' in the truck bleedin'. The ambulance driver took a look at me and said, 'Caller didn't say nothin' 'bout it bein' a colored boy. We kin't take him in our ambulance. Whites only.' Thom Jeff commenced to cussin' him out real good." Everybody laughed. "Sorry preacher," Mack said looking over at Brother Bob, who smiled. "Then he told Mama to get in his station wagon and loaded me in the back and drove us to the hospital. I was bleedin' all over Thom Jeff's car. Every time my heart beat, blood spurted out. I was purty much passed out and don't remember what happened next, but over the years Mama told me the story ag'in and ag'in. Thom Jeff, he took me into the 'Mergency Room. We was met at the door by a man who said, 'You can't bring that Negro in here—only he didn't say Negro—you'll have to take him to the Good Samaritan Hospital for Coloreds down in Charlotte.' 'The hell I will,' Thom Jeff said. 'I'm not gonna stand here and argue with you while the best damned sawyer in North Carolina bleeds to death.'" More laughter and another apology from Mack. "Dr. Fred Hubbard wuz the head doctor of the hospital, and Thom Jeff asked if he was there. The man said yes, and Thom Jeff said, 'Let's go see him.' And 'fore the man could answer, him and Mama done helped me into the 'Mergency Room past the man, who went inside and called Dr. Hubbard. Y'all might remember that ole' Dr. Hubbard started the hospital here in Wilkes County. Dr. Hubbard come to the ER, and once he seen me, Mama said, he told the staff to take me to a room right away, and he started workin' on me right then. I reckon if it warn't for Thom Jeff MacPherson, I wouldn't be here today, and

I'm mighty grateful to him and his family and mighty proud to call them my friends."

Ham felt tears welling up in his eyes. More stories he'd never heard. He thought about the day his daddy showed him Alexander Hamilton's grave and how his daddy told him he loved him. He sobbed quietly. He was going to miss his father more than he ever imagined.

On Monday morning, it was just Nina, Ham, Diane, and Michael Allen in the house. Nora was over at Cornelia's that morning to help clean up after all the visitors for the weekend. This was the first time the four of them had been alone since Thom Jeff's accident. They were sitting at the table when there was a knock on the door. Mack and Bill Fagg were standing on the back porch.

"Come in, Mack. Good to see you Bill," Nina said. "Would you boys like some coffee?"

"Yes ma'am, thank you," they said in unison. Nina poured them some coffee. "Diane, would you and Michael mind givin' the four of us a few minutes? Maybe you can start the wash?"

"Yes, Mama," Diane said. She and Michael Allen left the room. Ham thought how drawn and small they both looked now, especially Michael Allen.

"Hammie, we need to talk to you about the sawmill," Nina began. Ham noticed the three of them were sitting on one side of the kitchen table across from him, as though he were being interviewed.

"Ok, Mama. I want you to know I've been thinkin' about that, and I plan to quit Lowe's so I can help run the mill."

"You'll do no such thing, Hammie!" His mother declared. "Mack, Bill, and I have already worked it out. Mack is goin' to run the mill. He's already the sawyer and knows everythin' there is to know about runnin' the sawmill. Bill is goin' to deal with the loggers and manage the purchase of logs and negotiate the sale of lumber. Again nobody knows that part of the business better than Bill." Ham had to agree his mother was right about both of those things.

"And I will handle the books, writin' the paychecks and settlin' up with the loggers and sendin' bills to the lumber companies. I've done all of the payroll up til now, of course, and I know all the loggers. I can use a little help with the lumber accounts, but there is absolutely no reason for you to quit your Lowe's job or not to go to college in the fall."

Ham started to protest, but his mother held her hand up. "It's settled, Hammie. The sawmill business is goin' good, and as long as we keep things goin' like your daddy laid it out, we'll be fine. We're goin' to go in as partners. We'll keep 50 percent of the business, and Mack and Bill here will get 25 percent." Both Mack and Bill nodded. "There should be enough for all of us and to keep the other workers paid, too. It'll be tight for a while, but your daddy had a small life insurance policy that will tide us over til we can get our feet back under us."

Nina was firmly in control of the situation, and Ham was impressed. But he felt guilty. He knew the insurance policy was only for $5,000, and after the funeral expenses, there wouldn't be all that much left.

He tried to protest again. "But Mama, I can help. I know the business, too."

Again, she cut him off. "Hammie, I know you can help. I do. And I will depend on you to do that. But you've got a little one on the way, and I really want you to get your college education. Even your daddy came round to that way of thinkin' lately." Ham knew that was true, too. After all, Thom Jeff had given him money for college tuition, but, of course, Ham reminded himself, that was probably because Thom Jeff didn't think Ham could do much around the mill with one arm. Still, he decided not to press the issue.

"All right, Mama. I'll do whatever I can to help."

"I'll have John Brookshire draw up papers," Nina said. Bill and Mack stood and shook hands with Nina and Ham and then with each other; and just like that, a new partnership was formed.

CHAPTER 28

It was not long before the new partnership was tested. Nina continued to do the payroll for the mill on Thursday nights. In the past, Thom Jeff had taken the workers' checks and distributed them at lunchtime every Friday. Nina could have given the checks to Bill or Mack, but she thought it was important the workers know she was involved as a partner in this newly forged effort. So the first Friday after Thom Jeff's funeral, Nina showed up at the sawmill with checks and homemade biscuits and blackberry jam. She took them into the little one-room office Thom Jeff had built to meet with loggers and buyers from the lumber companies. The checks and biscuits with jam were both well received. On the next Friday, Ham had a half-day off and decided to go over to the mill with Nina to deliver the checks. She picked him up at the front door of Lowe's and drove over to the MacPherson, Smith, and Fagg Mill. Nina and Ham immediately felt tension in the air as they exited the station wagon, checks, biscuits, and jam in hand.

It was about 11:45 a.m.; Nina thought it best to get to the mill a little before lunch to get set up before the workers knocked off for lunch at noon. She and Ham heard shouting coming from the second of the two stationary mills, the one where Randy Motsinger, not Mack, worked as the sawyer. They walked down to see what was going on.

Randy had left his position as sawyer and was standing next to the chipper, holding a couple of blades in his hand. They looked like straight razor blades a giant would use; they were about a foot long and sharp on only one side.

"Boy, I asked you what the hell you did?" Randy was shouting at a black man, standing in one sock and one shoe beside the chipper. Nina didn't recognize the man.

"I done tole' you, Mr. Randy. This big ole' slab got stuck in the mouth of the chipper, and I was tryin' to get it loose," the man said.

"By kickin' it with your steel-toed boot, dumbass?"

"Yes sir. I din't know my boot was gonna come off. I'm just glad my foot din't go through the chipper, too!" The man laughed nervously.

"Well, your damn foot would have done less damage to the teeth of those chipper blades than your boot, with all that metal. Look at what you done!" Randy held up two blades in his hand. There was a big chunk of metal missing from its middle. Nina noticed now that the chipper was not running, and its hood had been raised. The blade in Randy's hand had come from the chipper.

"These blades cost a hundert dollars a piece! And I think you probably screwed up all six of 'em. You gonna pay for it?" Randy demanded.

"Why, you knows I don't have that kind of cash, Mr. Randy," the man said.

"Course, I know that, Melvin!" Randy shouted.

"Hey, what's goin on here?" Bill Fagg had gotten off his loader to see what all commotion was about. By this time, the other mill had stopped, and Mack and the other workers had walked over also.

"Stay out of this Bill!"

Mack walked over to the man with one shoe and said something too low for anyone else to hear.

"Hey Mack, what'd you say to that n—?" Randy demanded.

"That's enough!" Bill moved toward Randy.

Mack moved toward Randy, too. Randy dropped the chipper blade and picked up a tire iron. "You wanna piece of me? C'mon then."

"You're fired, Randy," Mack stated.

"You can't fire me!"

"Oh yes he can," Bill said. "Mack's part owner just like me and Nina. I reckon you better get your shit together and leave."

"I can't believe you'd go into partners with *him*, Nina." Randy pointed at Mack. "Thom Jeff would never gone along with that."

"You're wrong, Randy. Thom Jeff loved Mack," Nina said.

Randy dropped the tire iron. "Fine. I ain't workin' for y'all. 'Sides I got a job over at Edmonds's mill. I quit." Randy started walking to his truck, then turned around toward Nina. "You got my check?"

Nina was holding the biscuits. Ham had the checks. "Give Randy his check, Ham." Ham held the checks against his chest with his prosthesis and shuffled through the checks as quickly as he could. He found Randy's check and handed it to him. No words were spoken. Randy got into his truck and took off, dust flying everywhere.

"Anybody else feel like Randy is free to go now," Bill said. "No questions asked. But if'n you stay, you do so with the understandin' that Mack here is boss just like me and Miss Nina over there." Nobody moved. After a long silence, Nina said, "Well, it's lunch time, boys. Go on over and get your lunch and meet me at the office for checks and biscuits."

After everyone had received his check, Mack, Bill, Nina, and Ham gathered in the small office to regroup.

"I'm very sorry that happened, Mack," Nina began.

"Not your fault, Miss Nina. I'm used to it," Mack said.

"Well, you shouldn't have to get used to it," Ham declared. "This is 1976, for Christ's sake."

"Some things hain't changed all that much, Ham," Mack said. "Racist stuff is always just 'neath the surface. A black man can't never forget that. Are y'all still sure this is what Thom Jeff woulduv wanted?"

"Absolutely, Mack. Thom Jeff may not have liked all blacks, and he certainly had his prejudices, but he did love you, Mack. Besides you're the best sawyer around these parts," Nina said.

About that time, through the office window Ham saw a white Ford pickup truck roll down the dirt road toward the sawmill office. "Who's that?" Ham asked.

"Never seen that truck before," Bill said.

A tall, distinguished man wearing a straw hat got out of the truck and approached the office. The four of them walked out to meet him.

"Afternoon, folk, my name is Ward Oakman, and I'm a buyer from Home Lumber Company over in Asheville." They all introduced themselves.

"How can we help you Mr. Oakman?" Bill asked.

"Well, my boss over at Home Lumber has just signed on with a contractor in Asheville to provide building materials for a several condominium units goin' in around Blowing Rock. Seems everybody is wanting a first or second home in the mountains, and what with Tweetsie Railroad and the ski slope and well, just the natural beauty of the place, Blowing Rock has become hot property. Our current suppliers can't guarantee enough lumber over the next twelve to twenty-four months, so I've been commissioned to find some other mills who might help us. Your outfit has come highly recommended to us as one that is efficient and reliable."

"Thank you sir. We're real proud of our reputation," Bill said.

"How much lumber are we talkin' about?" Mack asked.

"We'd be looking for about 5,000 board feet of lumber per week from you for the first year. Can you handle that volume?" Mr. Oakman asked.

"Yes sir, we can do that!" Mack replied, looking over at Nina and Bill.

"We'll pay you 10 percent more than you are currently getting. I'll just need to see your most recent bill of lading."

Nina opened the side drawer of the desk and pulled a sheet of paper from the file. Thom Jeff kept meticulous records.

"Here you go, Mr. Oakman." Nina handed him a recent bill.

Oakman looked it over. "Fine, fine. I'll have a contract ready on Monday. Looking forward to working with you."

"We're lookin' forward to working with you, Mr. Oakman," Nina said. Ward Oakman got back into his truck and left.

"Wow, that's great!" Ham said.

"Absotively, posolutely," Bill said. "Reckon we better find us another sawyer, quick."

"Yeah, and one that likes black folk, evidently," Ham said.

"I know somebody," Mack said. "We'll be all right. We'll sell Oakman all the pine lumber he can use. We won't get rich. Nobody gets rich in this business. But we'll be okay now."

Ham heard that on Monday, Mack brought Travis Kite, a young sawyer whose reputation among loggers was growing. Ham was certain MacPherson, Fagg, and Smith Mill was the only sawmill in North Carolina with not one, but *two* black sawyers.

CHAPTER 29

Since Thom Jeff's death, Ham felt himself spiraling downward. Even the good news about the sawmill business didn't help much. He still managed to go to work at Lowe's, but when he got home to his grandparents' house, he had little appetite and no interest in conversation, even with Nora. He would go to the basement after supper and sit in the dark until Nora came downstairs and turned on the light. Then he would go to bed without saying much. He would lie in bed pretending to be asleep until he heard Nora's rhythmic breathing. He thought he had handled the grief and emotion of losing his arm pretty well, but losing his father had raised the grief level beyond the flood level, and everything came spilling over its banks. So much he hadn't said to his father. So much he wished he hadn't said to his father. Nightmares about red belly tractors and amputated limbs haunted Ham, and he didn't know what to do.

One thing he did do was to find the medicine bag his mother had given him at the hospital and fished out the bottle of hydrocodone Dr. Walker had given him to deal with the post-surgery pain issues. The prescription had a couple of refills remaining, and Ham had dropped it off at the drug store without Nora's knowledge. He had been taking a couple each evening to help him sleep. At least that was how he justified it to himself. In truth, Ham was sure the painkillers were contributing to the vividness of his nightmares.

On Monday, August 9, Ham excused himself from the dinner table and went down to the basement. Cornelia raised her eyebrows and asked Nora, "Is everythin' all right, dear?"

"I'm really not sure, Miss Cornelia," Nora confessed. "Ham won't talk to me ever since we buried his daddy, and he goes to bed every night right after supper. Like now." Without speaking, Dubya rose from the table and headed downstairs.

Ham heard the doorknob turn at the top of the staircase. He knew it was too early for Nora to come down, and he had just taken two hydrocodone pills. He opened the drawer on the end table and slipped the bottle in. He would return them to a safer hiding place later, he told himself. For a fleeting moment, he had the image in his mind's eye of his father hiding his whiskey bottles from his mother. But Ham quickly dismissed that unpleasant thought.

He heard the stairs creak, and soon Grandpa Dubya appeared at the bottom of the steps.

"Everythin' al right, Ham?" Dubya asked.

"Yeah, sure, Grandpa, everythin's fine," Ham replied.

"That's not what Nora thinks." Dubya walked over to the end table and opened the drawer. He must have heard it squeak when Ham opened it. He reached in and pulled out the bottle of hydrocodone. "What's this, Ham?"

"My painkillers from Dr. Walker," Ham said matter-of-factly.

"I thought you stopped takin' those? Made you constipated, and you didn't think you needed 'em anymore."

"Well, I started back."

"These pills are 'dictive, Ham. You can get in real trouble with them. Kinda like alcohol, they deaden pain."

"I'm not addicted to those pills, Grandpa!" Ham got defensive.

"You know your daddy 'self-medicated' with whiskey most of his adult life, all the while denyin' it."

"I'm not like Daddy that way," Ham raised his voice.

"Well, you can put pain pills to your head and pull the trigger if you want to Ham, but you won't do it with this bottle." Dubya slipped the bottle into his overall pocket. "And I suggest you commence to talkin' more to your wife and thinkin' about the child that's comin' in a couple of months."

Ham began to cry softly. "I know they said God won't put more on you than you can bear, Grandpa, but I think God has mis-figured in my case. I don't think I can handle losin' Daddy and my arm all at once."

"Well, I reckon I agree with you Ham. You've been given more than you can handle. By yourself." Dubya hesitated. He mindlessly ran his finger around the rim of the lampshade beside the couch. "Look, Ham, us

MacPherson men have never been particularly good 'bout talkin' things out. But if'n you don't, well, it can kill you. You need to talk 'bout it to Nora." Dubya started back upstairs.

"What was your daddy's name, Grandpa?"

Dubya turned around and looked at Ham. He came back into the room and slumped into an easy chair.

"Ham, I never told anybody else this but your grandma. 'Course, Magnum Fox figured it out with all his gen'logical investigations. Accordin' to my birth certificate, I was born, George Washington MacPherson on March 6, 1896, in Richmond, Virginia." Ham nodded. This much of the story he knew. "My mother, Cecilia, died givin' birth to me, and after a year, my daddy died, too. Of malaria. He was named Robert Elee MacPherson."

"Robert E. Lee, like in the Confederate general?"

"Yep. One and the same. 'Cept his middle name was spelled E-l-e-e. My daddy apparently was born in Stratford Hall near the homestead of Robert E. Lee. In fact, Robert Elee was born on October 12, 1870, same day General Lee died. Some folk round here, 'specially down at the church, wouldn't take too kindly to knowin' my daddy was named after a Confederate hero. 'Course others, like your daddy, might have been right proud of the fact. Since neither my daddy or Mama had any relatives livin' in Richmond, I was put under the care of the Friends' Asylum for Colored Children in Richmond."

"You were in an orphanage for black kids?" Ham asked.

"Yep, they started the orphanage after the Civil War for the children of former slaves who had been separated from their parents and abandoned by their former masters. Lady by the name of Lucy Goode Brooks was the head of the orphanage. She was the one who decided to take me in. I never met her, but wrote letters to each other over the years. She was a saint." Dubya's voice broke a little.

"Anyhow, she took me in, refusin' to abandon a baby because of the color of his skin. She's the one, what gave me the nickname 'Dubya.' She started lookin' for a relative who might take me in and found a reference in my mama's things to a cousin, Lois Jeannette McNabb, who lived here in North Wilkesboro.

"I knew her as Aunt Ginny. She was what ole' Roy Rogers would call a 'tumblin' tumbleweed.' She left Richmond and attended the University of North Carolina at Greensboro. It was called the 'Normal and Industrial School for White Girls' back then, and was started by the legislature to train girls—white girls, I guess you'd say by the name—to be teachers. There was a whole bunch of illiterates in North Carolina back then. Still are, I guess. Anyhow, once she graduated, she come here to North Wilkesboro in the 1890s, not long after the town was started, and taught in the one-room schoolhouse. Miss Lucy wrote Aunt Ginny and told her about me, and Aunt Ginny replied immediately that she would take me in. She traveled, all by herself—she never married—by train to get me. Back then, the Southern Railway ran from North Wilkesboro to Winston. Then she had to switch to the Raleigh and Western Line, which she took to Raleigh, and from there she caught the SAL, the Seaboard-Airline train, up to Richmond. Took her the better part of a week. Trains were faster and safer than the ole' horse and buggy. But they warn't easy by any stretch of the imagination. I remember Aunt Ginny tellin' me that the month before she left there'd been an awful train wreck near Pilot Mountain. The engine of a Cape Fear and Yadkin Valley train derailed and crushed the fireman and conductor who were caught up under the train. Anyhow, she brung me back to North Wilkesboro, and I've been here ever since." Dubya paused a moment as he reached back for memories he hadn't called up in a long time.

"Aunt Ginny made a good home for me. As I said, she never married—she was what we called in those days a 'spinster.' But she loved the kids she taught. And she loved the two rooms she rented from Mrs. Bordereaux. And she especially loved me. She tolerated an awful lot from me. I warn't easy to deal with." There was a creak on the staircase. Grandma Cornelia and Nora were standing, listening. They came into the room. Cornelia took Dubya's hand. Nora sat on the couch beside Ham.

Grandma Cornelia spoke. "Your Grandpa Dubya was a bit of a rascal, Ham. When I met him, he had discovered mountain brewed moonshine."

Dubya nodded and said, "That stuff'll make you see double and act single!"

Cornelia continued. "In those days, boys on the farm would go into town on a Saturday and look for mischief. Dubya'd be waitin' for 'em. It warn't unusual to see Miss Ginny—that's what us schoolkids called her—draggin' Dubya here by the ear down the street and back to Mrs. Bordereaux's boardin' house. I was just a young 'un, but we all knew Dubya MacPherson. He was six years older than me. And, oh my, was he handsome. When I was seventeen, I was quite smitten with George Washington MacPherson! He was half a head taller 'n anybody else, and just the sweetest thing in the world—when he warn't drinkin' that is." Cornelia looked up at Dubya and smiled. He leaned down and gave her a little kiss on the cheek and squeezed her hand.

"There was all kinds of Dubya MacPherson stories circulatin' in those days. Some of them true, I 'spect," Cornelia mused. Ham had heard some of these.

"Tell Nora about the ten-dollar bill, Grandpa." That was Ham's favorite story.

"Well, now this one is true." That was how Dubya began every story about his youth. "I was walkin' down Tenth Street one Saturday afternoon. That was where all the action was, and I might have been drinkin' a little."

"You were 'three sheets to the wind,' Dubya, as you always like to say," Cornelia corrected.

"Well, anyhow, I needed to take a 'whiz,'" Dubya said, "pardon my French, Nora." Nora giggled. "So, I dropped my trousers and relieved my-self right there on the sidewalk. Turned out that the sheriff was watchin' me and came over to me and said, 'Boy, there's a five dollar fine for urinatin' on the sidewalk.' I pulled up my pants, pulled a ten-dollar bill out of my pocket, and handed it to the sheriff."

"Here's a ten, sheriff. I might want to piss here again!" Dubya, Cornelia, and Ham all said in unison. They all laughed. It felt good to Ham to laugh.

"Nobody much knew what I saw in Dubya, other than he was a big, husky handsome feller," Cornelia said. "Especially my daddy, who did not approve at all. But I knew he was a diamond in the rough. We fell in love and married. I was twenty, and Dubya was twenty-six. It's been over sixty years. Lot of heartbreak and grievin'. But a lot of joy and love. And he's still the love of my life!" Cornelia kissed Dubya square on the lips. Ham looked away, uncomfortable.

Nora sighed, reached over and squeezed Ham's hand. "I hope we can make it sixty years, Ham!"

Dubya looked at Ham and Nora. "Well, that's the story of my daddy's name. Don't tell anybody. Robert Elee's daddy, who named him, surely would've crapped his pants if he knowed that I was taken in by the orphan-age for colored children in Richmond when Daddy died." They all laughed. Ham hadn't known about the orphanage. There was so much about his family that remained a mystery to him.

"But nothin' I can do to change it. Just glad I was named George Washington, I reckon, and not Jefferson Davis!" Dubya and Cornelia headed for the stairs. "Remember what I told you, Ham?"

"Yes, all right, Grandpa." Ham knew Dubya meant the painkillers. Nora looked quizzically at him. They stayed up talking til 2:00 a.m., and they made love for the first time in a week. Afterward, Ham cried really hard for the first time since he wept with his arm in the poker room.

The next morning, Ham met Brother Bob for breakfast at Susie's Diner and told him about the pills and the conversation with Grandpa Dubya and Grandma Cornelia. He said he felt angry at his father, and then he felt guilty about feeling angry.

"Why don't you write him a letter?" Bob asked.

"Write who a letter?"

"Your father."

"But he's dead . . . "

"Yes, he's dead—and part of your anger lies in the fact you can't talk to him. So write him. Obviously, it's more for you than for him."

Ham thought a moment, then lifted his right hand. "Write with this?"

"Get a typewriter. You're really good with that mechanical cash register down at Lowe's. I'm sure you can manage a typewriter."

That afternoon Grandma Cornelia dug out an old Remington manual typewriter and helped Ham thread a new ribbon into it after he got off work. That night, using just his index finger, Ham pecked out his first letter to his father, whom he called "Daddy T. J.":

August 10, 1976

Dear Daddy T. J.:

I am mad as hell at you! Why did you die? Why did you go out on a slick hill on that tractor? Why didn't you know better? Were you trying to fulfill that stupid MacPherson curse? I had a lot to tell you. I had a lot I wish I didnpt tell you, But I'm goinf to tellh you now. I just don't know when you will read this.

Ham

He felt better. He wrote a letter for the next two nights, telling his father how he felt about losing him. He found a lockbox in his grandparents' basement that had a key inside. He put the letters in the lockbox and hung the key on a string around his neck. He felt he had turned a corner. But before the week was up, he would have to turn another.

CHAPTER 30

That Friday was August 13. Cornelia was generally superstitious about Friday the Thirteenth, and her anxieties were doubled by another intuition she held firmly. "Tragedies travel in threes," she always said. And she was convinced Ham's accident and Thom Jeff's death would soon be followed by a third similar event. She just didn't know who it would happen to, but as Friday the Thirteenth approached, she was convinced she knew when.

Early in the morning on Saturday the fourteenth, the phone rang at Dubya and Cornelia's house. Cornelia answered the phone by the bed. It was Nina.

"Oh my God, Nina!" Cornelia said into the phone.

"What happened?" Dubya asked from the other side of the bed. Cornelia motioned for him to be quiet.

"Of course, Nina, of course. Dubya and me will come right over to stay with the kids. Hold on. I'll get Ham on the phone." She put the receiver face down on the nightstand. Dubya looked at her with a quizzical look. "Carl's dead," she said. "I've got to get Ham on the phone." She rushed downstairs and opened the door leading to the basement. "Ham, pick up the phone. It's your mama!"

Ham was roused from a deep sleep, one of the first he'd had in several weeks, by the sound of his grandmother's voice. "Ham, can you hear me?! It's an emergency! Pick up the phone!" Nora turned on her side away from Cornelia's voice.

Ham reached over with his hand to find the phone. He still found it awkward to shift his weight in the bed—his stump seemed to keep him in perpetual imbalance. Finally, he was able to raise the receiver to his ear.

"Hello? Mama?"

"Hammie? Oh, Hammie. Your Uncle Carl was arrested last night and now he's dead."

"What are you talkin' 'bout, Mama? What do you mean he's dead?" Ham was trying to shake the cobwebs from his brain. This couldn't be true.

"Last night, Hammie. The sheriff arrested Carl for public drunkenness. They put him in jail overnight and called this mornin' to say they found him dead in the jail cell when they went in to release him."

"Dead in jail? How'd that happen, Mama?"

"I don't know Hammie. They've taken the body down to the hospital for the medical examiner to perform an autopsy. I've got to go identify him as the next of kin. Maybe the coroner will know something."

"I'm goin' with you, Mama," Ham exclaimed.

"Okay, I'll come by there in about ten minutes." Ham rolled out of bed and got dressed.

When Nina picked up Ham, he could see her eyes were swollen from crying. He reached over and hugged her with his right arm as best as he could. "How did this happen, Hammie? First you, then your daddy, and now Carl?" She began crying again.

When they got to the Wilkes General Hospital, a nurse took them to a waiting area to wait on the medical examiner to meet with them. After a long while, a young doctor whom Nina had never seen before approached. "I'm Dr. Gavin. Are you the family of Mr. Carl Robinette?"

Nina nodded. "He's my brother—or was."

"Did he have respiratory problems?" Dr. Gavin asked.

"Yes, he had the beginnin' of what the doctor called emphysema. He had an inhaler for when it got real bad. He still smoked even though the doctor said smokin' made it worse."

"Yes, emphysema is a component of what we now call Chronic Obstructive Pulmonary Disease or COPD. And smoking does exacerbate the symptoms of COPD. It appears your brother had an episode while incarcerated last night in the county jail. Also his blood alcohol content was .16 or nearly twice the legal limit."

"What would have caused an 'episode' Dr. Gavin?"

"Well, I am not sure about that. Strenuous activity might contribute."

"You mean like a struggle or fight?"

"Yes, something like that."

"Did the sheriff say Uncle Carl resisted arrest?" Ham asked Nina.

"No, they didn't say nothin' 'bout that," Nina said.

"You said your brother used an inhaler. Did he usually carry it with him?" Dr. Gavin asked.

"Always," Nina replied.

"I should mention that no inhaler was found in his personal effects."

Puzzled, Nina looked first at Dr. Gavin, then at Ham. "That's odd. He never went anywhere without his inhaler."

"Even when he was drinking?" Dr. Gavin asked.

"Uncle Carl was always drinking," Ham replied.

The medical examiner had put "asphyxiation from COPD seizure" as the cause of death on Carl's death certificate, but Nina and Ham were not satisfied with that determination.

Nina and Ham decided to drive to the sheriff's office. There was a deputy there on duty.

"Excuse me, is Sheriff Palmer here?"

"No ma'am. It's his weekend off. Can I help you?"

"I'm Nina MacPherson. This is my son, Ham. Are you new to these parts?"

"Yes ma'am. I'm Euless Watson from over in Catawba County. Just started workin' here in the last month or so." Deputy Watson stood and came around from behind his desk and shook hands with Nina. As he shook hands with Ham, he stared at his prosthesis.

"What can I do for you?"

"My brother was Carl Robinette. I understand he died in your jail cell last night?"

Deputy Watson took a step back and stiffened. "Yes ma'am. He was real drunk when we picked him up last night. Put him in a cell and when we checked on him this mornin', we found him dead."

"Who's 'we'?" Ham asked.

"Me and Deputy Thomas. Jeb Thomas," Watson replied.

"Did you know he had a breathin' problem?" Nina asked.

"No ma'am. He didn't say nothin' 'bout that."

"Did you find an inhaler on him or in his cell?" Ham asked.

"An inhaler? What's that?"

"Little thing that helps you breathe," Nina replied.

"No ma'am. I don't recall seein' anythin' like that," Watson said.

"Could we look in his cell?" Ham asked.

"Well, no. I'm 'fraid I couldn't allow that. There's somebody in the cell right now."

"Was that person in the cell with Carl last night?"

"No ma'am. Carl, Mr. Robinette, was in the cell by hisself."

"Did he resist you when you arrested him? Carl can be pretty bull-headed when he's drunk," Ham said.

Deputy Watson hesitated. "Nope. He was gentle as a lamb."

"All right. Thank you for your time. Will Sheriff Palmer be in on Monday mornin'?" Nina asked.

"Yes ma'am. Eight o'clock sharp."

Ham and Nina left. Ham was convinced the sheriff's deputies had agitated Carl in jail, maybe causing him to have a seizure. And where was his inhaler? They both returned Monday morning and spoke with Sheriff Palmer. Yes, Sheriff Palmer knew Carl used an inhaler. No, they hadn't found one in the cell. Maybe it fell out before they arrested him. No, Carl didn't resist arrest. No, there was no struggle with his deputies. Yes, he trusted his deputies, even Watson, who was relatively new. They could not get anywhere with the sheriff and left as dissatisfied as when they arrived. Ham called his cousin Leo Jr., who was a highway patrolman, and he asked around with other law enforcement about Uncle Carl. He reported that if anything had happened between Carl and the deputies or an inmate, nobody was talking and weren't likely to talk. Nina and Ham always maintained that some kind of foul play, whether with the deputies or another inmate, led to Carl's death, but they were never able to prove anything.

Lots of questions were still swirling when Brother Bob performed Carl's funeral service on the following Wednesday afternoon. Brother Bob began by saying Carl was preceded in death by his beloved Pansy. Ham knew Pansy had died of cancer in her twenties. She and Carl had only been married about five years. It was around that time, Nina had told Ham, that Carl began drinking heavily and grew his hair out into a ponytail. Brother Bob's eulogy was laced with allusions to Jimmy Buffett lyrics; Uncle Carl loved Jimmy Buffet. Brother Bob said, "While the rest of us were moving through life head first at full speed, Carl was moving to his own beat cruising 'along in ¾ time.'" He told how Carl would explain his zany purchase of a hearse by saying, "Preacher, 'if we weren't all crazy, we would all go insane.'" He spoke of Carl's love of the ocean whose "belly held treasures that few had ever seen." Ham wasn't sure how many in the congregations caught the allusions, but he knew Uncle Carl would have appreciated them. Brother Bob spoke also of Uncle Carl's COPD and struggle with alcohol. Everybody loved Carl; he was the quintessential lovable town drunk. Brother Bob ended his sermon with these words:

> "Over the years, Carl and I talked about matters of faith. Carl believed in God. Not just the idea of 'god,' but the God of Abraham and Sara and Mary and Joseph, the God of Israel and of Jesus Christ. Like many of us and maybe more than most, there were times when he had difficulty in believing that God could love so flawed a creature as himself. But thankfully God's love does not depend on our feelings of worthiness to receive it. Carl now sleeps with the ancestors in the presence of a God whose *pursuit* of us is *unrelenting*, whose *forgiveness* knows *no end*, and whose *mercy* has *no limits*. Carl has been released from this life and rests in the arms of a Loving and Merciful and Gracious God, in the hope of the Resurrection to come. Amen."

It seemed only appropriate that Uncle Carl's body be transported from the church to the cemetery in Mr. Ed, and so he was. For the second time in less than a month, Ham had buried a male relative, a man who had profoundly shaped who Ham was, even though at the time he may not have been able to articulate clearly his indebtedness to Thomas Jefferson MacPherson or Carl Robinette.

A few days after the funeral and several weeks before college classes were set to begin, Ham got a call in the evening from John Brookshire, III, attorney-at-law, or J. B. as he was called. He was Ham's second cousin, since Grandma Cornelia and John Brookshire Jr. were brother and sister. He just called him J. B., and what little relationship they had—mostly at church—was cordial but certainly not intimate, nor had Thom Jeff and J. B. been particularly close. J. B. asked Ham if he and Nora could meet with him in his law office on the next Saturday morning, August 21. He said he had invited Nina and Brother Bob to be there, too. Ham agreed and was so startled by the lawyer's call he didn't think to ask why they were meeting.

At 9:00 a.m., Ham and Nora pulled into the parking lot of the two-story brick house that had been converted into the law office of John Brookshire, III, Esq. It stood across the street from the county courthouse. Nina and Brother Bob were already there, and Ham and Nora took seats beside them and across from J. B. at a large mahogany conference table. J. B. asked if anyone wanted coffee. No one did.

"Carl Robinette named me executor of his estate in his will," J. B. began. Ham was surprised Uncle Carl had a will. J. B. opened a file in front of him and placed horn rimmed reading glasses on the end of his nose. "The four of you were named beneficiaries in the will. Bob, you are here representing the interests of the Second Little Rock Baptist Church." Bob nodded.

J. B. turned to Ham and Nora. "Carl has left his house and everything in it, except his clothes, to the two of you as joint owners." Nora gave out a little gasp. The house was a neat, white frame house that sat on the edge of town. It had three small bedrooms and a picket fence. The landscape was immaculate. Whatever his other flaws, Carl took great pride in his home. It was the house he shared with Pansy for five years. Both of them were employees at Lowe's. Ham barely remembered Pansy; she died in 1963 when he was five. "Carl has left instructions that the balance of the mortgage be paid in full from his estate. He owed $10,000. You will receive a title to the home free and clear of any debt." Ham and Nora looked at each other in shock. "That leaves a balance of approximately $85,000 dollars."

Nina interrupted J. B., "$85,000?! Where did Carl get that kind of money?!"

J. B. looked up from the file. "Yes, frankly, Carl's holdings came as a surprise to us as well." J. B. took off his reading glasses, folded them, and placed them on the table. "Nina, as you know, Carl began working for Lowe's as a teenager, and the owner Mr. Buchan, was very fond of Carl. Lowe's went public in 1961 and began trading on the New York Stock Exchange. Employees were given the option of buying and/or receiving shares in the company in lieu of a bonus. Together, Pansy and Carl accumulated one hundred shares of Lowe's stock, and Mr. Buchan left Carl another one hundred shares in his will. The shares sold for $12.50 in October 1961. When we cashed out the stocks this week, the 200 shares had grown to 2,400 shares and traded at $40.50. That's $97,500. When we deduct the cost of the mortgage and legal fees, that leaves roughly $85,000."

Now all four of them—Brother Bob, Nina, Ham, and Nora—looked in disbelief at each other. Uncle Carl had nearly $100,000? Who could possibly have guessed that!

J. B. continued. "Carl left $10,000 to the church, Bob, and also all his clothes to the shelter. Nina, he left $25,000 to you, Diane, and Michael Allen. And he left $40,000 to you and Nora, Ham." Ham did a quick addition in his head, and asked, "What about the other $5,000?" The question was motivated purely by mathematical precision than any kind of greed on Ham's part.

J. B. chuckled. "Well, the remaining $5,000 is to go into a trust fund for the unborn daughter of Ham and Nora MacPherson."

"But we don't know if it's a girl or a boy," Nora said.

"Well, evidently Mr. Robinette was confident of the baby's gender."

"Will that be a problem if the child is a boy?" Nina asked.

"It will be a complication," J. B. admitted. "But let's wait until the baby is born before we worry about that. It will take a few days to sort out the paperwork, but I hope to have a check to each of you by the end of next week." J. B. stood. "Does anyone have any questions?"

Ham asked, "When did Uncle Carl write this will?"

"He came to me the week after you and Nora announced your wedding date, if I'm not mistaken."

"That was when he predicted we were gonna have a girl, Ham!" Nora exclaimed. Ham nodded in agreement.

"Oh, I almost forgot. Ham, Carl also left 'Mr. Ed' to you. Do you know what that means?" J. B. asked.

"Mr. Ed is Uncle Carl's hearse," Ham replied.

"Ah, that explains it. Well, that's all I have. I am sorry for your loss, but I am pleased that even in death Carl was able to help his family and his church."

They all walked out of the law office together. Ham found himself humming a Jimmy Buffet tune on the way home.

It's those changes in latitudes,
Changes in attitudes nothing remains quite the same.
With all of our running and all of our cunning,
If we weren't all crazy, we would go-o insane.

Uncle Carl was indeed crazy, and for that, Ham was grateful, and he felt an obligation to make Uncle Carl's investment in him pay off.

CHAPTER 31

H am and Nora moved into Uncle Carl's house over Labor Day weekend. Since they had a free place to live, they decided it would be cheaper to attend the local Baptist college than it would to move to Asheville to attend the state university, despite its much lower tuition and fees. Classes at Stearns and Marshall Baptist College began on September 7. Thanks to Uncle Carl's generosity, both Ham and Nora were full-time students. They loved Stearns and Marshall, which was named after Shubal Stearns and his brother-in-law, Daniel Marshall, who were important early Baptists associated with the Sandy Creek Association in North Carolina. There were several ironies here. Stearns and Marshall never reached the North Carolina mountains, but an exuberant group of Brushy Mountain Baptists in 1855 wanted to celebrate the one hundredth anniversary of the founding of the Sandy Creek church in North Carolina by naming a school of higher education after them. This despite the fact the Sandy Creek Baptist tradition was staunchly anti-education. Stearns and Marshall would not have approved of the school that bore their names. The official motto of the school, emblazoned on everything that bore the S & M logo, was "Where the Truth shall set you Free." During the cultural revolution of the 1960s, a more secularized student body coined an unofficial motto: "S & M College—where the truth shall set you free—unless you prefer bondage—whatever turns you on"! The administration was not pleased.

Both Ham and Nora were taking general education courses in English and History. Ham was going to major in Accounting, so he had a couple of math courses. Nora wanted to be a nurse, so she was pursuing a pre-health curriculum. They frequently saw Brother Bob on campus, though in that context he was known as "Prof. Sechrest." Ham planned to take a philosophy or ethics course with him in the spring semester. Both of them had part-time jobs. Ham was working at Lowe's in the evening and on weekends. Nora was working in the after school program for Second Little Rock Baptist as the secretary and receptionist. The plan was for her to work until the baby came. Her due date was late November; she had already worked it out with her professors to take her final exams some time after Christmas after the baby was born. It was a hectic lifestyle, but they loved it. Both were especially happy to be in school.

Most every Sunday, Ham and Nora would go to Dubya and Cornelia's for lunch. Nina and the kids were there. It was strange to be there without Thom Jeff, but everybody was managing to get by. The triumvirate of Nina, Bill, and Mack were keeping the sawmill going strong, especially now that they had the account with Home Lumber over in Asheville, and Diane was doing well, it seemed. Nina was worried about Michael Allen. At fourteen, he was at a difficult age to be without a father. He was sullen, didn't have much of an appetite, and had little interest in school. Nina knew he would take a lot of love and care. Grandpa Dubya was especially attentive to Michael Allen. He picked him up from school, took him fishing, and drove him around to various activities. He even gave him Thom Jeff's spot in the YOMCA. Nina hoped he would eventually be okay.

On October 3, Ham pecked out a short note on the Remington manual typewriter and locked the note in the metal box with the rest of his letters.

October 3, 1976

Dear HH,

I listened to your last game on the radio tonight against the Detroit Tigers. I was happy when you got a hit in your last at-bat, driving in a run. The announcer said it was your 2,297tg RBI of ypoir career. Thank ypi for all the joy you brought me and other fans. I wish we coulkd have been teammates. I wish we coulkd have met.

Ham

This "HH" was "Hammerin' Hank" Aaron, Ham's childhood hero.

Ham stayed busy. He still got sad thinking about the losses of the summer, but he had kept his promise to stay away from painkillers and other forms of what Grandpa Dubya called "self-medication" (though he did become a prolific letter writer). Jimmy Carter defeated Gerald Ford on Tuesday, November 2, in the presidential election. In the first presidential election in which he was a registered voter, Ham cast his vote for Carter, who carried North Carolina and the rest of the South and won 297 electoral votes to Ford's 240.

Ham rarely made it to the poker room that first semester. One Sunday evening in mid-November, Ham made an appearance at the poker room. Everybody was happy to see him. He was surprised to see the group had added Robert Strickland, CEO of Lowe's and the Harvard man. Strickland was Brother Bob's idea. It turned out the two Ivy Leaguers had a lot in common. There was a little tension between them that night because on the day before Yale had beaten Harvard 21–7 in football. Brother Bob sported his azure blue Yale scarf and sang a Yale fight song when Strickland entered the poker room that evening:

> *Bulldog! Bulldog!*
> *Bow, wow, wow*
> *Eli Yale*
> *Bulldog! Bulldog!*
> *Bow, wow, wow*
> *Our team can never fail*
>
> *When the sons of Eli*
> *Break through the line*
> *That is the sign we hail*
> *Bulldog! Bulldog!*
> *Bow, wow, wow*
> *Eli Yale!*

Strickland was not amused. Grandpa Dubya got up from the poker table and went over to the folding table holding snacks. He picked up a box situated in the back left corner and put it on the table in front of Ham.

"Got you a present, Ham. Been waitin' for you to show up to give it to you."

Ham opened the box and pulled out a battery-powered card shuffler. He put half a deck on one side and half on the other and turned it on. In seconds, the cards were shuffled and re-stacked into a single deck.

"It'll make it easier for you to shuffle, I think." Grandpa said.

"Thanks Grandpa, it's great!" Ham said.

Bill Fagg put his hand over the shuffler. "I told him not to get it, Ham," Bill said. "You can't really trust technology. AND, if you run the cards through the shuffler more than seven times, you'll unshuffle the cards."

"What are you talking about, Bill? You can't 'unshuffle' a deck of cards!" Strickland exclaimed.

"The hell you can't," Bill said. "I heard a report on TV. Fellow said they've banned these 'matic shufflers in Las Vegas because if you run the cards more than seven times, they 'unshuffle.'"

"What does it mean to 'unshuffle' a deck of cards?" Brother Bob asked.

"Why, everybody knows that an 'unshuffled' deck means it returns the cards to the original order before you started shufflin'. You Ivy League boys ain't really all that smart, are you?" Bill said. Dubya nodded in agreement. Bill continued, "Like I was sayin' before the 'Haaavard' man interrupted, you can't trust this new-fangled technology." That reminded Bill of a story. "There was a fellow drivin' down around Raleigh on Highway 70. He was cruisin' along about sixty-five miles per hour, when somethin' whizzed past him in the passin' lane. Must have been goin' ninety miles an hour. He followed it best he could and saw it turn right onto a research farm run by the State University department of engineering. He was curious, so he turned down the road and stopped at a booth controllin' traffic in and out of the farm. 'Say, did you see somethin' turn in here goin' 'bout 100 miles an hour?' he asked the man in the booth. 'Oh yeah,' the man said. 'That's the three-legged chicken the engineers and poultry experts been experimentin' with to increase production of chicken legs to make more money.' 'Three-legged chickens? Well, I be damned. How do they taste?' the man asked. Fellow in the booth said, 'Don't nobody know. Ain't nobody been able to catch one yet.' That's technology fer ya," Bill said, pointing at the battery powered card shuffler. Everybody laughed. Some things never changed in the poker room, Ham thought.

Ham and Nora decided to drive to Waynesville to visit Nora's grandparents for Thanksgiving the next week.

"Let's take Mr. Ed to your grandparents, Nora."

"Why Ham? I don't want to drive all the way to Waynesville in that thing!"

It'll be good for the engine, and your granddaddy would get a kick out of the hearse. Plus, I can listen to that new James Taylor eight-track you got me for my birthday." Ham turned nineteen on November 15, and Nora had given Ham the newly released *Greatest Hits* by James Taylor. Since he had sold the Studebaker Ham had no way of listening to the tape except in the hearse. Nora's VW didn't have a tape deck.

"Oh, all right, Ham." Nora gave in reluctantly. She knew her grand-daddy Culpepper would, in fact, enjoy the novelty of the hearse. And she liked James Taylor, too.

They listened to "Carolina in My Mind" and other hits on the way over to Waynesville, and they had a wonderful visit for two days and headed back on Sunday afternoon, November 28. A heavy snowstorm hit the mountains just as Ham and Nora left Interstate 40 and took US Highway 64 near Morganton. The snow was so thick Ham could barely see out of the front windshield, and the wipers were hardly up to the challenge of a mountain blizzard. An eighteen wheeler, traveling the opposite direction toward them, began to jack knife on the road. Ham swerved to miss it and hit the soft shoulder of the road. The truck recovered, but Ham did not. He spun out of control into a ditch. Luckily, both he and Nora had on their seatbelts. Unluckily, the force of the seatbelt against Nora's belly caused her water to break. She was well into her ninth month.

"Ham, my water just broke!"

"What does that mean?"

"It means I'm goin' to have the baby. We've got to get to the hospital—now!"

Ham tried to put the hearse into gear. The only problem was it was stuck in the ditch. The wheels spun in place, but the hearse didn't move. It was getting late. The weather was awful, and there was not another car in sight.

"I can't move the car, Nora. What do we do?"

"Let's get me in the back of the hearse. That way at least I can stretch out."

Ham left the car running and opened the sliding glass door to the back of the hearse. He turned the heater as high as it would go. That would help take off some of the chill in the air. He got out of the hearse and made his way over to Nora's side of the car. The door wouldn't open fully because of the bank of the ditch.

"Let me get you out on my side," Ham said. He went back around and opened the door. Nora slid over to the driver's side. Ham scooped her up in his one arm and carried her to the back of the hearse. Nora leaned down and opened the back door. There was the mattress with clean sheets and a blanket neatly folded on top of it.

Ham laid Nora gently onto mattress and crawled in, too. He shut the door behind him. Nora scooted as far as she could toward the front of the hearse to give Ham room at the bottom. Soon Nora began having labor pains. Still no passing cars.

"Ham, you're goin' to have to deliver this baby!"

Ham gulped. "All right Nora. We can do this." Ham took off his jacket and flannel shirt and lifted the harness of his prosthesis over his head. He placed the artificial arm on the side. He didn't want to accidentally scratch Nora or the baby with the hook. He grabbed the sheets and spread them beneath Nora. He helped her out of her skirt and panties. The hearse was cold. Ham put his jacket over Nora's chest, and the blanket over the jacket.

The contractions came harder and faster. Nora screamed; Ham tried to comfort her. Several hours later, Ham saw the baby's head crown.

"I see it, Nora! Push, push!"

The last thing Nora heard was the sound of a baby crying and James Taylor singing "Sweet Baby James." She saw blood everywhere. She remembered thinking, my baby is going to be born in the back of a hearse. Of course. How ironic; Nora had been in Miss Turnage's English class, too. She saw red lights flashing, then she passed out.

When she woke up, she was in the hospital in Morganton. Ham was sitting beside her holding a baby—her baby, their baby—in his arms. Ham saw Nora's eyes open. "Look, it's your mama!"

Nora's eyes widened. "Is it a—?" She hesitated.

"It's a girl," Ham beamed and placed her in Nora's outstretched arms. Nora had never seen anything so beautiful!

"What shall we name her, Ham?"

"Oh, I've already named her. James Taylor was singin' 'Sweet Baby James' so it seemed only natural to name her Jamie Polk MacPherson after James Polk. The eleventh president of the United States and a native son of North Carolina."

"What! You didn't! Is it too late to change her name?"

Ham feigned indignation. "What's wrong with namin' her that? It carries on a time honored MacPherson family tradition." Nora looked like she was going to cry.

"Of course, I didn't name her that Nora. Besides I wouldn't name her without talkin' to you first. I was thinkin' Carla Culpepper MacPherson. What do you think?"

Relieved, Nora said, "Oh, I think that's perfect, Ham. Carla Culpepper MacPherson, welcome to the world!" She snuggled her little bundle of joy close to her chest.

"What happened Ham? How did we get here and where are we?"

"Morganton Hospital. A state worker with a snowplow saw the hearse in the ditch and called the EMT on his two-way radio. They came and got us and brought us here."

"Was the baby already born?"

"Yep," Ham replied. "I clamped and cut the umbilical cord with my hook." Then a worried look crossed his face. "You lost a lot of blood. It's a good thing they got there when they did."

"How long have I been out?" Nora asked.

"Quite a while. Your parents came. They're around somewhere. And my mom. And JC. He went with Dubya to get the hearse, but it was gone."

"What do you mean 'gone'?"

"Vanished. I turned off the engine before I got into the ambulance, but I left the key in the ignition. Maybe somebody pulled it out with a chain, and we'll get it back. Or maybe it was stolen. JC thinks it just ascended into heaven to be with Uncle Carl."

"I like that explanation best," Nora said.

"Yeah, but I like thinkin' about Mr. Ed travelin' around the mountains lookin' for somebody else to help."

"You mean like Herbie the Love Bug?"

"Yeah, except Mr. Ed doesn't talk." They looked at each other and sang together, "Unless he has somethin' to say!" They laughed.

Ham smiled; he was happy. The Wizard of Wilkes County had a family. Not a perfect family or a holy family, but *his* family. Yes, his family. And with them and with help from his extended family of flesh and faith, both living and dead, and friends like JC, he knew they would make it. He kissed Nora on the cheek and Carla on the top of her head, and Ham gathered them, and all the hope they held, in his arm.

AFTERWORD

*M*y dear Reader. My name is John Quincy MacPherson, and I, along with family friend and religious studies scholar, Mikeal C. Parsons, narrated the story you just read. I am grateful to Rebecca Poe Hays, Mikeal's research assistant, for copyediting the manuscript for us. Against the advice of our publisher, I have decided to tell you a little bit about myself and the making of this book. I have written it as an Afterword because I am told readers do not read Forewords or Prefaces, and in any case, I did not want to prejudice your reading of the story with my meta narrative. Still there are some things I think you might like to know.

I am the second child of Ham and Nora MacPherson, born six years after Carla. Obviously, my parents decided to continue the MacPherson tradition of naming the first born male after a president. I'm glad they did (though I am grateful Dad did not name me Ulysses S.; I think my mother may have had something to do with that!). I hope one day a MacPherson may be able to name a first-born girl after a female president. As Brother Bob would say, "That day may not be far off!"

I've known the main outline of this story since childhood, and I've pieced together some bits through reading and research; others I just made up. I'm not a professional writer; I've been a trauma surgeon for about three years. I decided to tell the story now because most of the principal players are either dead or they never existed at all. In either case, neither group is in any position to protest. The former have gone on to whatever destiny they made for themselves or whatever mercies God has chosen to grant them despite that human-made destiny. The latter have no basis for protesting the timing of the story's release since their very existence depends on the story itself (though I do recognize even they could object to certain details once I'd blown breath into their nostrils).

Dubya and Cornelia are long gone, of course. Ham died three years ago at the age of fifty-six after a brief bout with pancreatic cancer. Paul Snyder attended Dad's graduation from Stearns and Marshall Baptist College and on the spot offered him a job in the Atlanta Braves front office as a staff accountant. So they moved to Atlanta, where I was born. Except for a year's leave of absence when we returned to Wilkes County to take care of Mom's mother, we spent the rest of our time in Atlanta. Dad earned an MBA from Emory while working fulltime and made his way up through the ranks. A couple of years before he died, he was promoted to Vice-President and Controller in the Accounting Department of Business Operations for the Atlanta Braves. Dad had made it to the "Show" after all. And he got to work with Hank Aaron, who joined the Braves' front office after he retired.

He and Nora had two children, Carla and me, and two grandchildren. He lived a full if somewhat shortened life, and he was surrounded by loving family as he drew his last breath. He lived well, was loved, and is missed. His last words were, "At least I beat the MacPherson Curse," which technically is true. Of course, it's possible the Grim Reaper was so busy he ran late in getting round to collecting my father. At any rate, at least Ham was not the victim of the Curse in the form of MacPherson stupidity. He did nothing wrong to deserve a death so wretched and painful as that caused by pancreatic cancer.

Before dad's funeral, Carla and I traveled to the old MacPherson homestead in Wilkes County, which now belongs to a different owner and no blood relative of ours. We asked for and received permission to remove the remains of Alexander Hamilton and our dad's arm. We re-interred Alex next to dad, and we placed the casket containing the arm in his larger casket (made a couple of feet longer to accommodate its new passenger). We also placed Dad's prosthesis (minus the hook) in the coffin with him, since it (or some earlier version of it) had been with him twice as long as his real arm, and we didn't know which one, if either, he'd prefer to spend eternity with. Carla found it all a bit macabre and refused the arm's grave marker. So I took it and hung it in my office at the hospital—it makes for quite a conversation starter! I also kept the baseball from Dad's last start on the grounds he placed it in a freezer bag to prevent its disintegration in the hopes it may one day be liberated. It sits on my desk in the study at my house and remains a prized possession. Because JC dropped the balls long ago, I don't know if it was the last baseball my dad ever pitched in a game, but I know it was the last time he signed anything *with his left hand. The signature was in a neat, small script. I placed the ball on the shelf beside the bat fragment with Jose Cardenal's signature on one side and the piece of fencing from his accident on the other. The hook from the prosthesis is also on the shelf. I offered it to Carla, but again she refused. In the game room at our house, I have the old Wurlitzer jukebox, the old Remington typewriter, and the 1921 National Cash Register, series 300. I guess I'm a kind of a pack rat, or so my wife says!*

After Dad's funeral, I discovered the key to the letter lockbox in his desk. Later, I found the box itself in the top of a closet. I opened the lockbox and discovered Ham's letters, all 153 of them! They were mostly short letters (some simply said, "Dear Daddy TJ, Still pissed, Ham"), but others were several pages long. I couldn't imagine how many hours it took to type all those letters with one finger! These letters had replaced the pain pills as his self-medication during the tumultuous events of 1976 and were the way he dealt with his loss and grief. A couple were written to his arm, H. H. (Howard Hughes), and there was one to Uncle Carl, thanking him for the inheritance he left Nora and him. But the vast majority were addressed to Daddy T. J. I guess the father-son relationship really is the most complicated and confusing one (rivaled only by the mother-daughter tango!). The letters to T. J. were very intense and raw and painful to read. All the letters, except one, were dated between August 10 and November 29, 1976 (the day after Carla was born). He wrote one practically every day, and on the weekends he would write four or five. They dealt with events between February and November of that year, though same gave background to events leading up to 1976. I wasn't sure if he had looked at the letters since writing them. They were all folded into thirds and beginning to yellow. Some water stains (tears?), however, were located on some of the letters in such a way that it would have been hard to explain while they were in the Remington.

I decided against printing the whole collection of letters in this book, thinking if Dad had wanted to share them he wouldn't have kept them under lock and key. The ones I have shared are reproduced with the original typos intact. My own guilt in reading them was relieved slightly by the fact they helped me turn a corner or two in my own life. Discovering their existence was probably the single most important factor in my decision to write these stories down. The longer ones were important sources of information as I wrote.

The last letter was addressed to my mother and dated July 2, 2011, the date of Mom's funeral. Mama Nora had received a bachelor's degree from

Stearns and Marshall and worked at the Emory University Hospital. She died suddenly of a heart attack, like both her parents before her. The suddenness of her death kept her from being surrounded by loved ones as she passed from this world into the next, but she was no less beloved. The letter was typed on the old Remington, despite the fact Dad possessed, and knew how to operate, a computer. It also had several "water stains."

> My Dearest Nora,
>
> Love of my life. I can't believe you are gone. Today is our thirty-fifth anniversary. I'm sorry we didn't make it sixty years like you wanted, but I wouldn't trade one second we had together for anything in the world> When I was broken and in pieces, you made me a whole man. You showed me what a family could be and do for each other> You believed in me and loved me when I couldn't believe in or love myself. There are so many things I wanted to tell you but you left so quickly. I miss you terribly and I cant wait to see you again.
>
> Until then, I am forever yours,
>
> Love
>
> Ham
>
> P.S. If you see Mr Ed, tell him I'll be there one day!

So I knew Dad had been back in the lockbox at least once since 1976.

After an illustrious football career at the State University in Raleigh and the NFL, JC moved to New York City. He found a life partner, Victor Gutierrez, a cellist in the New York symphony. After twenty years together, they were able to marry in New York on July 4, 2011, a month after same-sex marriage was legalized in that state, just as Brother Bob had predicted forty years earlier. I haven't heard from JC in a long time. I imagine him living a satisfied and satisfying life with Victor in the City.

Brother Bob was the composite of several progressive North Carolina Baptist pastors—Caryle Marney, W. W. Finlater, Warren Carr, Tom Roberts, and Bob Seymour—whose stories were mostly unknown until David Stricklin's fine study, A Genealogy of Dissent: Southern Baptist Protest in the Twentieth Century (2014), was published. I took Martin England's story from Stricklin's book. I have no idea if Rev. England ever used the story in a sermon, but he should have. There is a Little Rock Baptist Church, but sadly, *there is no Second Little Rock, though one can hope and dream there might still be one, if only in the New Jerusalem.*

There are some historical characters who may not have done what I reported them to have done or to have said what I recounted them to have said. Walter Rabb was the baseball coach of UNC in 1976; I don't know if he recruited Ham—he should have. Same for Coach Jim Brock of Arizona State University, who would go on to win several CWS national championships. Many consider the ASU team of 1976, with twelve players who went on to major league careers, the greatest college team of all time (even though they didn't win the College World Series that year). Ham would have fit right in. Paul Snyder, Director of Player Personnel for the Atlanta Braves, did (and does) exist; Stan Huffman, Major League Bureau of Scouts, does not. Historical anachronisms are sprinkled throughout the story. For example, the Village People did not release "YMCA" until 1978, so Ham could not have placed it in the jukebox when I report that he did; however, I am confident he would have done just that had it been available at the time!

There are also fictional figures whose historical counterparts did accomplish what is recorded in this book. For example, there was no Bobby Skeeter at Sylva High, but students of North Carolina baseball history and lore will recognize this character was based on Steve Streater, recently recognized as one of the top 100 male athletes in NC of all time. He led Sylva-Webster to the state title in 1975 (not 1976) and did, in fact, win twenty-three games that season, pitching in every one of Sylva's games. He was named the national High School Player of the Year, and the twenty-three wins still stand as the single season record for an individual high school pitcher. Streater had a distinguished career in football at UNC but tragically was paralyzed in an automobile accident on the same night he signed with the Washington Redskins in 1981. He was confined thereafter to a wheelchair and died in 2009 at the age of . . . . fifty.

After that the separation of fact from fiction becomes even less clear. Those who know me and who are industrious will try to disentangle the historical from the fictional. They will try to peel back the fiction of the story to get to its historical core. They will be surprised, perhaps, to find how many of the details of the story rest on historical bedrock. But this story is rather more like an onion. Fact and fiction are mixed together in balanced, if unequal parts, and the peeling back of the layers will remove both fact and fiction, and when one finishes the peeling back, she will realize she's accomplished nothing more than destroying the inherent shape of the story. It's so hard to distinguish between the "factual" and "fictional" anymore I've finally given up trying. Some of the stories remain disputed by eyewitnesses. For example, Uncle Michael Allen insists that the story of his daddy taking a cab from Carolina Beach to North Wilkesboro after his mama left him there is true, while Aunt Diane claims no memory of it (and until the day she died, Grandma Nina denied it ever happened). Some of the stories told to me by family members were no doubt already tainted with embellishment, and as I've said, I made some stuff up to keep the story from lagging. The extreme skeptic among you might even question my existence. Am I "real" or just the narrative voice of the story created by one who wished to remain anonymous? Only the Shadow knows.

What can I say? I can say there was an arm and it was lost, and its loss rippled through my family for several generations, complicating and destroying, enriching and restoring relationships and dictating vocations and careers, as in my case. There was also an Uncle Carl who was arrested for public intoxication and who died mysteriously in a jail cell. He did not live to see the birth of a child whose gender he predicted. Some losses, such as of life or limb, can never be recovered, and yet part of our own psychic and spiritual recovery paradoxically entails coming to grips with that irretrievable and irrevocable loss. The phantom pain is real, and it does not easily go away.

I can also say there was a hearse, and it was never found. Maybe Mr. Ed's disappearance, as JC suggested, was because the hearse ascended, Elijah-like, straight into heaven to join Uncle Carl in that great Hearse Club in the sky. With Dad, I rather like to imagine Mr. Ed is still traveling the back roads around the Brushy Mountains. Whether there's still a mattress in the back of it is anyone's guess.

Finally, I can say I believe the whole story to be true in the deepest sense, regardless of what really happened and what didn't happen, what was said and what wasn't said, and who really lived and who didn't. It's the story of human success and failure and frailty and a tribute to the human spirit buoyed by human community and relationships. I have tried to report and reflect upon these stories of human experience in the hope that in their telling we may learn to live more peaceably with ourselves and with each other. Regarding the success of this goal, dear Reader, you and only you can serve as judge and then only by the life you choose to lead.

John Quincy MacPherson (with Mikeal C. Parsons)
May Twenty-Second in the Year of Our Lord